RISE OF THE STRONGEST SOVEREIGN

RISE OF THE STRONGEST SOVEREIGN

BOOK 1

KAZ HUNTER

Podium

RISE OF THE STRONGEST SOVEREIGN

CHAPTER ONE

S ystem Message: System Loading . . .]
[Please stand by . . .]

[. . .]

[. . .]

I regard the messages with more than a bit of confusion, though, admittedly, with a bit of excitement. At the moment, I'm standing near Times Square, New York City. No, I don't live in New York, but I've always wanted to visit and see the sights.

[System Loaded. Apocalypse Protocol Engaged.]

All around me, people begin to gasp in shock. The messages are appearing in front of my face, just like in a video game. I reach out and poke the screen. It distorts a little as my finger passes through it. What does this mean? I've been hearing a lot about artificial intelligence and augmented reality; is this some sort of test? Am I about to be part of a corporate promotion? If so, this is going to sweep the gaming industry.

[System Message: Attention, humans! The Apocalypse Protocol has been initiated! Rifts will appear across your planet, unleashing hordes of monsters and opening gateways to dungeons filled with untold riches and challenges. As a result of the Apocalypse Protocol, certain individuals will be Awakened and will gain access to untold powers and abilities. These individuals will be able to fight the monsters and explore the dungeons. Selection of these individuals is at random and is not based on any merit or demographic.]

I'm no longer wondering if this is actually a promotion. All around me, people are screaming and running away. My phone is starting to ding too. I'm getting messages from my brother—and he's all the way in Kansas. Whatever this is, it seems to be worldwide.

[System Message: Those who Awaken will experience a surge of power and will suddenly find themselves with a connection to their abilities. We encourage all individuals to remain calm and work together in this time of chaos. Those who Awaken should use their powers responsibly and strive to protect their fellow humans from the dangers that have been unleashed. The Apocalypse Protocol is irreversible, and the world as you know it will be forever changed. As you face these new challenges, we, the System Administrators, wish you the best of luck navigating your new reality.]

"Oh, yeah?" someone shouts from just next to me. "If you're really bringing this on us, you don't care about us that much!"

I don't disagree, but I also find that I don't care. All around me, people are beginning to realize that something strange really is happening. This isn't just a test; this isn't just a promotion. Strange streaks of blue light flash through the sky, and, suddenly, a bolt of lightning strikes the exact center of Times Square.

[Now Opening: Times Square Dungeon.]

"What's going on?"

"Are you seeing this too?"

"Are we in danger?"

I have to laugh at the last question. Of course we're in danger! Anyone with half a working brain could see that much. As mothers begin to rush their children to shelter—and a few policemen start frantically calling out contradictory instructions—I ball my hands into fists. Whatever happens, I'm not going to fall. I might or might not wind up being Awakened, but I'm not going to let these System Administrators, whoever they are, get the better of me. My hand finds its way to my holster, a concealed carry that I've had on me for years now. As I pull it out, a few people scream and run, but I see other like-minded individuals doing the same thing.

Quite suddenly, the bolt of lightning that struck Times Square arcs back up into the sky. Now *that's* a strange thing to watch, let me assure you. Instead of hitting the clouds again, though, it stands still, flickering and flashing, forming a pillar about thirty feet tall. Then, it begins to pull itself apart, forming a portal of dark energy. I can't see through, as there's a screen of darkness across the entrance, but I *do* see a massive claw come tearing out.

With a screech, a massive gargoyle leaps out. It looks like a lizard crossed with both a frog and a bat, its ugly wings beating uselessly as it snaps jaws that drip either acid or venom. It stands about five feet tall. More soon follow. Somewhere around ten soon take up a defensive guard around the portal.

[System Message: Awakened Ability Detected! Initiating Awakened Process . . .]

[. . .]

[. . . Please hold, our servers are experiencing a larger-than-usual demand.]

I have a pretty good idea what the message means, but I don't have time to wait. I, along with everyone else holding a gun, cut loose on the monsters.

Bam-bam-bam-bam-bam-bam-bam-bam-bam!

The noise is deafening, and I see bullets slamming into the gargoyles up and down their ugly bodies.

[Damage Dealt: 1 HP]

[Remaining HP: 99]

I look down at my gun in amazement. It wasn't the most powerful handgun I could have purchased, but it wasn't the least powerful, either. All around me, people are realizing the same thing. Someone throws a grenade, which lights up the square with a flash and a resounding *boom!* The gargoyles seem largely unfazed, and one of them screams and starts lumbering toward me.

At that very moment, my hands crackle with a new and untold energy.

[Ability Unlocked: Monster Trainer. You have the power to communicate with and tame monsters. Tamed monsters will obey your commands.]

I decide I don't have time to perform a proper test, and simply point my hand at the charging gargoyle. A blast of reddish lightning flashes from my palm and strikes the monster dead in the chest.

[Gargoyle is resisting your efforts to tame it.]

I bring up my second hand and add a second blast of lightning. The creature snarls and takes another step forward, shaking the ground.

[Gargoyle is beginning to give in. Don't give up now!]

I grit my teeth, uncertain of exactly how these new powers work, but quite certain that if I don't figure it out, I'll die. I plant my feet and pour every ounce of my mind into subduing the creature.

[Congratulations! Lesser Gargoyle, Level 1 has been tamed!]

[Abilities: Razor Claws, Aerial Mobility]

I gasp in relief then give a nod to the creature.

"Kill all your little friends."

The gargoyle spins around. The others, distracted by the bullets, don't see the attack coming. I watch in satisfaction as the monster begins to tear through the other gargoyles. It doesn't take long, thankfully. As the gargoyle finishes the job, it comes stomping back over to meet me, and I take a look around.

A crowd is gathering around me. A little girl walks up; I don't see her parents. Her voice is only a whisper.

"Are you an Awakened now?"

"I think so." I smile and nod down at her. I send a mental command to the gargoyle, and it bends down and holds out a claw, which she strokes. While the crowd watches, I look around. I don't see anyone else who managed to take down one of the monsters. That means that I'm the only Awakened in this area. Not a problem, by my estimate, but it does mean that the number of people who are Awakened is pretty small.

"Thank you." A policeman comes running up. "We're in your debt."

"Get these people to safety," I order. "Find a place away from the rifts and lock them down." I give him my phone number. "Call me if you need help."

He gives me a nod then starts ordering people away. The gargoyle blinks at me and then teleports itself onto my shoulder, shrinking down to only about a foot tall. I turn toward the crackling dungeon portal. As I approach, the gargoyle speaks.

Master, you should not go in there. You will not survive.

"Don't tell me what I can and can't do," I respond, though I do pause. The gargoyle came from inside; it knows what's hiding there. "Will more monsters be coming back out?"

This Dungeon is F-Ranked. It will discharge monsters every twenty-four hours, until it gets cleared. A scream echoes off the building walls, and I turn to look. It comes from the direction of the ocean. *There are plenty of monsters in the city right now, if you care to find them. Once you've leveled up a bit more, you can start exploring.*

"Fair enough." I start walking in the direction of the screams, and I hear snarls echoing around as well. "I do wish I had a weapon, though. Not that I don't appreciate you, but . . . you know."

The gargoyle doesn't really have any good response to that. Suddenly, though, my phone buzzes. I look down at it, rather surprised that it's still working.

"Unknown number," I murmur. The text message doesn't show up, so I unlock the phone and open the message app.

[Welcome to Riftwatch! This is the Admin Group. We want you to broadcast your Awakened abilities to the whole world, to give a ray of hope in these dark times! Sign up now and become a livestreaming legend!]

My eyes narrow as I look it over. There's something fishy about the message, but I can't tell exactly what it is. After a moment, though, I nod.

"I'll do it."

I don't even have to respond to the text message before my phone goes dark again, and a new message appears in front of my face, just like the original ones.

[Congratulations! Your actions are now being livestreamed to the entire internet on riftwatch.com, handle JasonLee. No further action is required on your end.]

A little red light appears in the corner of my vision to let me know that I'm being watched. I know I can't waste any more time, and I start marching down the street toward the screams.

[ChaosRider: Wait, is this real? Does he have a monster on his shoulder?]

[RazorEdge: I bet it's just an illusion.]

[FireStorm: My system says that it's a Lesser Gargoyle! That's super cool!]

I smile at the messages. Right below the red dot, a number appears indicating my viewership. It ticks steadily upward as I walk along, despite me doing absolutely nothing.

[ChaosRider: Guys, guys, calm down. Let's see him do something before we go crowning him king or anything.]

[GoldenShield: Come on! Don't be a sourpuss. Have you seen anyone else with monster-taming abilities?]

[ChaosRider: There's a guy in Jersey who has fire powers! That's pretty cool!]

[FireStorm: Then go watch his chat! Stop mucking things up around here.]

I let out a long breath and ball my hands into fists. A moment later, I reach an intersection and look out into a small sort of square. Frost covers the ground, the fire hydrants, and the broken storefronts. I frown as I look at it all. A good deal of blood covers the ground, too, now frozen as hard as ice. I walk over next to a car that's been crumpled up like a tin can, and I let out a long breath.

"Any chance that an Awakened did this?"

[GrendleH8tr: Not a chance!]

"Figured as much." I look around and notice a flickering light a few streets down. That was the portal, and I look in the opposite direction. There, the frost leads across the ground, marking a trail of destruction before turning a sharp corner. I start in that way, and the gargoyle teleports itself back to the ground next to me.

[Riftwatch: A Mysterious Benefactor has sent you a gift!]

I hold out my hands and, with a flash of light, a small, ornate box appears in my palms. It's made of wood and *solid*. I smile, then hold it for just a moment.

[FireStorm: Open it! Open it!]

[LunarEclipse: OOH!!! I wonder what could be inside!]

[ChaosRider: I bet it's boring.]

I decide I've waited long enough, and I flip the latch. The box dissolves in a flurry of blue sparks, and a large dagger settles into my hand. It has a blade as dark as night, about six inches long, and I heft it for a moment.

[Weapon Acquired: Shadow Dagger]

[Class: F]

I give it a twirl and then, feeling a bit more confident, start walking down the street once again.

"Thank you, Mysterious Benefactor," I speak out loud, my voice sounding just as dead as the buildings I pass. Here and there, terrified faces peer out through the destruction. I'm being watched, in more ways than one.

As I turn the corner, I find my prey. There, a pack of five wolves stands tall, their fur white as snow. They turn to glare at me, and I find myself looking into eyes as black as the void of space. Behind them, a few civilians scream and make it to safety, as I prepare myself for battle.

"Gargoyle, make mincemeat of these things."

My gargoyle launches itself into the air, rising up on the cold winds. Cold? Yeah, the temperature starts dropping almost immediately. The first wolf bounds forward, claws eating up the pavement. Ice explodes from under each paw, and it leaps one final time, opening its jaws wide.

[ChaosRider: This is the end of Jason Lee!]

I leap forward then drop to the ground, sliding on the ample layer of ice. As I slide underneath the wolf, I lash upward with the dagger. It cuts deeply into the bowels of the monster, and the thing lands with a crash on the ground just behind me.

[Monster Defeated: Lesser Frost Wolf, Level 1]

[You have earned 10 XP]

[You have Leveled up!]

More messages appear, but I don't have time for them. I charge forward at the next wolf, blade flashing through the air. A few moments later, I leap past his head and slam the blade deep into his neck. My gargoyle drops down onto a third wolf, raking and tearing at it with its claws.

That, though, is when things take a turn for the worse.

A fourth Frost Wolf opens its mouth and howls, and the air chills rapidly. I shiver as the second wolf falls to the ground, dead, but the gargoyle, a cold-blooded creature, slows to a crawl. The fifth wolf takes the opportunity to leap up and pounce on the monster, smashing it into the ground.

I snarl, then leap at the howling wolf and drive my blade deep into its chest. It falls backward, and I turn and throw the dagger at the one my gargoyle injured. The blade sinks in up to the hilt, and the wolf drops as well. That leaves only the one that my gargoyle is fighting . . . Or, rather, *was* fighting.

My heart sinks as I watch the Frost Wolf stepping away from the now-frozen body of the Lesser Gargoyle. I grit my teeth. I have no weapon, and I have no gargoyle.

[ChaosRider: *Now* this is the end of JasonLee!]

The wolf springs forward, eating up the ground in great leaps and bounds. I have exactly one chance, and I hold out my hands. Bolts of lightning erupt across the distance and hit the wolf in the chest.

[Frost Wolf is resisting your efforts to tame it.]

I ignore the message and keep focusing. The monster, far from slowing, keeps coming.

[Frost Wolf is resisting your efforts to tame it.]

I grit my teeth. The Frost Wolf gives one last spring, flashing through the air. It's now or never.

[Frost Wolf is . . .]

CHAPTER TWO

ow tame!]

[Congratulations! Lesser Frost Wolf, Level 1, has been tamed!]

[Abilities: Chomp, Frost]

I smile as the wolf gives me a big lick before slowly stepping back. I climb to my feet, and I notice that my followers have climbed to almost five thousand.

[ChaosRider: Alright, I have to admit, that was cool.]

[DarkCynic: Yeah, Jason!!!]

[ShadowDancer: He deserves another gift for that!]

[GrendleH8tr: What he needs to do is level up.]

Right! I glance at the other side of my vision, where a level-up message is waiting for me. I reach out and touch it.

[Congratulations! You are now Level 2!]

[Please accept from the following rewards:]

[Level E Weapon]

[Level E Monster]

[Monster Trainer Skill]

"What should I do?" I smile as I look at the chat. "Any thoughts?"

[RazorEdge: Take the weapon! Take the weapon!]

[FireStorm: Are you kidding? The weapon will only last for a little while. Getting more and more monsters is going to be how he succeeds in this world.]

[GrendleH8tr: Dude, take the skill. If monster training is how you succeed, amping that up is going to be your best bet.]

I decide to take the advice of GrendleH8tr: "I'll take the skill."

[Skill Acquired!]

[Pocket Dimension: Create a pocket dimension where you can store your unneeded monsters.]

I smile and decide to test it out. With a wave of my hand, a crackling portal appears in the air in front of me. It isn't large—not nearly the size of the dungeon— and it doesn't seem quite so dark inside.

Master, if you don't mind my saying so, you don't want to put me in there. Not yet, anyway.

I wasn't sure if everyone else could hear the beast, which seemed to project itself straight into my mind. "Now what should I do, my pet?" I scratched the wolf behind its ears. "You need a name."

I have a name. Bjorn.

"Bjorn sounds like a good name for you." I smile and nod.

[GrendleH8tr: The words of the wolf appear in subtitles. We know you're not crazy if you talk to it.]

I sigh in relief. "Perfect! Then what do I need to be doing, Bjorn?"

The dungeon I came from was D-Ranked. Monsters come out every six hours, but, more importantly, a boss came out as well. You'll want to take it down quickly.

"Any chance you know where it is?"

Bjorn simply padded off down the street, and I followed. I kept my dagger at my side, and I dissolved the portal. All around me, the streets seemed to become more and more destroyed. I could hear more explosions and screams coming from elsewhere in the city. Things would settle down, but it was going to take some time.

[ShadowDancer: Jason shouldn't be traveling with the monster who killed the gargoyle!]

[FireStorm: I don't disagree. Jason, that thing murdered your friend!]

"Yes, it did." I shrug as I continue to follow the beast. "But you do have to realize that we're in a strange, new world. That gargoyle almost ate me before I managed to tame it. We have to take what we can get and not worry about things beyond that."

[RazorEdge: That's a good way of looking at things, I think.]

[ChaosRider: Seems rather bleak to me.]

"Besides, Bjorn is a good boy." I shrug. "We just need to—"

A dull roar echoes through the air, and all the buildings around me shudder. It doesn't sound quite like the roar of a monster—more like the enraged roar of a human. A *big* human.

[IceQueen: OOH! That sounds like a boss!!]

[ViperQueen: I'm watching it over on BossTracker! It's going to crush Jason for sure!]

Ahead of me, Bjorn pads along a bit faster. I rather wish

that my gargoyle was still here, since he could fly, but I decide to make do with what I have. I race along a bit faster as well, and the two of us soon start threading our way through the winding streets of the city. Suddenly, we round one final corner and stop.

A group of civilians—ten or fifteen; it's hard to tell—are hiding in what looks to be a diner of some sort. Standing just in front of the shop is a huge, hulking mass of meat.

[The Frozen Butcher, Level 8 – Boss]

[System Notification: Defeating bosses will provide rewards galore!]

[RazorEdge: Rewards galore? Go for it, Jason! Quick, someone send him another care package!]

I know I don't have time to wait for a care package. The Frozen Butcher must stand at least fifteen feet tall, and is *quite* obese, with thick folds of fat hanging down from his belly and his arms. He has at least five chins, maybe six, and in his right hand he has an enormous meat hook. As I stand there, he slams it down through the roof of a car and hefts the whole thing off the ground. The people inside the diner scream, and I point my arm forward.

"Go, Bjorn!"

Bjorn bolts down the street and lets out a howl. A piercing blast of freezing air hits the butcher from the side, and a thick layer of frost grows across his body. He smashes through it in a moment and turns toward us, snarling. Before I can close the gap, he slings the car at us, sending it crashing down the street like a boulder.

Bjorn, nimble as a cat, leaps up and over the car. I dodge to the side and let it go crashing past, then race toward the butcher once more. Bjorn leaps up and latches his teeth onto a thick, flabby portion of the butcher's belly, which jiggles under the impact.

"*Rarhhhhh!*" the butcher screams then swings his left hand down to smash my wolf. Bjorn lets go just in time, and the butcher merely slaps himself powerfully. Ripples spread across his fat, and I smile. I draw out my dagger and rush forward, ready to end this guy for good.

Follow my lead, Master.

I don't necessarily like being told what to do by a pet, but he knows the butcher, so I decide to oblige. Bjorn backtracks next to me, and we charge forward together. Our movements synchronize, and we both leap up into the air as one. The butcher snarls and attacks, but he's too slow, and we hit him in the side. I strike him several times with my dagger, while Bjorn mauls him as best he can.

We both fall to the ground, and from that point, utter chaos breaks loose. The butcher slashes outward with his hook, intending to batter me into jelly. I drop to the ground and let the hook pass over my head, slashing upward with my dagger as I do so. Bjorn, meanwhile, bites deeply into the butcher's calf and causes the boss to let loose a massive roar. I then duck closer, driving my knife into his belly and drawing it along the monster's gut. The butcher responds by kicking me firmly in the stomach, and I'm thrown backward into a car.

I find it mildly amusing as the car crumples around me like aluminum foil. As I pull myself out of the wreckage and take my stance once again, the butcher leaps forward, performing a body slam. I step out of the way, but as he hits the car, metal and glass are blasted sideways in an immense shockwave. I'm hit by bits and pieces of the chassis, windshield, rearview mirror, and a great deal more, and am tossed into a nearby wall.

Now *that* one hurts. I groan and sink to the ground, and the butcher climbs back to his feet. In the corner, I watch my health drop down into the orange.

[System Notification: If your health hits zero, you will be considered defeated, and you will die.]

"Not today." I rise once more and charge at the monster. This time, though, I'm a bit more ready. The butcher lifts his massive hook up over his head and brings it crashing down. I leap backward, and the hook slams into the ground just in front of me, sticking in the asphalt. Before the butcher can respond, I run up his arm, raise my dagger, and drive it down into the base of his neck. He roars and rises up, thrashing about, and I hang on desperately for my life.

My body is thrown about like a rag doll, and I'm battered against his flabby back and arms. My health drops more, down to the red, and I groan. With all my strength, I pull myself up onto his shoulders and grab hold of the monster's ear. Pulling out the knife, I take a deep breath, then raise it up and bring it crashing down onto the beast's skull.

The butcher chooses that very moment to turn his head upward, and my knife slams into his eye. *That* makes the butcher howl in pain and thrash about—though I consider it a minor victory, as I had hoped to just kill him outright. Down below, Bjorn attacks with frost once more, targeting the butcher's legs. It seems to slow the immense beast down, and he staggers a bit. I decide to take my chance: I pull out the weapon and drop down to the ground, slicing down the monster's back as I do so.

When I land, I roll away, and the monster snarls and tries to stomp on me. I manage to roll away just in time, though the shockwave does pick me up a bit at the end. Bjorn snarls and rushes to stand in front of me then leaps up and latches his jaws down around the butcher's wrist. That makes the monster howl with pain, and he begins to shake his wrist rapidly. This time it's Bjorn who's tossed around like a rag doll, and with one final snarl, the butcher flings my wolf through the window of a nearby department store.

[ChaosRider: No!!!]

[FireStorm: Did you see that? Bjorn was totally going to give himself up for Jason!]

[LunarEclipse: Going to? He *did!* Justice for Bjorn!]

I stagger back to my feet, though in the corner of my vision, I can see that Bjorn's health isn't quite gone. The butcher seems to realize this too, and he snarls . . . then turns and staggers away. His gait is slow, and he leaves a long trail of blood behind him. I thump my chest, then turn and run to Bjorn's side.

I leap through the broken window and find my wolf lying in a pool of blood next to an overturned rack of clothes. Suddenly, a message appears.

[Riftwatch: A Mysterious Benefactor has sent you a gift!]

I hold out my hands once more and, with a flash, a red box with a white cross appears in my palms. I flip it open quickly and find two items. First, a bottle of Monster Medicine. I hold that up to Bjorn and, with a flicker, it dissolves into green sparks.

[System Notification: Your tamed Lesser Frost Wolf will be healed in 30:00.]

I nod and look at the second item. It's an energy drink, the Pumped! brand. I shrug, twist open the cap, and down the contents without bothering to read the item description.

[System Notification: Pumped! will heal you 10 HP per minute for the next 15 minutes.]

"That'll have to do." I wave my hand, and my flickering pet portal appears. "Alright, Bjorn. In you go."

Bjorn doesn't comment, but he rises and limps inside. The portal closes after him, and I rise and face the path that the butcher took.

[ChaosRider: Woot woot!!! Bjorn lives!]

[ShadowDancer: I wonder what happens if Jason dies while Bjorn's still inside. Will Bjorn die, too, or just be trapped in the pocket dimension forever?]

It's a good question, and one that I don't intend to answer. I leap back out through the window, then race off down the street. I can see my health bar slowly rising back toward the green, so I take it slow, but I do want to catch the butcher before he gets to wherever he's trying to reach. I assume he's trying to make it back to his dungeon, but I don't know that for sure.

Thankfully, the trail of blood is easy to follow. It leads through the streets, all the way to Central Park. There, make-shift walls are being set up, and several people wave at me as I jog along. I don't wave back, as I'm trying to stay focused. The blood seems to show that the butcher didn't attack anyone while fleeing, which is good in my estimate.

I soon round the corner and find myself facing a flicker-ing portal, on the same street where I first found the ice. The butcher is limping toward the portal and dragging his hook along the ground, which sends up a flurry of sparks. I take a deep breath, then plant my feet.

"Hey!" I call out. "Stop!"

The butcher pauses and turns back to me. A thick, flabby grin spreads across his face, and he turns and lunges through the portal. Dark energy closes around him, and I start racing after him. Before I can reach the location, though, shadows flicker around the exit. Suddenly, forms start to emerge.

Dark, evil-looking forms.

They hit the ground, thin and wiry things, each about three feet tall and sporting long claws. Beady eyes stare out at me, and long, toothy mouths all scream in unison.

[Monsters Detected: Lesser Imps, Level 2]

[Notice: Dark-class creatures may not be tamed.]

[RazorEdge: May not be tamed? What a joke!]

[GoldenShield: Ahh, old Jason will figure a way out of this!]

[GrendleH8tr: Stay calm, kid, and use your head.]

As the Imps all charge at me, I nod and take a deep breath. Now isn't the right time to get angry. I grip my dagger a bit more tightly and charge forward. I have no pets to help me; all I have are my blade and my skill.

It'll just have to be enough.

CHAPTER THREE

The fight against the Imps doesn't take long. That isn't to say that it's easy because, frankly, those things have tough skin, and it takes a few chops with the knife to hack through them, but they all fall before me.

[LunarEclipse: Look at him go! I've never seen someone take on so many Imps at once!]

[ShadowDancer: I have. Keep an eye on Firemaster's feed!]

[GrendleH8tr: Don't listen to those guys. Just focus.]

I push it all to the side and lunge forward. More Imps are still coming, even after I've chopped through at least a dozen of them. I fall back a bit then glance around. I need to kill them faster, but I'm not sure exactly how.

"*Scree!*" One of them jumps at me and I lash out, cutting him clean in half. The bits of his body hit the ground and I rush forward, cutting the heads off two more. As they thump to the frozen asphalt as well, I notice a lamp post nearby, teetering a bit after the butcher came through. An idea rises in my mind and I rush forward, slashing at the base of the structure.

My blade, true to form, cuts clean through the base of the post, which comes crashing down. Five Imps at least are crushed beneath it, their little voices screaming in pain as they're flattened.

[RazorEdge: Whoa!!! Now that was cool!]

[IceQueen: Do it again, Jason. Do it again!]

I glance around the area. Yet another one jumps at me, and I slash it through the chest. It staggers back, not dead yet, and I kick it as hard as I can. It staggers backward and slams into another one, and I finish it off with a quick strike. Then, catching sight of a series of collapsing escape ladders hanging from a nearby apartment, I rush over and cut through some wires. There's a sharp *whir* as the ladders come crashing down, and the Imps scream as they're all flattened beneath them.

That move only leaves a few Imps left. Some of them start to run toward Central Park, but I chase them down, not letting a single one escape. Even one free monster means a danger to someone. That's the simple reality of our world now. With that, I turn toward the portal and slowly walk up. Energy flickers around my body as I stretch out my hand, and, to my surprise, I encounter something solid.

[System Notification: This is a Rank-D Dungeon. You are only Level 2. It is advised to be at least Level 10 before entering a dungeon of this rank. Do you still want to proceed?]

"Yes." I nod firmly.

There is no response, but the solid form seems to give way under my hand, and I slowly step forward and into the dungeon. A wave of freezing cold air washes over me, and I suddenly find myself inside what can only be described as a longhouse.

The walls are made of wooden logs—logs that have rather wide gaps between them, through which blows an icy wind. Snow drifts lightly across the floor and several bloodstained footsteps lead across it. There are tables all around covered with food, plates, and more. Burnt-out candles mark the center of some of them. Of course, my eyes are particularly drawn to all the dead, frozen bodies that seem to be statues, depicting a feast not fully finished. All the bodies seem to be Vikings, complete with horned helmets, large fur capes, and a good deal of axes.

[GrendleH8tr: Watch yourself, Jason. These were cultists who worshiped the Frozen Butcher. They gave themselves to him, and he accepted their sacrifice.]

[ChaosRider: What are you, the loremaster?]

[GoldenShield: I think it's a cool tone to set! Let me make up some! Let's see . . .]

I keep my eyes on the frozen warriors, but mostly just start toward the door at the back of the room where I know the butcher went. In front of that door is a head table, where a jarl and his wife are seated with the other royal guests. I draw out my dagger and slowly start to slip around the side.

Screeeeeeeeeeeeeeeeeeeeeeech!

The sound of a rusty knife on a rusty plate echoes loudly, and the jarl slowly rises. His features are impassive, but the knife in his hand is anything but. All around me, the warriors start to move, and I know I'm in for a fight. Battle axes are picked up; knives are readied.

Before anyone else can move, I charge forward, dagger flashing in my hand. The jarl reacts instantly, throwing the knife into my shoulder. I scream in pain, and blood trickles down my shirt, but I do my best to ignore it. With every last ounce of strength in my body, I lunge forward and drive my blade into his chest.

The weapon crushes bone beneath the strike, and the draugr stumbles backward. He doesn't die, though, and a moment later, an axe hits me from the side. I'm knocked into one of the cracked walls, and I groan in pain. The queen then rises and punches me in the gut with her frozen fist, driving all the air from my lungs.

[FireStorm: Jason's in for it now!]

[ChaosRider: Can we please cut out that refrain? I've thought that myself a dozen times, and he keeps coming through.]

"I appreciate the . . . confidence," I murmur. Then I reach up, grab hold of the knife hilt in my shoulder, pull it out, and stab the queen in the face. She slumps to the ground, and I pull myself up. I can see my health bar dropping, and I feel myself weakening, but I know I'm not out of the fight just yet.

Another warrior lunges forward, raising a massive battle axe over his head. Before he can react, though, there's a flicker of light, and Bjorn explodes from the pocket dimension, striking the warrior in the chest. All around me, draugr stagger and fall. Bjorn latches down onto the warrior's frozen wrist and gives a quick twist. There's a *crack* that echoes through the air, and he hands me the axe.

[Weapon Acquired: Viking Axe]

[Level: E]

[ShadowDancer: See! It was best for him to take the skill! Now he has an E-ranked weapon anyway!]

I don't take time to read any more of the messages. Instead,

I simply rise and lash out with the axe, carving my way through three of the draugr at once. Warriors fall backward before me, and I take the fight to them. Not one can stand before me or my weapon, and I soon chop the frozen zombies up into little bits and pieces. As the last draugr falls to the ground, Bjorn comes padding over, and I scratch him behind the ears.

Master! Are you alright?

I reach up and feel the knife wound. It's deep, but the bleeding seems to have stopped. The rest of my body aches from the beating I've taken, but I'm not dead yet, in any case.

"Yeah, well enough." I nod. Together, we turn toward that last door. "Let's go butcher this butcher."

Okay, so it's not the best line I could have come up with, but I'm kind of on the spot here! We slowly step toward the door, and I reach out and pull it open.

[IceQueen: Stay safe, Jason! We're rooting for you!]

I nod then pause. "If anyone else has any more gifts they'd like to send, now would be the time."

There's a flash, and I get a few more healing items. I say thank you, and I heal myself and Bjorn. Then, slowly, axe in my hand, we step inside.

The door opens into a throne room. I imagine that this is where the jarl must have once held council. Tattered tapestries hang over the gaps in the walls, fluttering in the wind. A few coats of arms lie on the ground, battered and almost unreadable. There, high on the wooden throne in front of me, sits the butcher.

He's huge and grotesque, his fat spilling over the edges of the chair in a great, blubbery waterfall. I grit my teeth and draw back my axe, ready to do battle. He merely laughs then begins to speak. Whatever he's saying, though, I can't understand. All that comes out is "*Wub lubblu blub,*" or something similar, and I decide that I've had enough.

"Die, Butcher!"

I draw back the axe and fling it at the monster. It sails through the air and slams deep into the monster's belly, sinking in up to the shaft. The chat erupts in cheers, and the butcher slowly pulls himself up.

[Originalgoth: Idiot.]

[LunarEclipse: Go, Jason! Show that thing who's boss!]

[Originalgoth: He just gave up his weapon. This is fun to watch, but . . . Jason, you're just a newb, and you're about to pay the price. Even babies know that bosses, when they're sitting, can't be harmed.]

"Maybe so." I shrug as the butcher pulls himself up. "But that weapon will still be there when the system decides he *can* be harmed."

The butcher lumbers down from the throne, shaking the ground. I only barely manage to keep my footing as the monster reaches down and grabs hold of the hilt of the axe. When he rips it out, he deals far more damage to himself than I ever could have, and collapses back on the throne, blood and gore leaking down onto the ground.

[DarkCynic: That was cold, Jason!]

[ViperQueen: Finish him off!]

[Originalgoth: That was . . . boring. Now, Shadowstrike: *there's* an Awakened to watch. He doesn't have to resort to trickery to get things done.]

[GrendleH8tr: Ignore her, Jason. Just go finish him.]

I decide to do just that, and I rush forward. The butcher,

trembling, tries to pull himself up, but I give him no chance. I leap up and over his blubbery carcass and slam my blade into his throat as Bjorn latches his teeth down onto an arm. A few moments later, the corpse goes still, and we step back and gasp in relief.

[System Notification: You have defeated a Boss!]

[Reward: Butcher's Hook – Rank D]

[Reward: 500 XP]

[Reward: Rank-D Loot Box]

[You have leveled up!]

[Congratulations! You are now Level 5!]

[Please accept from the following rewards: (3)]

[Level E Weapon]

[Level E Monster]

[Monster Trainer Skill]

I smile as I peruse the options. This is going to take me a little bit of time. First, I gather up my dagger and my axe and place them both in my inventory. Bjorn watches the entrance as I make my next selections. I leveled up three times, so I get three rewards.

[ShadowDancer: Get three monsters!!!]

[FireStorm: No, Jason, get more skills!]

[Originalgoth: I think he should just leave them alone and go back to civilian life. He's nothing more than a loser pretending to be an Awakened.]

I scowl at that last message. Originalgoth seems to have only cropped up a few moments ago, but she—or he—is already getting on my nerves. I ignore it for the time being, though, and get to work.

"First, I want a Level E monster."

[New Tamed Monster Acquired!]

[Lesser Gargoyle, Level 3]

I break into a smile as a gargoyle, identical to my last one, appears. It bows to me, and I bow back. What a polite little thing. As it steps to the side, I know what I'm going to do.

"One more monster."

[New Tamed Monster Acquired!]

[Major Locust, Level 1]

With a flicker, a large, insectile creature appears on the ground. It stands on its hind legs, about four feet tall, and appears vaguely humanoid, with a number of sharp, pincer-like things ready to tear anything it meets to shreds. Large, compound eyes stare out at me, and it cocks its head to one side.

"Now, you're not something I'd like to meet in a dark alley at night!" I laugh and hold out a hand. It gently places a claw in mine, and we shake for a moment. "Good to meet you."

With that, I'm left with one reward left, and I look at the skill.

"I'd like another skill."

[Skill Acquired!]

[Rapid Heal: Heal a tamed monster! Warning: Overuse of this skill will have consequences.]

That ends all my level-up rewards, so I go to the loot box. As I select it, there's a flash, and a large, wooden chest appears on the ground in front of me. A golden key materializes in my hand, and I slowly bend down and insert it into the lock. There's a flash as it dissolves, and in its place appears a . . . sleeping bag?

[Item Acquired!]

[Thermal Sleeping Bag – Level 80 (Mythic)]

[Sleep anywhere you want! You will be immune to environmental effects as well as to monster attacks.]

[Originalgoth: LAME!!!]

[FireStorm: Hey, it's not Jason's fault!]

[RazorEdge: Yeah! Loot boxes are random! Just like getting these powers. I could be just as cool as Jason if I had been chosen.]

[Originalgoth: You don't *want* to be as cool as Jason, trust me.]

I scowl once more as I read the chat then nod. "Ban Originalgoth."

[Riftwatch: Originalgoth has been banned from the chat]

[ChaosRider: Go, Jason! We don't need that negativity in here!]

[ShadowDancer: Yeah, right on!]

[GrendleH8tr: Probably smart, but ... watch yourself, Jason.]

I nod. "I'll be careful." After a moment, I glance around. "Does anyone have the time?"

[RazorEdge: It's 10:00 PM, EST]

"Then I'm going to make good use of this sleeping bag." I haul it to a corner of the room where the butcher's stench isn't quite so bad then stretch it out and crawl inside. To my delight, it's really quite warm, and I feel myself nodding off. "Thanks everyone for watching! I'll see you again tomorrow!"

As my eyelids flicker shut, I see one final message.

[Riftwatch: Livestream will deactivate while sleeping. Enjoy your rest!]

CHAPTER FOUR

When I wake up, I find a large number of things happening all at once.

[Warning: Dungeons will close after their boss has been defeated.]

[Warning: You have stayed in the dungeon longer than necessary.]

[Warning: You will be trapped in this dungeon if you stay here any longer.]

[. . .]

The warnings go on for some time, delivered every fifteen minutes or so for the previous eight hours. I rise, gather my sleeping bag, and head for the main entrance. Behind me come my three monsters, and I form the portal to the pocket realm.

"Best stay inside for now."

They all enter without question, and I close it up before stepping back out onto the streets. The moment my feet hit the asphalt once more, there's a brilliant flash, and the portal closes behind me. I'm left alone with only the corpses of Imps to keep me company. That said, it gives me time to look at the rest of my messages.

[Riftwatch: A Mysterious Benefactor has sent you a gift!]

[Riftwatch: A Mysterious Benefactor has sent you a gift!]

[Riftwatch: A Mysterious Benefactor has sent you a gift!]

[. . .]

There are about ten gifts in all, which I start to open. Most are healing items and food. I take an apple and munch on it happily as I start walking toward Central Park, eager to see what else is around for me to fight today.

[ChaosRider: Glad to see you up and awake, Jason! It's another great day in the apocalypse, wouldn't you say?]

"Indeed it is, ChaosRider." I nod and take another bite out of the apple. "Time to crush some more monsters, I'd say. What should I do today?"

[LunarEclipse: Go clear another dungeon!]

[ViperQueen: Go to Central Park! It's really grown up overnight.]

A hunch tells me to check out Central Park, so I start heading in that direction. The chat continues to spill onward, advising me what to do today and giving me some highlights from other parts of the world. I ignore it for the time being, though, and focus on the last set of things that have built up from the night before.

[Riftwatch: You have unopened messages from Originalgoth.]

"Open," I mutter.

[Private Message: I don't see why you had to ban me. I was

just stating my opinion, and there's nothing wrong with that, you know. You're a fool, and you're going to get yourself hurt out there. Give up now, before you embarrass yourself and the whole human race. It won't matter anyway.]

The message goes on for quite a while longer, but I ignore it. Ahead of me, the park appears, and I do have to admit that it's impressive. Massive walls now rise around the entire perimeter. Busses, cars, sheets of metal, even piles of debris help form the barricade to hold back the tide of destruction that threatens to come sweeping through. I see a fence not far away, with two wrought-iron gates that I think I recognize from a zoo, but I don't have time to go check. As I start to approach, there's a loud screech, and the ground begins to rumble.

[LunarEclipse: Ooh, what's this? It's going to be good, I'm sure of that!]

[Originalgoth: You're going to want your monsters, Jason! Get Bjorn!]

[ChaosRider: No, get the locust! I'd love to see what it can do! Or do the gargoyle!]

"Let's see what we're dealing with first," I answer as I take my stance. I draw out my dagger and look around. It's smaller and does less damage than the axe, but it's a whole lot faster. The asphalt continues to rumble, and then, with a crack, a manhole cover is blasted up into the air.

Emerging from the sewers is a massive snake. It hisses and spits at me as it hauls its bulk up from the ground. It's almost two feet thick and must be at least fifty feet long by the time it finishes heaving itself up. I grit my teeth as I look at it. It won't be an easy fight, but it'll work well enough.

"Bjorn! I need you now!"

There's a flicker of light, and Bjorn steps out of the portal and joins me. Together we face down the serpent, which drops down to the ground and starts writhing across the street, hissing and twisting back and forth. I nod to Bjorn and send him a mental command.

Bjorn leaps forward, creating a layer of frost beneath his feet as he charges. The snake rises up, and I throw my dagger as hard as I can. It *thwacks* into the underside of the snake's neck and makes it draw back sharply. Bjorn tilts his head back and howls.

The howl shakes the buildings around, and sharp wind blows down the street. Snow falls, and the snake is driven back as ice grows all around it. I can see the cold-blooded monster beginning to slow, and I take my shot. Rushing forward with all my might and speed, I draw out my axe—which, I know, I had just decided not to use, but give me a break—and I launch myself up into the air.

[Originalgoth: Here comes a guillotine move!]

Ignoring her return to my chat, I bring my axe crashing down, fully intending to just chop off the snake's head, but it draws back before I can manage it. Instead, my blade slams into the asphalt and sticks there, and I have to jump backward as the snake strikes at me. I see my dagger, still embedded in its throat, and think about what to do.

"Locust! Your turn!"

The locust comes skittering out of the portal a moment later, and it regards the snake with a bit of apprehension.

What would you have me do, Master?

"I need my dagger back. I'm hoping you can sneak around and get it," I answer hopefully.

You'll need a distraction.

"I have one," I answer again. "Just skirt over to the side."

The locust nods and scampers off toward the wall while the snake rises up and opens its mouth. Long, pointed fangs look down at me, and I brace myself. Its eyes flick down to the axe, still waiting down below. It knows I don't have a weapon, so it's trying to bait me.

The joke will be on it.

I slowly raise my hands then call on my Monster Tamer ability. Lightning explodes from my palms, flashes through the air, and hits the snake dead in the face. Even in its cold and sluggish state, it reacts swiftly and bears down upon me with a mighty hiss.

Now I know, even as I try it, that the attack won't succeed in taming it. Though I haven't confirmed it yet, my suspicion is that you can only tame monsters of an equal or lower level than yourself. I'm a level five, and while I don't know it for sure, I'm fairly certain that this guy is at least an eight or nine. In any event, the distraction works, and the monster heads straight for me.

[Lesser World Python is resisting your efforts to tame it.]

"Tell me something I don't know," I mutter, trying to maintain my focus. The snake rushes closer and closer, and then . . . at the last moment, I cut off the attack and dive to the side, and the snake snaps down on the spot where I was standing. The massive head knocks me to the side, and pain flares through my body.

As I stand up, though, I spot the locust, who has grabbed hold of the dagger and is busy carving a long line down the snake toward its tail. I cheer, only for the snake to spin around and attack the locust. It spreads its wings and attempts to fly, but the snake is too fast. It hits the locust dead-on, and the dagger clatters to the ground as the head rises into the sky to attempt to devour the creature.

Bjorn reacts instantly, though, and bounds forward to grab up the dagger in his jaws. Meanwhile, I snatch up the axe and swing it with all my might. I hit the trunk of the snake, and the blade bites through bone and sinew, cleaving all the way to the street below. The back fifteen feet of the snake are now disconnected, but that's *still* not enough to kill it.

Bjorn, dagger in his mouth, stabs the creature in the belly. My locust falls to the ground from above as the snake screams and spins around to strike at Bjorn. Bjorn nimbly leaps out of the way, and the snake smashes into the street hard enough to crumble part of it into the sewer. I rush forward, ready to end this, and Bjorn gives a twist of his head to toss me the dagger.

I catch it then throw myself forward. The snake hisses and spins to meet me, opening its mouth wide. From tip to tip, it must be four feet across, with long fangs extended. I decide to make those my target. I step to the side and slash my dagger through the left fang, catch hold of it near the top, and drive it down into the bottom of the snake's mouth. It screams and withdraws, shrieking loudly, and I brace myself.

A moment passes, and the snake brings its body crashing down. It hits the ground hard enough to crumble a good bit more of the street into the sewer then begins thrashing back and forth in a dance of death. I try to run, but the great coils of the snake hit me from the side and knock me down then come crashing down on top of me. I can't tell if it's on purpose or by accident, but it feels like it's crushing me into the pavement.

Before I can die, though, I take a deep breath and kick upward with all my might. The snake moves *just* enough, and I roll away and get my footing. Bjorn bounds toward me, leaping across the coils of the snake, and I grab hold of his fur. A moment later, we land safely away from the monster as it continues thrashing back and forth.

Master, it's resisting the venom. Soon it will be able to attack again.

"Then how do we stop it?" I frown. "I can't get close enough to cut off its—Wait." My eyes settle upon a small, rather black lump of chitin not far from the snake's head. "Skill: Rapid Heal."

[Your Locust is fully healed!]

A flash of greenish light shoots down from the sky, and the locust rises back up. It looks around then pounces on the back of the snake's head. I see claws tearing away scales as it desperately fights to bring an end to the thing. Bjorn howls, sending down another blast of cold. Finally, slowly, it gives in.

[Monster Defeated: Lesser World Python, Level 12!]

[You have earned 140 XP!]

[XP needed to level up: 1]

[FireStorm: That's the way, Jason!]

[ChaosRider: Yeah, keep up the good work! You're my favorite, by far!]

[B9: Ahh! Only one more point to level up? That's the worst! Quick, go kill a sparrow or something!]

"I couldn't do it without my faithful friends." I pat Bjorn on the head then motion for the locust to come back over to me. I open the portal, and they both step back inside. After a moment, though, I have the gargoyle step back out. He shrinks himself down and lands on my shoulder, and we turn and start walking toward the main gate.

No other monsters appear to challenge us, which I appreciate. As we come up to the gate, I find several policemen standing guard, all armed with oversized weapons that look like they came from a military armory. Just outside the gate, a priest in a long, black cassock has a large jar of salt, which he's sprinkling in a ring across the entrance.

"Watch the salt," the priest warns as I carefully step across. He steps across as well and gives me a nod. "Wouldn't want to mess it up."

I can't help a bit of a snort. "That works?"

In response, a large, scaly lizard-bird of some sort comes shooting down out of the sky. It stretches out its talons, aiming for the policemen . . . only to hit an invisible wall as it reaches the salt.

Thunk!

It sounds like a bird hitting the thickest pane of glass ever. Its neck snaps rather loudly, and the whole thing falls to the ground, dead.

"Well enough." The priest shrugs then holds out a hand. "Father Brown."

"Jason Lee." I shake his hand back. "I appreciate it."

"If you appreciate it that much, you'll do me a favor." Father Brown smiles. "St. Patrick's Cathedral has been rather overrun by some nasty little gremlins. I won't go along with you and cramp your style, but I'd appreciate it if you could retrieve some items for me. I can write up a list."

I blink then glance at the chat. "What do you all think? Should I take on a fetch quest?"

[FireStorm: Don't do it, Jason! It's beneath your dignity!]

[ShadowDancer: Give him a break! He can do what he wants. We're just watching.]

[GrendleH8tr: Following fetch quests is a good way to locate some really nice loot, instead of just wandering around randomly . . .]

I decide to take GrendleH8tr's advice. Whoever he is, he seems to have a level head on his shoulders. "Just point me in the right direction."

"Wonderful." Father Brown nods and starts to walk away. "I'll be back in a moment."

While I wait on him, the policemen seem to take an interest. "If you're heading out, there's a boat in the harbor with loads of weapons on board. Bring back as much as you can carry, the big stuff only, and you can have your pick of the lot, so long as we get most of it."

Now *that* doesn't take long to get picked up in the chat.

[ChaosRider: Do it, Jason! Do it and you're cool!]

[DarkCynic: Yeah!!! WEAPONS!!!]

I smile and nod. "I'll get it done."

"Excellent."

Father Brown returns a moment later and hands me a long list of items. I whistle as I look over it all. There's salt, crucifixes, and a handful of words that I don't really recognize, which I'll have to look up later. After a moment, I fold the list and tuck it into my inventory.

"You seem like you're trying to go on the warpath, Father."

Father Brown merely shrugs. "In all fairness, most of those items are simply for my ministry here, though . . ." He points as a snake, five feet long, comes up out of a nearby sewer and charges headlong across the street. He makes the sign of the cross through the air, and the snake flops on its back, dead without needing to land a single blow. "If I were to go through and number the *saints* who have battled monsters, we would be here for some time. You might say it's all part of my natural duty as a priest."

"I'll take your word for it." I smile, then turn away and march off into the city, being careful to step over the salt. "I'll be back by sundown!"

"Don't make promises you can't keep," Father Brown calls from behind me.

"I never do," I call back.

With that, I'm off into the city. Fetch quests or not, they were taking me to hordes of monsters and hoards of weapons, and . . . well . . . I figure that on days like this, I can't really ask for much more than that.

CHAPTER FIVE

All around me the cityscape rises, a bit more chipped and desolate than it used to be. Most of the windows are broken now, though some of them have already been replaced by large pieces of cardboard or sheets. I guess people are trying to survive in this world as best they can! Here and there, I see cars that have been pulled back into alleys with their escape routes cleared of debris. People are trying to make sure they can escape if need be, but they are holding tight for the time being. *Interesting.*

[FireStorm: Hey, Jason, you should go explore that bank! I bet there's a dungeon in there!]

[ShadowDancer: And you could pick up some cash while you're at it!]

[ViperQueen: Dummy, money won't be worth anything these days. We'll have to settle on a new unit of exchange.]

[LunarEclipse: Dummy to *you*. I just went out and bought some fried chicken, so there.]

I smile as I read the messages. They're all lighthearted and, as they continue to scroll, are commenting on my various surroundings. I do pause outside the bank and look up at the immense edifice for a moment. It's an old building—one with big Greek columns and wide, now shattered, windows. It certainly looks like the sort of place where monsters would hide, but I already made a deal, so I need to see it through.

"Sorry, guys." I shrug as I turn away. "A deal is a deal. You like when I work with cold efficiency, so that's the nature of things now. If I make a commitment, I go with it."

[GoldenShield: Thattaboy, Jason! Keeping up some morals in the time of the apocalypse!]

[Originalgoth: That sort of talk will get you killed.]

[IceQueen: Wait, didn't Originalgoth get banned?]

[ShadowDancer: You're only just now noticing?]

[GoldenShield: Oh. I thought we were just ignoring that she was back.]

I scowl at the chat, but at this point, I'll admit to being a bit intrigued by the fact that Originalgoth was back. Creating a new account with a new handle is the oldest trick in the book when it comes to getting around streamer bans. But to have the exact same handle? That sort of thing usually isn't allowed, and it means that Originalgoth is either a hacker of some sort, or Riftwatch has a whole lot of problems. Neither one bodes well for me.

"Ban Originalgoth," I speak up quickly. I frankly don't think it will do a lot of good, but I do have to maintain at least an appearance of caring, and I'd like to monitor how long it takes them to get around the ban a second time. Call it an experiment, then.

A moment later, Originalgoth has been banned once more, and I turn my eyes back to the road ahead of me. The cathedral isn't far away, and I draw out my dagger. It's not as large as my other weapons, but it feels somehow nicer, like an extension of my own body.

"Alright, guys," I say as I reach a major cross street and turn to face toward the building. "What do you think I'm going to encounter here, and how many do you think I can take down? I want to see your guesses and then, after the battle, I'll send a shoutout to whoever is the closest."

[ChaosRider: Ooh! I think it's going to be snakes, and you'll kill 20.]

[FireStorm: WAY higher! At least 50! And . . . dwarves.]

[GoldenShield: Wolves again. Definitely wolves, and 12.]

The guessing goes on and on. I give my dagger a twirl, and soon I come into view of the enormous cathedral.

Now, I'll admit, I'm not the type to go to church all that often, but let me tell you: that building is *impressive*. It's surrounded by loads of modern-style skyscrapers, so it almost looks small in comparison, but the *detail* is incredible! There are columns, and arches, and spires, and flying buttresses, and stained-glass windows—all sorts of things that those pillars of glass and steel around it are distinctly lacking. Oh, and statues! Several statues of saints, I think, and then up on top: statues of great big gargoyles!

Fun history fact: Originally, gargoyles were ornately carved downspouts that helped control runoff from the roofs of old churches. I learned that in my history classes back in college!

Fun here-and-now fact: *these* gargoyles appear to be substantially larger, almost ten or fifteen feet tall, and seem like they're primarily there to help crush humans into dust or chew them up into little bits and pieces.

With a piercing roar, two of them jump off the roof and come crashing down onto the front steps, shaking the ground. I brace myself, and I analyze them as best I can.

[Furious Gargoyle, Level 5]

[ChaosRider: Ooh! They're getting bigger and stronger!]

[FireStorm: Who guessed gargoyles? Did anyone?]

I size up the monsters as they take up their positions in front of the door. Suddenly, there's a skittering noise, and more monsters begin to appear from the rooftop. They look like spiders, with long, black limbs that make a clicking sound against the stone. One of them jumps down and lands on a gargoyle, which doesn't really seem to mind it.

[Direwolf Spider, Level 4]

I give my blade another twirl. I'm growing stronger, but I'm becoming concerned that my current pets aren't really going to be of any help here. Well, at least most of them. I open the portal and call one of them forward.

"Bjorn! Heel!"

Bjorn bounds to my side, sizes things up, and tilts his head back and howls. Immediately, a blast of cold air roars through the street, and I rush forward.

[System Notification: Furious Gargoyles are resisting the cold.]

"Then we'll just have to do this the hard way." I reach the steps and pound upward. The spider jumps down, stretching out its claws toward my face. I reach up and grab one of its legs then spin and throw the spider as hard as I can. As it turns out, my strength is starting to get up there, and the thing splats against a nearby skyscraper hard enough to cause greenish gunk to explode across the windows like a bug on a windshield.

[FireStorm: Nicely done!]

The gargoyles snarl and leap at me, and we come together with a great crash. I throw my shoulder into the first one, knocking it backward a few steps then turn and plunge my dagger into the chest of the second. It roars, ignoring the pain, and slashes its claws across my chest. Blood flows freely down my shirt, but I ignore the pain and pull downward as hard as I can. The blade draws a line all the way down through its knobby skin, and I step back as the creature sways and comes crashing down into a growing pool of blood.

The second gargoyle snarls and lunges next. It's still quite close to me, so I take a hit across the shoulders and am sent spinning. I fall headlong down onto the sidewalk, struggling back to my feet as it rumbles downward. Suddenly, I hear its wings flap, and a blast of wind hits me and sends me rolling. As I come out of the roll, I see it flashing downward through the air, aiming straight at me.

I only barely manage to jump out of the way in time, and it smashes into the pavement hard enough for its claws to stick. As I rise back up, the spiders hit, leaping up on me in a great black wave. There are a *lot* of them, and I feel them tearing at my skin, at my clothing, at my bones. I cannot express how badly this hurts. Suffice it to say that I would rather visit the DMV every day for a month than go through it again. Still, though, this is what I'm faced with, so it's what I deal with.

"Enough!" I scream, and I throw my hands out. I activate my Monster Tamer power, and lightning explodes from my palms and begins arcing through the crowd of beasts. Now *this* is where I'm surprised yet again, because instead of just targeting one of them, it starts affecting *all* the spiders that get struck. You know the way lightning jumps from thing to thing, so you can imagine how it worked.

[ShadowDancer: Whoa!!! Is Jason going to get a whole herd of spiders?]

[LunarEclipse: I think it would be a pack of spiders.]

[ViperQueen: No, totally a flock of spiders.]

[ChaosRider: Guys, I just looked it up, and a group of spiders can be either a cluster or a clutter!]

[RazorEdge: A clutter of spiders! I like it! Go, Jason!]

I have to laugh in spite of myself, and I pour every last ounce of energy into my attack.

[Direwolf Spider is resisting your attempt to tame it.]

[Direwolf Spider has been tamed!]

[Direwolf Spider has become enraged!]

[. . .]

The messages come so fast I hardly know what's going on. Behind me, the gargoyle gets its claws out of the pavement and comes lumbering toward me, and I know I don't have much time.

"If you're currently loyal to me, attack something that isn't!"

I know, I know, it's not the most specific command, but it works. A moment passes, and the horde of spiders seems to more or less explode. I can't see what each individual spider is doing, but I can see little bits and pieces of spider getting thrown up into the air or smashed to the ground. Suddenly, I'm not being attacked anymore, and I turn to face the gargoyle. It lumbers ever closer, and I raise my hands once more.

"I already have one of you, but I'm sure he wouldn't mind a buddy. Plus, you're more powerful. I promise this won't hurt. I think. Okay, honestly, I don't know, but—"

I quit talking and activate my power. Several small sparks of energy flicker from my fingertips and die away, and I scowl.

[Monster Taming has been exhausted. Wait 30:00 to use again, and 2:00:00 for full potency.]

"Alright, then. I suppose this will hurt." I shrug then point at it. "Attack!"

Blood drips from my arms as the spiders swarm past me and leap onto the gargoyle. I hear it stumble backward and fall with a crash to the ground, but I admittedly can't see it through the thick clutter of spiders. Blood leaks out from underneath them, though, and I soon get a message that the monster has been defeated.

[You have leveled up!]

[Congratulations! You are now Level 6!]

[Please accept from the following rewards:]

[Level D Weapon]

[Level D Monster]

[Monster Trainer Skill]

I glance at the rewards then up at the cathedral. More monsters are swarming down, both spiders and gargoyles. I point at them and send my clutter of spiders up to face them. I can't count them exactly, but I think there's somewhere around fifty under my command, and a *whole* lot more that are coming down to meet them. We'll see how this battle goes. In any event, though, I have a few spare seconds, which is all I need.

[LunarEclipse: Get a weapon!!!]

[GrendleH8tr: Think, kid. You've got this.]

I nod, ignoring the flurry of advice that comes pouring through, and make my choice. "I want another skill."

[Skill Acquired: Dual Leveling]

[A designated tamed monster will level up along with you! This will not decrease the XP that you receive. The monster may be in a pocket dimension at the time.]

"Perfect." I nod then turn to Bjorn. "Alright, buddy, back inside." He leaps into the portal, and I make my decision. "I want to specify the gargoyle."

[ShadowDancer: Why not Bjorn? He's so cute!!!]

"I have my reasons." I nod to the chat. "For now, though, I need to get moving. I have a job to do."

I run toward the building. My army of spiders has worked about halfway up the edifice, where they're meeting the descending clutter. XP continues to roll in, and I briefly consider climbing up the side of the cathedral, but I decide that it'll be better to wait. Instead, I walk beneath the battle and up to the doors of the church then slowly push open the doors and step inside.

At this point my breath is taken away once more. Inside, it's almost dead quiet, with only a few muffled sounds of chaos from outside and shadows passing across the stained-glass windows. There are actually people in the pews, a lot of them, praying in front of the grand marble high altar. I stop for a moment, and a monk in a brown habit slowly walks up to me from the side.

"Is there anything I can help you with?" he asks, as if nothing at all were the matter. As I stand there, several nuns walk over and begin applying bandages to my wounds, which are dripping blood all over their floor.

"Father Brown asked me to get some things for him." I pull the list out of my inventory and hand it to him. I then take out some medicine and chug another bottle of Pumped! energy drink. My wounds heal as I'm standing there, and the nuns move to cleaning up the blood on the floor.

"I'll have these to you in just a few moments." The monk bows. "Please wait here."

He marches off, and I'm left to stand there, listening to the distant sounds of battle outside. About five minutes pass, and the monk returns. He has a large, cardboard box in his hands, which he passes to me. I slot the whole thing into my inventory, and he bows. "Thank you. Your service is much appreciated."

The nuns bow as well, and they all go back to their prayers. With that, I step back outside, where I find a massive pile of spider corpses that have apparently been raining down this whole time.

There are only a few of them left alive, all hostile to me, and they jump down. I bring out my dagger and cut them to pieces then walk back out into the street. As I do, though, my eye catches sight of something.

Marked out in the middle of the street, beneath the bodies, is a blast mark. At least that's what I think at first, but . . . it's more than that. It's a burn mark, to be certain, but . . . the more I look at it, the more I realize that there's a whole series of them, a pattern, etched across the street.

"Did I not notice that thing before, or is it new?" I ask the chat.

[ChaosRider: Totally new! I'm certain of it.]

[IceQueen: I agree. I don't know how it was burned into

the street *below* all the bodies, and the bodies aren't harmed, but ChaosRider is right.]

More affirmations come from the chat, and I pause, thinking. I can't tell exactly what the symbol is, due to all the obstruction, but to me, it looks sort of like a tree.

"Can someone with good photoshop skills work on cleaning that up?" I ask as I start down the street in the direction of the harbor. "Now, in the meantime . . . it looks like ViperQueen predicted spiders, while FireStorm had the closest guess, so you're both winners!" I smile and give my dagger another twirl, trying to perfect a signature spin move. "Now, start guessing again for the armory ship, because this is going to be a doozy!"

CHAPTER SIX

The air begins to smell salty the closer to the harbor we get. Salty and fishy. I pass several overturned trucks that had been carrying fish from the water up to grocery stores and other such places. Now, only bits and pieces of the fish are left. Apparently monsters like eating raw fish.

[LunarEclipse: Gross! Bleh, fish guts everywhere! I hate fish!]

[ShadowDancer: There are some fresh ones over there, Jason! You should let your monsters out to have a snack!]

I shake my head. "No time for that." The sun is setting in the sky above, so I push onward a bit faster. "We need to clear out that ship before darkness falls. I don't want to be fighting amidst high explosives when I can't see what I'm hitting."

There are a few nods of affirmation in the comments, along with one particular downvote.

[Originalgoth: I think you ought to try it. I'm in the area, and I wouldn't mind seeing a good explosion.]

Amid all the other comments, no one else notices Originalgoth's return, so I refuse to give any particular acknowledgement of it, either. I'm still trying to feel her out, and I want to know what she'll do if I *don't* outright ban her. Build up until she becomes obnoxious again, or just watch from the sidelines?

In any event, I soon come down to the docks, where long rows of metal piers stretch out into the salty ocean. Waves crash and lap against the boats, most of which are actually still intact. A few of them have sunk or capsized, but given the number of tails and fins I see leaping up from the water, I have to be impressed by the boats that are still hanging on.

[ViperQueen: Jason! Turn right, it's the big black boat with a zillion American flags!]

I nod in acknowledgement and turn to follow the sidewalk to the right. As I do so, there's a loud splash, and a fish-ape-thing comes splashing up from the waters. It walks on long fins and snarls at me with a mouth full of teeth. Slowly, purposefully, it lumbers toward me, and I draw back my dagger.

"Time to fillet this fish!"

The dagger slams into the monster and sinks in up to the hilt. There's a sharp gurgle from the fish, and it slowly slumps over to the side and lands on the street with a thud. I walk up and draw my dagger back out then move along at a bit faster of a trot.

[FireStorm: That's the way to do it, Jason! Another cold kill!]

[RazorEdge: I'd like to see some more excitement, frankly.]

[ChaosRider: Just give him time! It'll come!]

"I'm sure we'll have plenty of excitement soon," I answer

as I reach the end of the pier with the boat. It's the only boat that could be the target. There are dozens of flags flying all across it, and the thing has to be the length of three football fields. I smile and start walking down the pier toward it, just imagining all the riches that will be held inside. My feet clang on the metal walkway, and I see the waters below me beginning to swirl.

Suddenly, a sea serpent explodes up from the water and punches a hole straight through the metal! It hisses and spits at me, but I don't give it time to do anything else. Instead, I lunge forward and slash my blade clean through its neck, and the head falls to the walkway with a loud *thunk*. The neck flops down, limp as well, and slowly slides back into the waters. I give my blade another twirl and look down into the waters as more fish and monsters swirl around.

"Bjorn, I could use you again." I open the portal to my pocket dimension, and Bjorn bounds out. "Freeze this place up, would you?"

Bjorn tilts his head back and howls, louder than I've ever heard him do before. Ice explodes across the surface of the water, freezing waves even as they crest against the walls of ships. It also seems to go downward, and I see a much larger sea serpent, with a mouth at least three feet wide, freeze solid only an inch below the waves. It stares up at me through the ice, furious in every sense of the word, until its eyes glaze over.

[You have leveled up!]

[Congratulations! You are now Level 7!]

[Please accept from the following rewards:]

[Level D Weapon]

[Level D Monster]

[Monster Trainer Skill]

I'm a bit surprised by that. Bjorn must have taken out more creatures below the waves than I thought! Though, in fairness, my clutter of spiders also did quite a bit of damage back at the cathedral. I can hear hooves pounding on the ship, so I know I don't have much time, and I make a quick selection.

"A weapon."

There's a flash, and a long blade materializes in my hands. It's a sword made of obsidian, and I give it a twirl. Now *that's* a weapon! I can feel the power held inside of it, and I suspect that it has a few hidden abilities, but I don't have time to figure out what those are. Ahead of me, monsters begin to appear on the deck of the boat, and I rush forward to meet them, ordering Bjorn back into the portal as I do so.

The monsters that come stomping down the deck look rather like minotaurs. Dark flames seem to wreath them, though not quite visibly. I know that sounds weird, just . . . imagine a reflection of fire on the surface of a lake, surrounding an object floating in the lake. That's the best I can describe it. In any case, they look quite furious, and they come pounding down to meet me.

I draw back my newfound sword and meet the challenge. The first one doesn't have a weapon, so I simply drive my sword deep into his chest. He gasps and staggers, then slowly falls to the side, dead before he crashes through the guard rail and falls into the water. I draw the blade out then spin and jump up into the air. My sword cleanly cuts off the head of the next minotaur, and I land and rush forward.

There are a *lot* of minotaurs rushing to get down at me. Thankfully, the ramp leading up to the ship bottlenecks them, which allows me to really use the full set of my abilities. I hack and slash, carefully peeling them apart, cutting up one after another after another. Minotaur body parts soon litter the ground, though there's no end to the horde in sight. Suddenly, I notice that the planks are beginning to sag, so I draw backward. The minotaurs, sensing blood, pile onto the ramp faster and faster.

That proves to be their undoing. The metal snaps and, with a loud crash, dozens of the monsters fall into the sea. They start floundering for shore, but they are quickly gobbled up by monsters in the waters. I smile before I realize that now I have no way of getting onto the ship. I frown . . . at least for a moment.

[RazorEdge: Use your gargoyle!!!]

It seems like good advice to me, so I open up the portal. The gargoyle steps out, drool falling from its jaws, and I notice that it seems to have gotten a bit bigger.

[Lesser Gargoyle is now Level 4!]

[Added Abilities: Mega Flight, Fireball]

"Alright, then." I walk around and climb up onto the gargoyle's back. "Mega Flight me over to that ship, then maintain a safe distance and Fireball those things!"

[ChaosRider: Do you really want to use fireballs around high explosives?]

"I do *not*! Thanks!" I quickly change tactics. A moment later, the gargoyle launches itself into the air, and I find the air nearly sucked from my lungs.

Mega Flight is *fast*. We go shooting up into the air like we were shot out of a cannon then come crashing back down just as quickly. When we land, a shockwave blasts several of the minotaurs off the edge and into the drink, and I leap free while my gargoyle takes to the sky once again. All around me, massive minotaurs gnash their jaws and come charging for my blood, and I rush to meet them.

My obsidian blade flashes in the waning daylight, and I begin systematically hacking my way through the beasts. One after another, they all fall around me until, finally, only a single one is left standing. It turns and starts to flee, so I draw out my dagger and throw it with all my might. The blade slams into the monster's back, making it stagger and fall. I cheer.

"How many minotaurs am I at?" I ask as I retrieve the blade and start looking for a hatch to enter.

[FireStorm: 35 by my count!]

[DarkCynic: No, he's totally at 51.]

[IceQueen: I counted 73!]

I smile as the debate rages. My gargoyle comes crashing down, and it joins me as I reach a padlocked door. Carefully, it reaches out and rips the door off its hinges, and we enter the dark interior of the ship.

I say *dark*. It's actually quite bright where there are still lights, but, unfortunately, there aren't a great deal of lights to go around. Many of them have been smashed, and those that *are* still around are flickering badly enough to hurt my head. On top of that, I can't tell exactly what might have done it, as there are no real identifying marks. No insect claw scratches, no claw marks from gargoyles or griffins or anything like that. I keep my sword and my dagger close at hand, and I steal through the ship as best I can.

It takes me quite a while to find the cargo bay. I'm not terribly familiar with the layout of ships—my only real experience being a handful of video games I've played in the past. I find abandoned bunks, control rooms, radar rooms, a mess hall, and a handful of other rooms whose purpose I can really only guess at. Finally, though, I find a large, sealed bulkhead, and call out my gargoyle once more.

He has to shrink himself down slightly in order to fit through the hall but, soon enough, he manages to rip the door open. With that, I step into a darkened interior, and I find myself looking at enormous piles of green boxes.

Ammo.

Explosives.

DANGER!!!

The boxes are covered in warning labels, and I smile. Slowly, I walk up to the first one and pop it open. Inside are dozens of machine guns, along with belts and belts of ammunition.

[ChaosRider: AAAHHH! So cool! Take it all!]

"Nah. These are too small." I shove the box aside then walk to one of the ones labeled *Explosives*. There, as I flip open the latch, I find bricks and bricks of C4, complete with detonators and switches and all sorts of other things. I smile, then close the lid and slot the whole thing into my inventory. "Time to find out how much I can carry at once."

As it turns out, I can carry quite a bit, and manage to fit ten whole crates of grenades, grenade launchers, bricks of C4, and a few bazookas inside, before I get a rather annoying message.

[System Notification: You have reached the carry limit. To increase this limit, level up!]

"Working on it." I flash a salute to the mysterious and

distant system then turn and start making my way back out of the ship. That, of course, is when I notice that my path is being blocked by a giant tentacle.

Not like a tentacle from a giant squid or something, I mean a *giant* tentacle that fills the whole hallway. It's poking around a bit as it pushes inside, like it can't quite see where it's going. All around me, metal creaks, and I have the distinct feeling that some sort of large, kraken-like thing is trying to crush the ship—and us—like a tin can. This is confirmed a moment later as some of the metal on the outer hull starts to crumble inward, and a bit of water sprays up.

Almost instantly, my chat explodes with suggestions, but I ignore it. I have to work fast if I'm going to succeed. "Bjorn! I need you!"

Bjorn hops out and, responding to my mental instructions, he howls. The ship grows frightfully cold, the lone tentacle that I can see freezes over, and I can hear ice cracking and freezing outside the ship. The slow crumpling of the hull ceases for a moment, and the gargoyle steps up next to me. He grows to his full size, and I climb onto his back. Bjorn hops back into the portal and, with that, the gargoyle spits a ball of fire upward and then activates Mega Flight.

The ball of fire blasts a hole through the upper deck of the ship, and we flash out. As we arc up into the sky, the setting sun casts a blood-red sheen over the land, and I look down at the ship. Sure enough, dozens of tentacles, each at least five feet thick, are wrapped around the vessel. I give one more command, and the gargoyle spits several more balls of fire down at the doomed arsenal.

Four of the fireballs either strike the tentacles or the frozen ocean around the ship. The fifth, though, is dead-on and flashes straight through the hole from which we just emerged. As I said earlier, the ship has a *lot* of ordnance stored on board, and it shows as the whole thing explodes into one enormous fireball.

Oh, how I wish I could describe it in better terms! Metal is torn apart under the sheer explosive power, shredded to bits and pieces, and then vaporized as the wave of heat comes right behind. Fire rolls across the harbor, blasting apart dozens of nearby ships—and then, with one final *boom*, a great column of fire erupts upward like a volcano. The gargoyle speeds away but I look back, watching as the fire fades into smoke. Soon we land on the roof of a building, where we can watch the chaos.

[System Notification: You have defeated a Boss!]

[Reward: Kraken's Ink – Rank A]

[Reward: 5000 XP]

[Reward: Rank-A Loot Box]

[You have leveled up!]

[Congratulations! You are now Level 12!]

[Please accept from the following rewards: (5)]

[Level D Weapon]

[Level D Monster]

[Monster Trainer Skill]

I watch it all with a grim satisfaction then slowly pull out my sleeping bag and spread it out.

"I have a lot to do, and I'm quite tired from the day." I crawl into my sleeping bag and address my fans, "Check back tomorrow morning, and we'll get on with the fight!"

CHAPTER SEVEN

Riftwatch: Welcome to Day 3 of the Apocalypse Protocol!]
I blink as the early morning sun rises, and I stand up and tuck my sleeping bag back into my inventory. I'm still on top of the skyscraper; I glance down at the harbor, where an immense patch of debris and fire damage still marks the destruction of the ship. I smile at the sight, then I turn my attention back to the assorted rewards.

"Alright, folks, everyone ready for me to see what I got?"

[ChaosRider: I've been waiting all night! Go for it!!!]

[ViperQueen: Yeah, Jason!]

[Originalgoth: I bet it's all stuff he's too weak to use anyway.]

The first thing I do is take out Kraken's Ink. It's a small bottle, like you'd see on an old-fashioned writing desk.

[Kraken's Ink]

[Effects: A target will be blinded for 3:00.]

"That's not bad." I nod in approval then tuck it back into my bag. "Now . . . let's save the loot box for last, eh?" I glance at the familiar choice of a weapon, a new monster, or a new skill. I have five I can use, so I'm certainly not lacking for options. "Let's start with a new monster, shall we?"

With a flash, a white horse appears in front of me. I blink for a moment and then smile. It tosses its mane, then leans down and snorts softly against my cheek.

[White Mare, Level 12]

[Abilities: Speed, Mega+ Flight]

"You're a nice girl, aren't you?" I stroke her neck a few times. "You're going to be nice to ride, I think. Alright, step to the side, and let's do another."

The mare obediently steps back, and, with a flash, a large squirrel appears on the rooftop. I'll admit, I do a bit of a double-take, and a flurry of laughter comes from the comments.

[FireStorm: What's that? That's ridiculous! What good could possibly come from that?]

[ViperQueen: A *squirrel?* I thought he was going to get something good!]

I ignore the comments for the time being and look at the label.

[Ratatoskr, Level 12]

[Abilities: Hide, Taunt]

"Interesting." I stretch out a hand and stroke the little critter. He purrs a bit under my palm then leaps into the portal. "Alright, then. I'd say that's enough new monsters. Let's go with a new weapon for number three."

There's a flash of light, and a shield appears in my hand. It has a glistening, rainbowy sort of sheen to it, and I frown. The front side is embellished with the symbol of a tree, something that looks vaguely familiar, though I can't place it.

[Shield of Might, Level 15]

[Abilities: Damage Protection, *Locked*]

I sigh in disappointment but sling the shield onto my back, nonetheless. A shield is still useful, and in only a few more levels I'll be able to use it. For a moment, I ponder my last two selections and decide to go ahead and get two more skills.

[Skill Acquired!]

[Interrogation: You may now speak to monsters you have not tamed, though they may not be willing to talk.]

[Skill Acquired!]

[Random Strikes: You may now spontaneously tame a monster during combat. This is random and is not affected by any factors.]

"Nice!" I pump the air with my fist as the comments explode with a wide range of approving cheers. I pause for a moment then slowly pull out the Rank-A Loot Box.

This one appears on the ground with a massive *thunk*. It's made of solid granite and is embellished with gold and jewels. Whatever's inside is going to be something cool, I'm certain of it. Slowly, carefully, I reach down and flip open all three latches, letting the lid spring open. There's a flash of light, and the box dissolves to reveal a helmet. It's obviously Norse, with the slanted eye holes that define the look, but it seems to be distinctly lacking in the horn department.

[ViperQueen: That's lame! It should have horns!]

[LunarEclipse: Actually, real Vikings didn't have horns on their helmets. True fact.]

[ViperQueen: Doesn't change the fact that it would look cool!]

I laugh, then stand up and slowly drop the helmet over my head. To my delight, it vanishes as it lands, though I can still feel it sitting firmly on my head.

[Helm of the Norse]

[You now have increased damage protection.]

[Your strength has been increased.]

[You speed has been increased.]

[Your stamina has been increased.]

[Any skills that you utilize will be treated as though you were two levels higher.]

No one in the chat comments on the messages, so I can only assume that they've been hidden from them. I'm not exactly sure why, but I decide not to look a gift horse in the mouth. There was probably a reason for omission, and that's good enough for me. Quickly, I gather up my things and order all my monsters except the mare back into the portal.

"Alright." I climb up and take my seat. "We need a new name for you, I think. Do you have a name?"

Lightfax.

"Then, Lightfax: onward!"

The horse stomps her hooves, then crouches and leaps forward. I can't really say that she's *flying*—since she doesn't have wings, and she doesn't exactly glide or fly or anything—but she certainly does have a powerful jump. Buildings flash by all around us as she leaps down from the top of that skyscraper, passing by dozens of streets all at once. As she comes down for a landing, just a few blocks from Central Park, I can't keep a wide grin off my face. Now *that's* cool. What's more, Lightfax isn't even breathing hard as we come trotting up to the entrance of the settlement.

Over the last day, the walls have grown even higher, and I see a ring of salt encircling the whole thing. The policemen look at me in awe as we trot through the gates, and I swing myself down.

"Lots of weapons, as requested." I give a bow and open my inventory, pulling out all ten crates. "I think you'll find more than enough to suit your tastes."

"Thank you!" One particular policeman—I can only assume that he's the chief based on several patches on his uniform—beams as he comes walking up. "When we saw the explosion last night, we just assumed . . . Well, it's good to see you alive and in one piece."

"And you as well." I nod at the boxes. "Hopefully these will keep you alive and in one piece too."

He thanks me again, then joins his friends in looking through all the weapons; I can hardly blame him for his excitement. I start walking away through the settlement, and I must admit, it's turning into quite the place. There are loads of tents set up everywhere, though permanent structures are already beginning to rise as well. Hammers and saws are almost constantly echoing around me as society rapidly rebuilds itself. Even still, I can see that there aren't *that* many people. Some folks seem to like the safety of the park, but others are just staying in their old apartments. I look up to some of the nearby buildings, and I see women hanging out their laundry. For some folks, it's the end of the world. For others, it's just another rather average day in New York City.

"Jason! You're back!"

I turn as Father Brown comes bustling over. I smile and hold out my hand, and he shakes it once more. "I told you

I would be. You'll also be happy to know that nothing has breached the interior of the church, and you had quite the congregation inside, praying."

"Bless them all." Father Brown takes the box as I pull it out of my inventory. "You've done me a great favor, and I'll make sure it gets rewarded. For the time being, I'm afraid I must run. Monster-hunting duty and all that."

I give a slight bow. "Then from one monster-slayer to another, I wish you the best of luck."

Father Brown doesn't say another word, but instead simply takes the box and walks off toward a small group of buildings. I don't follow him. Instead, I mount up Lightfax and prepare to take off once more. The hour is still early, and I imagine that I can clear out at least a dungeon or two more before I have to call it quits.

"Hey! You're Jason Lee?"

The voice is loud and not tremendously friendly. That's not a problem, really; I've never exactly had my share of friends, but it does set me on edge. I turn and Lightfax turns as well, allowing me to look down on what could only be another Awakened.

He stands a good six feet tall, and he has rippling muscles that look as though he were a bodybuilder before this all started. Admittedly, as I look at myself, I've put on a bit of bulk from leveling up ever since this all started, but this guy looks like he could walk through a brick wall without flinching.

"Yeah, I am," I nod. "Who are you?"

[RazorEdge: Who is he? What's Jason talking about???]

[LunarEclipse: That's Harold Min! Hothead!]

[Originalgoth: I keep telling you folks that Jason is only a poser and not the real deal.]

"Who am I?" Harold Min snorts and looks at me as though I have multiple heads. Sidenote: acquiring a skill that gives me an extra head would be really cool. "Who am *I?*"

"Sorry." I shrug. "I've been too busy out fighting monsters to keep up with all the new celebrities. My chat says that you're named Harold Min?"

"Ming!"

[LunarEclipse: My bad, missed a key.]

"Ahh." I hop down from Lightfax. "Harold Ming, then. It's a pleasure to meet you."

"It's not a pleasure to meet you," Harold Ming snarls. "What are you doing here on my turf? I claimed Central Park and all the areas around it! Me! Other Awakened can't be here!"

"Dogs claim territory, too, but that only lasts until another dog with a full bladder comes along." I shrug. "Claim what you want. I'm working here, and I'm not likely to stop."

Harold seems to become angrier. "You'll regret this, Jason Lee!"

"Somehow, I rather doubt that." I slowly pull my hand back, which has been hanging in the air for some time now. I climb back up onto Lightfax, and I turn the great horse toward the city. "Now, unless you'd care to actually stop me, I'm going to go get back to work."

"What's your level?" Harold pulls up his shoulders. "I don't think you want me trying to stop you."

"Twelve," I answer, coolly.

That seems to freeze Harold in his tracks. He blinks a few seconds, and I soon see why.

[ShadowDancer: Harold Ming is only a Level 8! He's good, but not as good as Jason.]

[Originalgoth: If Jason hadn't gotten lucky with that ship, Harold would be better.]

[GrendleH8tr: Are we forgetting that Harold is only a Level 8 because he accidentally blew up a gas station?]

"A level eight, huh?" I cross my arms. "Let's let this be a lesson, then. First, don't insult people if you don't know how powerful they are. Actually, that's terrible logic. Just don't insult people. Secondly, don't get in my way, or I'll crush you like a bug. There are monsters out there that need a proper beating, so it doesn't make sense for us to fight each other. Third . . . No, that pretty much sums it up."

"I challenge you to a contest!" Harold calls out as Lightfax prepares to spring away. "The person who can clear the most dungeons wins! It doesn't count if you kill a boss that's stumbled out into the wild."

I roll my eyes. "And what are the stakes?"

"If I win, you stay away from my territory."

"And if I win, I get . . . something of an unspecified value from you." I shrug, wanting to be done with the petty conversation.

"Deal!"

We don't bother shaking hands. Harold snaps his fingers, and flames erupt around his whole body. He flies up into the air, sort of like a superhero, and goes whooshing off into the city. I watch him go then pat Lightfax's neck.

"Alright, girl. Let's get this done."

Lightfax leaps forward, sailing through the air once more. In the blink of an eye, she shoots straight past Harold as he's flying over the edge of the park. Harold lets out an annoyed cry, but I ignore it. A few moments later, Lightfax touches down a few blocks out from the settlement, and I pat her neck.

"Take me to the closest dungeon."

With that, Lightfax explodes through the streets like a streak of light. She's even faster on the ground than in the air, and I have a distinct feeling that Harold is going to regret ever having posed such a challenge to me.

CHAPTER EIGHT

Lightfax comes screeching to a stop just in front of a massive, rippling gate. Lightning pulses and flickers, and horrible screams come from inside. Some of the screams sound like torture victims; others sound like enraged monsters. Whatever the case, I'm sure I can handle it.

"Alright, girl." I hop down and pat Lightfax on the shoulder. "Best if you head back inside. Garg?"

There's a flicker, and Lightfax ducks back into the pocket realm. As she does so, my gargoyle comes stomping out, and I whistle.

[Lesser Gargoyle is now Level 8!]

[Added Abilities: Mega+ Flight, Inferno]

"You're really beefing up." I pat his arms, which are a good bit thicker than they once were. For that matter, where he once stood only about five feet tall, he now rises to a height of almost ten feet. He's a giant, no doubt about that, and I'm certain that he'll be of immense value in a fight. "Are you ready?"

Garg nods, and we take our stance.

[ShadowDancer: Alright, here comes Jason's rise! First dungeon, let's have at it!]

[Originalgoth: I hope he dies.]

[ChaosRider: Can we ban her again?]

I give a brief nod to the chat. "Ban Originalgoth." I receive a notification that it's been done, and I stride forward. As I reach the portal, I slowly reach out my hand and step through.

Wham!

A dark body collides with me, and I'm blasted back out from the portal and onto the street. Standing astride my chest is a goblin: a nasty, black-skinned creature that looks to be more bones than skin. It opens a wide, toothy mouth and leans down to chomp my face off.

"I don't think so!" I stab upward with my dagger, spearing it through the chest, which does the job. As I toss the corpse to the side, more of the creatures come running out, laughing and chittering and stretching out their little claws.

Garg doesn't give them any quarter.

A brilliant swath of flame erupts from his mouth, burning the asphalt and melting the concrete. Goblins dissolve into ash under the immense blast and, after a moment, the flames die away, leaving only a few drifting flakes. The portal seems clearer now, and this time I step through a bit more carefully.

My foot comes down on the wooden deck of a ship with a loud *plunk.* I smell the salty air even more strongly than at the harbor, and find myself on a Viking ship moored to what looks to be a dark rock protruding up out of the waves. It's hardly even big enough to be called an island: it's just a single chunk of gray slate with a gaping cave mouth. All around, as far as I can see, is water. Dark, foamy, frothy water, with bits and chunks of ice bobbing about here and there. I shudder as a cold wind blows across the landscape, and the sea makes a mournful howl.

"Alright, everyone." I try to keep my composure, and I walk forward toward the islet. As I reach the end, I have to hop to make it onto the stone. My feet slip on the wet slate, but I catch myself, and I haul myself into the cave entrance. My gargoyle, just behind me, shrinks itself down just enough to follow. "Keep a close eye out. I don't want to miss anything."

[ChaosRider: You've got this, Jason! I'm taking loads of screenshots so we can go through it all later!]

[LunarEclipse: Can you send those screenshots to me? I'm watching on my sister's computer, and she has her shortcuts all rewired.]

A torch hangs in a sconce just next to the entrance, which I pick up and hold before me as I start downward. There are no stairs, but the floor slopes steeply, and I struggle to keep my balance. I manage, though, and turn my eyes to the walls, which are covered in Norse runes. At least I assume that they're Norse. They look like something that would be written in a dwarven mine, and from what little I know, most artists base dwarves on the Norse culture, so . . . it's an educated guess?

[FireStorm: Wait! Jason, stop! Go back! I can read this!]

"You can?" I stop and take a few steps back, until I'm near the entrance.

[FireStorm: Yeah! This script was invented by the internet a few years ago. Or maybe the System Administrators gave it to us early so we could prepare! *EEEEEK!*]

"Just translate the words," I mutter. I'm freezing and about to enter the depths of who-knows-what; I really don't want to stand here and listen to a history lesson on how the internet came up with something. From my experience, the internet comes up with something new every few days. It's not worth keeping track of.

[FireStorm: Just a moment . . .]

[FireStorm: . . .]

[FireStorm: Got it! It says . . . I am a dwarf, and I'm digging a hole!]

"What?" I frown. "That's it?"

[FireStorm: Yep! It just repeats it over and over!]

"That's interesting." I start humming as I slowly make my way downward. "Sort of catchy, I'll say that. Someone ought to—"

A moment later, I learn a lesson about idly chatting as I reach the bottom of the slope. I was expecting a much longer descent, though I'm not complaining. There's a wooden door barring my way, and I gesture at it. The gargoyle steps up and smashes it to bits, and with that, I step through into a dwarven mine.

At least, that's what it has to be. It's a massive space— one that I don't *really* see fitting under an ocean, but let's be real: map consistency likely isn't a concern for System Administrators who are busy trying to trash Earth. Anyway, it's a natural cavern, though there are large marks on the ceiling and floor where stalactites and stalagmites were carved away, making the area smoother. Additionally, on the walls, tunnels and buildings have been carved into the stone, revealing a wide assortment of locations to visit and plunder. Sconce torches light the whole area, and I slowly lower my own.

Instead of a torch, I draw out my sword and prepare myself for battle.

The monsters themselves—the dwarves—come marching toward me. There are loads of them, probably at least a hundred, and they are coming from all directions. They're not like normal dwarves; they're tall and slender and have black skin. Really, they just look like taller versions of the goblins that jumped us outside. A few of them are holding hammers, and several have drawn swords.

"Alright, Garg! Let them have it!"

Garg steps forward and opens his mouth, unleashing a great blast of fire that sweeps through the area. Dwarves twist and writhe in the flames as they're engulfed, and I smile in grim satisfaction. Before I can react, though, one of the dwarves throws his hammer at me. It goes by my head and slams into the wall, cracking the granite, and I lunge into motion.

Garg quits exhaling fire, and as the dwarves come charging up, he joins me as I tear into them. I draw my sword and slash it through the torso of the closest dwarf. Instead of flesh or blood, a smoky sort of substance pours out, and the dwarf just sort of dissolves into thin air. Makes cleanup easier, I suppose. I duck as another dwarf throws a hammer, and the projectile hits a dwarf behind me, killing it instantly.

"Hey! That was my kill!" I spin and lash out, carving the monster from top to bottom. It screams and falls backward, dissolving into smoke before it can hit the ground. My gargoyle suddenly flaps his wings and launches himself into the air then gives a mighty *crack* with those same wings. A powerful, concussive blast of air slams into the ground and creates a shockwave that flattens dwarves all around.

Steel meets steel, and on we fight. All in all, despite the great numbers, it doesn't take long to subdue them all. As the last one falls below Garg's claws, I look around. The buildings along the wall largely appear to be functional—dining areas, forges, that sort of thing. They'll be cool, and likely have some good loot, but I don't have time to deal with them right now. Instead, I turn my attention to several dark tunnels that lead downward into the earth. They're all marked with similar runes, and I cross my arms.

"Alright, FireStorm, give it to me!"

[FireStorm: Go to the one on your right! It's marked as a forge, so that's probably where the boss is.]

"That seems logical to me." I walk up to that door, where I find an impossibly steep slope leading downward into the abyss. I test it with a foot and feel my grip slip almost instantly. "Lightfax? I think I need you."

Garg stays out of the portal as Lightfax appears, and I climb up onto her back. With that, Lightfax steps forward, and we go sliding down into the darkness.

Just as I was hoping, Lightfax is able to keep her footing as we go shooting down an impossibly steep slide. For a little bit, we stay inside a tunnel, but soon shoot out into an immense cavern, which is crisscrossed with other slides and stairs. The path narrows to only a few feet wide, and I become certain that a single slip means death. Far below, at the bottom of the cavern, I see only sharp rocks. Suddenly, Lightfax springs forward, jumping away from the slide as we reach a turn, and she sails across a great gap to land next to a small doorway. Garg flies over and lands next to me with a *thud* and, with a bow, Lightfax vanishes back through the portal.

"Alright, folks," I whisper as I slowly walk into the darkened doorway. In the distance, I can hear a hammer pounding. "I think this is it! Stay tuned for the greatest, most epic boss battle you've seen yet!"

As I come to the end of the tunnel and peer out, I find a large, domed room. At the center is the biggest forge I've ever seen—so big that the flames from its fire are what keep the place lit. Hunched over the forge is a hulking mass of a man, who pounds away with a hammer the size of my body.

"Who's there?" he rumbles and pulls himself up. I take a deep breath then slowly step out and square my shoulders.

"I am."

The man scowls then slowly starts to chuckle. "And here I thought it was Loki, coming to check on me again! Ahh, nothing more than another ankle-biter."

"Are you the boss of this dungeon?" I demand.

The blacksmith shrugs. "I suppose you could say that I am, yeah. So what's it to you?"

"I'm here to defeat you."

"Oh, you are?" The blacksmith laughs. "Son, you want my advice? Just—"

My blood begins to get hot. "I said I'm here to challenge you!"

"Alright, alright, don't get your dander up." The blacksmith sighs and pulls himself upright then turns to face me. He's at least twenty feet tall, and he has muscles to spare. Where the butcher was overweight, this guy is solid steel. "Tell you what. You beat me, and I'll forge you something or improve one of your items. Get beat by me, and I'll feed you to Odin's ravens. Deal?"

[LunarEclipse: Odin? Loki? SQUEEEEE!]

[ViperQueen: They're actually keeping it somewhat accurate to the myths.]

[GrendleH8tr: Meh. I see a lot of inaccuracies.]

[Originalgoth: Just wait until you meet Loki's sister.]

"That works for me." I nod and take my stance. "Garg? Let him have it."

Garg launches himself up into the air and spits an enormous fireball at the blacksmith. It explodes across his immense frame, doing absolutely no harm whatsoever. As the flames trail away, he laughs.

"You must be a bigger fool than I thought! I work with fire all day long. I'm immune to—"

By this time, I've made good use of the distraction and have almost reached him. I jump up and drive my sword into his chest . . . Or at least I try to. The blade bounces off a plate of armor underneath his leather forge clothes, and he shrugs as I come down to land.

"Okay, somewhat clever—but not enough."

Before I can move, he swings his hammer and *whacks* me with it as hard as he can. Now, the head of that thing is the size of my torso, so I don't have to tell you that it hurts. A lot. I'm flung across the room, where I slam into a wall hard enough to crack the stone behind me. I slump to the ground, my health bar dropping down into the yellow, and slowly pull myself up.

"Bjorn? If he's immune to heat, he might be weak to cold."

Bjorn bounds from the portal, tilts his head back, and howls. The room instantly cools, and the fire dies down a good bit. The blacksmith chuckles then draws back his hammer.

"Not a bad move, but it won't save you."

He throws the hammer, and I dodge out of the way. The weapon smashes deeply into the wall, but I'm already moving. I know I'll need every ounce of my strength to defeat him, so I pour out all the speed I have. I draw out my shield and throw it as hard as I can, and it bounces off his face. With that, I start to feint right, then spin and dodge to the left. Good thing, too, as the blacksmith stomps a foot down where I was planning on running.

Now that I'm close to him, I draw out my sword and plunge it through his clothing once more. This time, I aim for a spot that's not usually protected by armor, right at the place where his leg meets his torso. It sinks in deeply, and blood spurts forth. He howls in pain, and I yank it free. He stumbles and falls to his knees, with me behind him, and I swing the sword at his neck.

Clang!

The blade crashes against an invisible helmet, much like my own. It jars the sword from my hands, and I gasp. The blacksmith is quick and he reaches back, grabs me, and flings me up through the air toward the forge. I come crashing down on the red-hot plate used for pounding metal, and he slowly rises. The hammer flies out of the wall and back into his hand, and I get the distinct feeling that I know what he's about to do.

I don't give him the chance to do it. As he approaches, I roll off the plate then reach into the forge and grab hold of a hot coal. It burns my hand intensely, but I know I can heal so long as I survive. As the giant comes stomping up, I pull the coal back out and fling it with all my might.

My aim is perfect, and the coal—which is about four inches across—bounces up the giant's nose. He howls in pain and drops his hammer then stumbles back and falls to his knees. Before he can react, I jump up and race forward, toward him. I don't have a weapon in my hands, so he doesn't seem too concerned . . . until I suddenly open my inventory and pull out my axe. I swing it with all my might, and there's a clean *chop* as I sever his head from his body.

The body falls to the floor with a *thump*, and I gasp for air for several long moments. The axe goes back into my inventory, and I give the head a kick.

"I know it's a bit more than a pound of flesh. But, in fairness, I'm *not* Loki."

[LunarEclipse: BURN!!!]

The head simply chuckles. After a moment, the body rises up, picks up the head, and puts it firmly back on his shoulders.

"I've wondered what that would feel like, ever since my old buddy the Green Knight had his fun with old Gawain. Not pleasant, I'll tell you that." I watch as the head heals to the neck once more, and the blacksmith picks up his hammer and starts in at the forge again. "Well, I'm true to my word. Tell me what you want, and I'll get this dungeon closed down." He winks at me, and I feel a surge of something like power rush through me. Power? No . . . *confidence*. "If what I've seen is any indication, even Hel herself is going to have problems taking you down."

CHAPTER NINE

ell herself?" I chuckle a bit. "I thought Hell had already been defeated. You know, the whole harrowing business? Plus, I always thought of the devil as more masculine."

"One 'L,' not two." The blacksmith chuckles as he holds up a hand as if to catch something. "Now, what's it going to be? New weapon, or an improvement to something you already own?"

I pause for a moment then pull out my shield. "Can you tell me what this does? I'd like to know before I decide."

I toss the shield to him, and he catches it out of the air. For a moment, he looks down at the object then shrugs and tosses it back to me. "Bifrost summon. Rather overpowered for a level twenty-five, if you ask me, but that's the way the System Administrators are doing things these days, I suppose."

I frown. "I thought it was a level fifteen."

"The item is a level fifteen. The skill takes a level of twenty-five." The blacksmith shrugs again. "Now, come on. I don't have all day. I mean, technically I do, but—"

"Here." I pull out my dagger and toss it to him. He catches it expertly then places it on the forge. "Do something with this."

[ShadowDancer: OOH! What do you think he's going to make with it?]

[DarkCynic: I bet he's going to turn it into a longsword!]

[Originalgoth: He should just smash it while he has the opportunity.]

"Ahh! Shadow Dagger." The blacksmith whistles as he looks down at it. "That's a nice weapon. Way more powerful than you should have been able to get so early on. About the only weakness it has is that it's so small. Let's see . . . What can I do to get you some more . . . Ah-ha!"

He lifts his hammer then brings it crashing down. There's a responding blast of light, and he picks it up again. Then, suddenly, he throws it into the wall. It slams into the stone, cracking the ancient rock, and he holds out his hand once more. With a flicker, the knife slides out and flies back to his hand, and he turns and hands it to me.

"That ought to do you good. Just be careful. I didn't spend as much time with it as I do with some of my other weapons, so watch which end is pointed at you when it's coming back. Wouldn't want you to accidentally stab yourself or something."

I nod then slide the weapon onto my belt. "I'll be careful." I start to leave then pause. "This Hel. Can you tell me about her?"

"Ahh! She's a scary one, I'll tell you that much." The blacksmith grabs a piece of metal and starts hammering it once again. "Odin's eldest daughter. Thor and Loki's older sibling. You probably know her as Hella; her name gets Anglicized a lot. Nasty bit of work, I can assure you. Once, she locked me up in an ice prison and had me tortured by ice wyrms for a few centuries just because I used a fork incorrectly at a big family dinner."

"Where do I find her?" I demand.

[ChaosRider: That's our Jason, taking the fight to the gods!]

[DarkCynic: They're not gods. This is all just some program. They're like mega-bosses or something.]

[Originalgoth: Don't be so sure.]

[Goatrider: Yeah! You never know what sorts of powers are lurking in the world.]

"Ahh, you don't find Hel. She finds you, usually before you realize that she's there." The blacksmith laughs. "If she takes a liking to you—or more likely, a disliking—you'll feel it. Most likely, though, you're just a little bug in her estimation. I'm sure she's keeping eyes on all the Awakened, but you'll just be one among them. And even then, heroes aren't usually something she worries her head about too much."

I try to think. The chat begins to explode, but I can already see the implications of all of this. These entities—whether they're gods or not, I'll leave up to the way things pan out—are likely behind all this chaos. That means that they'll be coming through the portals at one point or another, trying to crush the world underfoot.

And that means that I: (a) need to become more powerful so I can crush them instead; and (b) need to get to them before they get to us.

"Alright." I cross my arms. "Let's talk, then. If I don't find Hel, who can I find? Which of those entities, or some of the others, would I be able to find and destroy?"

"You're setting yourself up to be a godslayer?" The

blacksmith laughs and rubs the back of his neck. "Oh, this will be interesting. Might even cause as much chaos as that Patrick guy did when he came running around knocking over all their temples. You know what? I'll throw you a bone. The guy you'll want to hunt down is Thor."

[FireStorm: You're going up against the god of thunder?]

[RazorEdge: Boo! I'd rather see him take down Loki.]

[Goatrider: Yes, take down Loki! Loki is much better.]

[TotallyNotLoki: No, I don't think Loki would be a great option. Besides, Thor will be an easy target to take down.]

[Goatrider: WHAT? No, it will be an immense battle! Thor is mighty and will totally crush this guy!]

I roll my eyes at the chat then nod at the blacksmith. "Why Thor?"

"Because I think you actually stand somewhat of a chance against him." The blacksmith shrugs. "Hel will crush you like a bug. Odin would hardly even blink, if he bothers to challenge you at all. Loki . . . I don't know. No one ever knows quite what that guy does. Thor, though, he'll just face you in a straight-up fight." The blacksmith chuckles and goes back to his work. "Plus, he buys all his hammers from me, so even if you do lose and he finds out that I sent you to him, he won't do anything to me."

[Goatrider: Is that so? Is that . . . Hmm. That may just be so.]

[ShadowDancer: Go, Jason! Go take down that lousy Thor!]

[Originalgoth: Yes, go get him! I'd love to see his hammer smash you into jelly on the street.]

"How do I find him?"

"Head to the Empire State Building," the blacksmith answers. "That's not where his lair is, but the dungeon there is full of his minions. With your skills, you'll be able to inter-rogate someone."

I wave at the blacksmith then slowly turn around and walk to the door. As I reach it, Lightfax steps out from my pocket dimension, and I climb onto her back. A few minutes later, we're dashing up and out of the dungeon, into the street. The sun is setting, and I blink in surprise. Apparently, more time passed in the dungeon than I thought. Harold flies overhead, trailing fire behind him. He's followed by several large raptors, and I chuckle as he smashes through the window of an office building in a desperate bid to escape.

"Can anyone tell me how many dungeons he's managed to clear thus far?"

[ChaosRider: Two! Admittedly, he got really lucky and ran into a micro-dungeon, but he's going to count it.]

[FireStorm: You'd better get moving!]

"I agree." I look around, but the buildings around me are too high. "Does anyone know which direction the Empire State Building is in? I'm afraid I don't know New York well enough."

[ChaosRider: Go left three blocks then turn right and go across the river.]

[ViperQueen: What? No! Five blocks then left!]

[IceQueen: Left will take him back to Central Park!]

I watch the chat for a time then pat Lightfax on the shoulder. "Do *you* know where to go?"

Lightfax gives a snort, and she shoots off through the city as though we were shot out of the barrel of a gun. All around me, concrete and steel become a blur, and I find it hard to breathe. We go racing over several bridges, navigating around several large bosses I glimpse stomping around through the streets.

[DarkCynic: Hey! Jason! You should go stop those things!]

[GrendleH8tr: That would only be a Band-Aid fix. Jason has the right idea. He needs to go straight to the source.]

"See? Someone gets it." I nod to GrendleH8tr then lower my head. We plunge onward and soon come racing around to a large street that runs right up to the Empire State Building.

Now, I'll admit that I know essentially nothing about the structure other than the fact that King Kong once climbed it. Though I'm quite certain that in the past, it hasn't had a giant, swirling portal overhead. Lightning lances down from the sky, striking the pinnacle in a constant flow of energy, while a portal seems to have appeared on the roof itself. I can see strange lights inside, and I know that this is where I need to be.

"Alright, folks." I come up to the base of the building and pause. I catch a glimpse of fire among the nearby buildings, and have a sinking feeling that Harold Ming is going to take a stab at clearing the portal before I do. "What should I do? I know! Command: Launch a poll. Option A: Climb the inside and fight everything. Option B: Just go up the outside."

[Option A: 51%]

[Option B: 49%]

The numbers come in after a few seconds, and I pat Lightfax's neck and climb down. "Back inside you go, then." She bows and steps into the portal, and I draw out my dagger. "Before I step inside, I'd like to give this a try. Anyone think I can get it on the first go?"

I don't wait for an answer but draw back my arm and throw the dagger as hard as I can. It sails down the street and slams into a wrecked car, sticking firmly in the metal. I nod then hold out my hand. There's a teeth-rattling screech, and the blade leaps free and comes flashing back through the air toward me.

I squint, trying to watch the weapon as it returns to me. It's only a few feet out when I realize that, just as the blacksmith warned, it's coming blade-first. I yank my hand back, and the dagger flashes right past me. There's a muffled scream and a thud, and I spin around to see several minotaurs stealthily sneaking up behind me. Their leader, a real brute of a fellow, groans and collapses, and I draw out my sword.

The next minotaur lunges at me, but before he can reach, I slash my blade through his chest. He groans and collapses in a heap, blood trickling over the pavement, and I step back and charge once more. This time, I drive my sword deep through the chest of the third, pushing him as hard as I can so that he falls over backward instead of forward.

With that, I hold out my hand, calling to the dagger. I forget, for that moment, that the weapon is stuck underneath the first minotaur. There's a rumble, and the whole body is lifted into the air and thrown at me. Once more, I'm forced to dive out of the way, and the last two monsters are flattened under the corpse of their leader.

I jump back to my feet as soon as I can, and I find the last two minotaurs struggling to stand up from underneath their newfound burden. Thankfully for me, this means that they're unable to strike back, and I quickly cut them down. With that, I turn toward the building, take a deep breath, and charge forward, dagger in one hand and a sword in the other.

Yes, I know it's poor form to dual-wield, and that it means

I have less control, but . . . well . . . it's an immense amount of
fun, and with my heightened strength, I find that it's less of a
burden than I might have thought. I crash through the glass
door at the front and find myself surrounded by a wide variety
of creatures: monsters that must have wandered in from all
over the city. A grim smile grows across my face, and I start
forward.

[ChaosRider: Yeah! Look at him go!]

[FireStorm: Jason is EPIC!!!]

The lobby doesn't take me long to clear and, as I drop the
last giant spider, I hear a crashing noise from the stairwell. The
elevator dings as well, and I glance at the chat.

"Alright, new poll. Elevator or stairs?"

[A: Elevator: 10%]

[B: Stairs: 90%]

"You guys just love punishing me, don't you?" I run to
the door and kick it open, flattening a sprite, and then charge
upward. Here, I find that my blades are a distinct advantage.
The stairwell is so crowded that none of them can really get
any of their attacks together before I cut them down. Below
me, monster parts rain down the open central column,
making a pile down below. I catch a glimpse of worm-like
monsters slithering out of the basement to gobble up all the
monster droppings, and I decide that I don't really want to go
down that way.

I forge steadily upward, fighting my way through monsters that pour out of the different floors of the building like a
never-ending wave. Up above, there seems no end, but I keep
pressing.

[You have leveled up!]

[Congratulations! You are now Level 13!]

[You have leveled up!]

[Congratulations! You are now Level 14!]

By the time I reach the top, my arms ache from how many monsters I've carved through, and I'm certain that my sword and my dagger have both grown dull. Not actually, of course, but it feels like they *should* have. I gasp as I stagger out onto the roof and find the area cleared. A handful of dead monsters lie scattered about and, on the horizon, the sun casts a long, red glow across the city.

"Any idea how many monsters I took out?" I ask as I tuck the weapons back into my inventory.

[ChaosRider: At least 1000!]

[ViperQueen: I installed software that keeps track of it. 1576, over the course of an hour and a half.]

"Not bad." I smile then let out a long breath. "Consider the Empire State Building cleared." I nod toward the portal. "Is Harold already inside?"

[RazorEdge: Yep!]

[DarkCynic: Don't sweat it, though. He hasn't leveled up since you talked to him. Even if you don't look as good on paper, you're crushing him!]

[GrendleH8tr: You really need to rest, kid.]

"What's he doing inside?" I debate running inside to try and clear the dungeon first.

[ShadowDancer: He's trapped!]

[IceQueen: Yeah, they used some ice crystals on him to nullify his fire powers and then locked him up!]

"Then I'm going to get a bit of rest." I pull out my sleeping bag and spread it across the ground then slowly crawl inside.

"Goodnight, everyone! Sweet dreams, and join me bright and early in the morning as I take on this next dungeon!"

The chat goes dark, and I let my eyelids fall closed. I'll take on the dungeon tomorrow . . . And, hopefully, knock Harold down a few pegs.

CHAPTER TEN

Riftwatch: Welcome to Day 4 of the Apocalypse Protocol!]

As I slowly wake up and find myself feeling quite refreshed, I also find myself staring into the eyes of a large, rather slobbery-looking dog. Well, more than a dog: something more akin to a warg. It's huge, it's green, and it's standing right over top of me. Thankfully, my sleeping bag prevents me from any and all harm, so I don't think it notices me, *but. . .*

[IceQueen: Better watch out, Jason, or you'll be eaten for breakfast instead of eating it yourself!]

[Originalgoth: This will be interesting to watch.]

"Indeed, it will," I concur then slowly draw out my dagger. The warg still takes no notice, and I give it a small toss. It sails up and over the monster, landing on the other side with a clatter. Almost instantly, the warg spins around and leans down to sniff it.

At that moment, I raise my hand and call the dagger

back to my palm. It leaps up into the air and strikes the warg through the heart, and the warg drops down to the rooftop. I let out a sigh of relief and slowly climb to my feet . . . and *then* I notice the two other wargs looking at me.

The first one pounces and I leap to the side, punching it as hard as I can as it goes past. My fist doesn't seem to do a whole lot of damage—but it does make the warg stagger—and I spin to the next. That one jumps as well, and I raise my hand and fire a bolt of lightning into its face. Just like always, that makes it stumble as it goes blind, and I punch it in the shoulder as hard as I can.

The warg staggers off to one side, near the edge of the roof, and begins sniffing. I don't give it time to locate me with scent and rush forward to kick it with all my might. The great beast is lifted off the ground and sent sailing off into the air, where it plummets to the ground far below. I then spin back to the first warg, which is charging headlong at me. A simple dodge roll is all it takes to get it to leap off into open space, and I watch as they both fall far below to their deaths.

"Done and done." I draw out my dagger then slip it into my belt and ready my sword. "Is everyone ready for me to enter this dungeon?"

[FireStorm: Go, Jason!]

[LunarEclipse: We're here for you!!!]

I let out a long breath then stalk forward and step through. Energy warbles around me, as always, and a blast of freezing cold air hits me. Still, I push onward, and I emerge into a cold, wooded glade. The trees on the outside of the glade have grown together so thickly that I can't possibly pass through, though I see a small archway made of vines that seems to be a doorway. Snow drifts down gently, and there's no wind. I look around for any foes then slowly walk forward and duck through.

As I enter the next section of the dungeon, I find that things are a bit more dungeon-esque. I'm still in the glade, to be certain, but the area is at least fifty feet wide and probably two hundred feet long, with hide-covered tents standing here and there throughout the area. Cold fires slowly yield themselves to the snow, while at the far end of this strange village, I see a dark cave. I can hear annoyed yells coming from within, though I can't quite tell what they're saying.

I stride forward slowly and purposefully, looking for signs of trouble. I find bones scattered all over the ground, most of which are scorched and burned, though it's hard to tell what they might have come from. Reanimate skeletons? If so, that doesn't bode well for me. I can communicate with monsters, sure, but not magical ones. I need to find someone to talk to, and that means I need to find a monster of flesh and blood.

When I reach the cave, the noises have grown loud enough for me to hear properly, and I pause for a moment.

"You won't get away with this! When I get out of here—and I will—I'm going to crush you all like bugs! I'm going to scatter your little bones from here to Timbuktu! I'm going to—"

There's a sharp *crack*, and I chuckle as I slowly step inside. There's a brief moment where everything goes dark, and then, as it clears away, I find myself standing in a small, circular cave, with a handful of smaller caves branching off. One of these small entrances leads to a simple depression in the wall, where I find Harold standing behind bars made of thick, white ice. Marching around through the middle of the room are skeletons—likely cultists who gave themselves over to the whims of their chosen deity.

"Alright." I clap my hands and clear my throat. "Who'd like to be first in line to get smashed to bits? Any takers?"

Dozens of dead heads swivel in my direction, and they all take up their stances. Some of them have shields, others have swords, some have armor, and some have nothing. One of them, near the back, has a satchel that seems to be filled with crystals. That one draws out an ice crystal, and the whole room seems to chill.

"You know what goes well with ice?" I ask, not really expecting an answer. "Fire! Say hello to my little friend!"

With a flicker, Garg steps out of the portal and opens his mouth. By this point, I think he must be a level ten, and he lets out an enormous gout of flame. Fire crackles and roars around the room, blasting the skeletons into bits. Snow melts outside the cave and comes trickling in. My faithful creature lets off the attack as the last of the enemies die. He steps back into the portal as Harold slowly steps out of the prison, and I walk down to meet him.

"This dungeon is mine!" Harold snarls as I approach.

"I have a Frost Wolf. I can lock you up again just as easily as I got you out," I comment as I walk past him toward the entrance that I'm fairly certain leads to the boss chamber. "Now, you can either come with me and help me clear this place, or you can go run home and let me have all the fun. I'm honestly okay either way."

Harold grits his teeth so loudly that I can hear it, but he follows along. We slip through the darkened cave entrance and begin to descend. After a short distance, the air grows even colder, and we step out into a large pit.

The pit has an open top, through which snow is drifting down lazily. Ice clearly rims the lip of the pit, preventing anyone from jumping up and escaping that way. As we enter, a stone comes crashing down across the entrance, and I look a bit more closely at our foe. There's not much in the pit except for a throne—and upon the throne, the skeleton of a man who must be at least ten feet tall. Bones click together as the body pulls itself upright and draws up an enormous axe. I scowl.

"No! I need someone I can talk to!"

"You can talk to me," the skeleton rumbles.

"And who are you?" I demand. "You don't look like anything but a lackey of Thor, someone who gave up their life needlessly for him."

"I wouldn't say *needlessly*," the skeleton banters at me. "I find this body quite useful, actually."

Harold has the realization at the same time I do. "Thor is speaking through that thing!"

"Then we'll just have to tear it apart and figure out if there are any clues we can follow." I grit my teeth and charge forward. "Don't hit me with your fireballs!"

Harold snaps something, but I'm not listening. Behind me, he rises into the air and throws several large fireballs at the skeleton, which the monster causally bats away with his axe. Our foe then draws the weapon back and sweeps it across the ground in a great arc, trying to hit me.

I jump upward as the weapon nears, and it passes under my feet. As I arrive at the skeleton, I draw out my sword and bring it crashing down on the creature's right arm. Bone shatters under the blow, and the whole limb drops to the ground.

[ChaosRider: Alright, Jason! Great dismemberment!]

[DarkCynic: WATCH OUT!]

I heed the warning and try to jump back. Several things happen at that moment, though. First, the skeleton's arm, which I had ignored, grabs hold of my heel, making me fall backward instead of jumping. Meanwhile, the skeleton's other arm, which is still holding the axe, makes another swing backward at me.

The blade passes narrowly over my body, so close that I can feel the wind from the attack. I shake off the skeleton's hand and jump back up then charge forward and bring the sword up once more. Before I can attack, though, a fireball hits me from behind and makes me stumble, crashing down to land at the thing's feet.

The skeleton doesn't hesitate, and it stomps down on me with all its might. Bone slams against the invisible helmet, and though I do still feel a good bit of the impact, I survive, which I suspect may not have happened if I wasn't wearing it. This seems to stupefy the skeleton, and I jump back to my feet, then grab hold of one of the leg bones and give it a yank.

The bone splinters under my grasp, and I flip it around to hold like a club and smash it over the skeleton's head. It staggers backward once more, and I throw the weapon aside, then draw out my own axe, lift it up, and bring it crashing down. My aim is true, and it shatters the skull and splits the whole desiccated body down the spine. Bones clatter to the ground left and right, and I let out a sigh of relief. Slowly, I take a step back . . . and then pause as the bones begin to shudder.

I watch, annoyed, as the pile pulls itself together. Bone fits back into bone and, within a moment, the whole thing has reassembled itself. The construction chuckles loudly then picks its axe back up.

"You may try to defeat me, but without the right weapons, you cannot harm this body!"

Harold lands next to me and thrusts out his hands. An immense inferno explodes across the ground and wreaths the skeleton in flame, but as near as I can tell, the fire seems to hit some sort of a barrier just a few inches from the bone itself. The structure is being protected, likely by its connection to Thor. I scowl for a moment, trying to think then glance at the chat.

[LunarEclipse: Oh no! Jason doesn't have any blessed weapons! If only Father Brown was here!]

[Goatrider: Behold! The mighty Thor will now win this battle!]

[Originalgoth: He's not fighting Thor, you idiot.]

[Goatrider: Oh! Right! He's . . . um . . .]

A thought strikes me, and I scratch my head. "Is there anything that would allow the gods themselves to access the livestream chat?"

[GoldenShield: Um . . . Don't know why they wouldn't be able to!]

[Goatrider: I'm very certain that they cannot!]

[TotallyNotLoki: They totally can.]

"Alright, then." I think for a moment. "Would someone tech-savvy be able to ping Goatrider's location?"

At that, the skeleton lets out a roar and lumbers forward once more. Harold continues blasting the thing with fire, which continues to not do a thing. It gives me an idea, though, and I put my hand on Harold's back.

"Whatever happens, just keep blasting fire, alright?"

"Alrigh—"

Before he can think about what's happening, I shove him forward. He crashes into the skeleton, a move that surprises both of them. His fire, pushed through the protective barrier by my attack, suddenly burns through the dried bone like kindling, and in a mere instant the whole thing is reduced to ash.

[System Notification: You have defeated a Boss!]

[Reward: 1000 XP]

[Reward: Rank-A Loot Box]

I smile and take a bow as my livestream chat explodes. I hold out my hand to accept the loot box and, with a flash, a chest appears on the ground.

"Hey!" Harold snaps. "I was the one who made the kill!"

"You were the weapon that got the job done. I don't know if that counts." I shrug. "Still, though, you probably should get something. Let's see what we've got here . . ."

I flip open the chest and, with a flash of light, I find a bow lying on the ground. It's an elegant weapon, made out of a dark, stained wood. As I pick it up, I find that it's as light as a feather.

[Weapon Acquired!]

[Elven Bow, Level 30]

I smile, then raise the weapon and draw back the string. An arrow appears to fit into my hands, and I point it upward and fire. The arrow, made of wood just as dark as the bow itself, flashes up into the great void of the sky, and I whistle as it vanishes.

"Ahh! Just a stupid old bow," Harold mutters as he stalks away. "You can keep it. I'm at three dungeons now; you're at two."

I shrug as he vanishes. "Not my problem now, I suppose. You can keep track. I'm just going to focus on getting to Thor. Any luck with that handle?"

As I walk back through the dungeon, trailing a bit behind Harold, an answer suddenly comes.

[IceQueen: Yes! I was able to hack into the location software, and it looks like Goatrider is located at the MOMA.]

[ShadowDancer: What's the MOMA?]

[IceQueen: Museum of Modern Art.]

I blink. That's right next to Central Park! It's one of the few landmarks I do happen to know. A few moments later, I'm out on the roof. Harold flies down toward what looks to be a smaller dungeon, but I have bigger fish to fry. If he beats me in his little dungeon contest, so be it. I never exactly accepted the challenge anyway, and . . . well . . . I'd rather take down Thor. Lightfax steps out onto the roof next to me, and I climb up.

"Away, my fair steed!" I order. "Let's go catch us the biggest boss of them yet."

CHAPTER ELEVEN

've been to the MOMA before, back on a high school trip years ago. It's down by Central Park and, as Lightfax and I flash past the walls, I reflect on what I know of it. It's an odd building, from what I remember. You actually go inside and start at the top then work your way downward. The art is oldest at the top and newest at the bottom. In that way, I think the whole building is set up as an allegory, an art piece in and of itself, depicting Dante's layers of hell.

Have I mentioned that I hate modern art? I mean, come on. A banana duct-taped to a wall is just a piece of fruit that's going to rot. I digress, though. As I come racing up to the entrance, I find myself feeling apprehensive. Why would the god of thunder make his domain here, of all places? There are so many great landmarks in New York; why come *here*? I assume I'm about to find out, though, and I hop off Lightfax and take my stance in front of the doorway.

[ChaosRider: Alright, this is the showdown of the century! Jason vs. Thor!]

[Originalgoth: Jason is going to get crushed like a bug.]

[Goatrider: Behold, the mighty THOR!]

There's a long pause, and no one dares to type anything else into the chat. I keep a close watch, looking for anything, but nothing appears.

[Goatrider: Hang on for just a moment. Left my hammer back in Asgard. It'll be here in a second.]

"Then now's my time to strike." I run forward and call out Garg. He appears, huge and scaly, and launches a fireball that blasts through the main entrance.

I go charging inside, only to find that it's a bit different than the last time. The whole building has been hollowed out, with all the assorted pieces of artwork piled together to make a sort of throne at the far end of the building. Seated upon the throne is a hulking mass of a man with long, flowing, golden locks of hair, and muscles to spare. The only odd thing about him is the smartphone in his hand and the soft tinkle of music.

"Ahh! Just a second. Sorry, thought that door would be stronger." Thor slowly stands up, his fat fingers struggling to type on the tiny phone. "They should really make larger versions of these things for us giants. Just . . . ahh . . . have to send Heimdall a text . . . This is really embarrassing, let me tell you."

"Are you . . ." I blink a few times. "Are you playing a match-three game?"

"Match four! I upped the challenge level, since, you know, I'm a god," Thor chuckles, continuing to refuse to look up from the phone.

"Alright." I'm a bit confused, and Garg steps in behind me. "Come on. Let's take this guy on."

I throw my dagger with all my might and charge forward. Garg launches a fireball at the same time, and together we race toward the mighty Thor.

At least . . . we try to.

Thor simply raises a hand and catches my dagger then drops it to the ground. The fireball detonates harmlessly against his body, and a bolt of lightning erupts from his forehead and hits me in the chest, knocking me to the ground. Let me tell you, that *hurts*. My limbs spasm a bit as I try to get them working again and slowly force myself back to my feet.

"Patience," Thor scolds me. "Just . . . just a minute . . . and . . . there we go!"

[Goatrider: Now you will face the wrath of the mighty Thor!]

[Originalgoth: e_e]

[Originalgoth: I can't believe we're related.]

I sigh, then order Garg back into the portal. Thor tosses the phone to the side and comes down to meet me. I draw back my sword then rush forward.

CRAAAAAAASH!

A blast of rainbow light explodes through the room, and the ceiling caves in under a brilliant explosion. The light hits right in front of me, and I'm thrown backward under the impact. As I climb back to my feet, I find a large hammer sitting on the ground, rather like the blacksmith's but a bit smaller. Thor holds out his hand, and the hammer flies up to smack into his palm.

"There we go!" Thor smiles. "Now, let's get this beatdown started!"

I grit my teeth. Something tells me that this is going to be a bit harder than I anticipated. Still, I rush forward, ready to give it my all. As I near him, Thor lashes out with the hammer, trying to hit me squarely in the chest. I drop to the ground and slide under the attack, but just *barely*.

The other bosses that I've fought have all been slow. Their attacks, though large and powerful, come slowly and predictably. Not so with Thor. I haven't even come up from my slide before I find the hammer arcing down to meet me on the floor, and my life flashes before my eyes. Desperately, I kick to the side, and the hammer hits the ground where I was just lying. A shockwave rolls out from the point of impact, picking me up and throwing me backward across the ground.

"I told you!" Thor crows. "You'll never defeat me!"

"Pretty sure you haven't told me that." I climb back to my feet and stretch out my hand. My body already hurts, but I make sure to hide it. The dagger sails back and smacks into my palm, and Thor's face becomes angry.

"He actually gave you that enchantment? That's *my* thing!"

"And now it's mine." I shrug. "Catch!"

I throw the weapon once more, though I'm hoping it will mostly just serve as a distraction. Thor whacks it with his hammer, sending the dagger zinging out through a wall as if the concrete were mere paper. I hear other things cracking and smashing under the impact, but I ignore them, and I bring up my sword to strike. Power seems to surge through it. Thor swings at me once more. I duck, and I drive the sword into his leg.

Thor screams in pain, and I push the blade in as far as I can. This, unfortunately, leaves me very close to him, and he punches me with his free hand. I'm thrown backward, feeling the impact in every part of my body. I instinctively stretch out

my hand for the sword, but it doesn't have the same enchantment and stays right where it is. Thor slowly stands up, fire
in his eyes. No . . . lightning in his eyes. Electricity begins
to burn up and down the length of his arms, and he comes
charging forward.

Quickly, I pull out my shield and come up to meet him.
He lifts the hammer and brings it crashing down, and I catch
it. Now *that* hurts. I keep my footing, mind you, but pain and
electricity burn through every sinew of my body. I'm driven
backward, and power suddenly explodes outward. As I stagger backward, I find the walls start to crumble, and my shield
flickers with suppressed energy. Thor snarls and raises his
hammer once again and, without any other options, I throw
the shield into his chest.

When it hits, a blast of energy rings out, and a Bifrost bolt
explodes upward, catching Thor in the face. He's lifted off
the ground, and I catch the shield, spin, and throw it at him
again. This time, it hits him in the chest right as he lands, but
the energy of the shield has been depleted. I can only assume
that the lightning charged it up and activated the skill even
without my consent. Works for me, in any case. As Thor is
struggling to rise, I rush forward, grab up the sword, and raise
it over my head to strike.

I bring the weapon down, and Thor blocks with the hammer. Lightning explodes along the length of the blade, and I
struggle to maintain a grip. I feel my hands starting to burn
under the attack, and I gasp. Finally, I disengage, then stab
downward as Thor stands. The blade pierces his chest, but
he whacks me with the hammer again. This time, I'm blasted
right through the crumbling wall and out onto the street,

where I land in a heap next to a manhole. There's a flash, and the hammer comes crashing through the wall just below where I came through, causing the whole wall to crumble. Thor stalks through the rubble, the hammer hits the street just next to me, and I have an idea.

It's not a good idea, but it's something.

Desperate, I hook my fingers into the manhole cover, rise, and throw it with all my might. Being little more than boring old Earth metal, it crumples like a piece of paper when it hits Thor in the face, and he laughs, reaches up, and peels it away. At the same time, though, I hold out my hand for my dagger. I hear crashing noises from a distance, but I can't tell exactly where it's coming from.

"Give up now, and I shall think about letting you live." Thor holds out his hand, and the hammer flies back up to his palm.

"Never." I grit my teeth. A moment later, a flock of pigeons explodes up into the air from a nearby rooftop, and my dagger comes back to land in my hand. I take a deep breath and bolt forward, aiming for my shield, which is still lying on the ground.

Thor laughs then holds up his hammer. A single bolt of lightning flies up into the sky, and dozens come crashing back down, striking all over the square. An idea hits my mind, and I throw my sword at the giant. It hits him in the shoulder, and while it doesn't stick *well*, it does turn into a lightning rod for a brief moment. Thor yelps in pain, and I dodge around him and reach my shield. Quickly, I scoop it up, then jab my dagger into the straps on the backside. With that, I charge back toward Thor, holding the weapon tightly.

Thor reaches up and yanks the sword free then snaps it with his hands and tosses the shards away. I respond by throwing the shield up at his face again. Unsurprisingly, he simply bats it away with his hammer, causing an explosion of lightning as he does so. That uses up his movement as I duck around behind him and leap up onto his back. Desperately, I grip the folds of his clothing and haul myself up onto his neck. Thor simply laughs then throws his hammer out into the street. He stretches out his hand, and I get the feeling that I know exactly what trick he's about to use.

Thankfully, I have my own trick first.

My dagger, still stuck in the straps of the shield, whirs back to my hand, bringing the shield along with it. It hits Thor in the face and detonates again. Now, Bifrost energy is nothing to mess with—especially when it's not being directed—and I'm knocked off his back and sent tumbling through the rubble. As I struggle back to my feet, blood drips down into the dust. Thor, however, looks in almost as bad of a condition. He's lying on the ground as well, and slowly struggles back to his feet. The handful of wounds I've inflicted are all dripping blood, and he snarls and turns to me.

"That was a mistake, boy!"

He strides forward, and I hold out my hand once again. My dagger, free of my shield, lands in my hand with a *smack*, while his hammer returns to his own hand. He starts to run then leaps up into the air. His hammer flickers with electricity, and I have the distinct feeling that I'm the target for every last kilowatt.

"Not . . . today . . ." I groan then draw out my Kraken's Ink and hold it up. "Target Thor."

The bottle dissolves, and Thor's eyes suddenly go dark. Now, if he had only continued on his trajectory at that moment, he would have easily smashed me into the ground without a thought, but being temporarily blinded startles him enough that he overshoots. Instead, he lands on a pile of debris just a few feet away from me, crushing concrete down into dust. The shockwave picks me up and tosses me away again, lowering my health down to just a sliver above the red. As I open my eyes, though, I find myself just a foot away from his hammer.

[ChaosRider: This is gonna be great!]

[Originalgoth: Indeed, this is going to be a battle worth watching. I'll enjoy seeing his blood spill through the streets.]

[TotallyNotLoki: Grab the hammer!]

[GrendleH8tr: Kid, take your time, think this through, and—]

I'm pretty sure that last message would be helpful. GrendleH8tr always has great advice, but . . . well . . . I'm in a hurry and about to die, so I stand up and do the only thing I can think of.

I grab the hammer.

Now, I won't lie: it hurts. Lightning explodes down my arm. The hammer is heavy, but I lift it, nonetheless. Thor staggers to his feet and, still blinded, stretches out his hand. Suddenly, the hammer starts to pull toward him, but I brace my feet and hold on tight. It pulls against me, and I fight it with every fiber of my being.

"Come on," Thor rumbles. "Come on! I can feel you! Come back to me, my weapon!" Thor keeps his hand stretched out for a moment then slowly lowers his hand. "Kid must have run. I bet the hammer is stuck in the sewer again. I'll have to tell that serpent down there to stop eating everything that—"

Before Thor can say anything else, I draw back my hand and throw the hammer with all my might. It connects with his head, and an immense blast of light explodes upward. Really, it's a proper sky beam, in every sense of the word, with Thor at the exact center. As it fades away, the hammer falls to the ground, and Thor sways, weary.

"Away!"

I don't know what the word means, at least not for a moment. Suddenly, there's a flash of Bifrost light, and a sleigh appears in the sky. It looks rather like Santa Claus's sleigh, though it's pulled by a herd of goats rather than reindeer. With a flash, it comes shooting down, and Thor leaps upward. The goats fly underneath him, catching his bulk perfectly. With that, he goes shooting back up into the sky. I watch my prey leaving, and I ball my hands into fists.

[Originalgoth: What a coward!]

[ShadowDancer: Agreed! Run like a little whelp, and never come back!]

"I'm not letting him go," I mutter. I hold out my hand, and my dagger flies back into my palm. I then locate my shield, which isn't far away, and watch the sleigh fleeing through the sky. "If he runs, he'll only hurt more people, and I'm not going to tolerate that. I'm tracking him down, and I'm going to kill him."

CHAPTER TWELVE

I walk away from the ruined MOMA, trudging through the debris back toward the entrance of Central Park. As I do, something catches my eye: perhaps the only painting that I've ever actually cared about from the modern era. Slowly, I bend over, and my hands find purchase on *The Starry Night*.

[ChaosRider: WHOA!!!]

[FireStorm: Is that what I think it is? You should keep it!!!]

[LunarEclipse: Don't worry, we won't tell!!!]

[ShadowDancer: You've earned it!]

I shake my head as I walk toward the gate once more. "First off, what would I do with a painting? It would only take up an inventory slot that I can't afford to waste, and I don't think it'll be terribly useful in taking down monsters." After a moment, I continue, "Besides, if I take it, no one else will be able to enjoy it ever again. Isn't that the point of this livestream? So everyone can enjoy these exploits? This belongs where people can all view it."

[RazorEdge: You said it!]

[GoldenShield: Who do you think you'll give it to?]

I don't give any further answers to the many questions that come my way and soon come walking up and into the gate. I carefully step across the ring of salt then hold up the painting as people begin to gather around. I see their jaws dropping in shock, and I have to allow myself a bit of a smile.

"Lucky you!"

"I want it!"

"I've got . . . one hundred bucks, right here!"

"No." I shake my head firmly. "Where's . . . where's a good public place to put this?"

Dozens of suggestions are thrown out. I offhandedly reject some of the outdoor map kiosks, as the people suggesting those places are quite obviously just wanting to steal it for themselves later. In the end, we settle on a small theater nearby and place it in a dressing room for the performers, where it's safe from the weather; several policemen set themselves up as guards and start working on charging an admission fee. It's an odd thing, but it feels a bit like the old world is still hanging in there.

Actually, as I leave the theater and start walking around the park, I'm noticing that it's really a *lot* like the old world. As the shock of things is wearing off, people are starting to leave the park and venture back into their old apartments. I even see several people carrying a window across the street to start fixing things up. After all, the monsters mostly stick to the streets, and as the Awakened are getting their feet underneath them, those very streets are becoming a whole lot safer.

"Hey! You!"

I look up to see Harold Ming dropping down from the

sky. He lands with a flourish—a perfect superhero pose—and stands up. I raise an eyebrow at his theatrics, but don't comment.

"How many dungeons have you cleared out so far?" He strikes a pose. "I'm up to five!"

[FireStorm: Three of those are micro-dungeons, and one of them is the one you saved him from.]

"Depends on your definition of the word, which seems to be somewhat of an issue with you," I answer, not really wanting to engage him. "Now, do you actually want something, or are you just going to stand in my way and blow hot air?"

"I just wanted to see how our little competition was going." Harold continues to stare down at me as if I were a child.

"Alright. Well, now you know." I step around him and start walking across the park once more. "Now, if you'll excuse me, I'm going to head back out there and try to get some work done. Save the world, all that jazz. You know the deal."

[System Notification: Now that you've all been given some time to adjust to this new world, we are pleased to announce that the very first Rift will be opening!]

"What's a Rift?" Harold frowns, looking confused. I'm pretty sure I can figure it out, but I hold my breath nonetheless as I wait for confirmation.

[System Notification: This first Rift will be F-Ranked. Easy peasy, to continue helping you get your feet wet. In addition, all dungeons outside the Rift in this part of the world will close in order to allow Awakened to focus more on taking it down. This grace will not be repeated in the future, so take advantage of it while you have the chance.]

As the notification fades away, there's an earsplitting

crackle-squeeeeeeeeeee, and a bolt of lightning brighter than the sun flashes across the sky. I make the mistake of looking up at it, and it takes several seconds before the spots clear from my vision. As my sight returns, though, I find myself looking down toward the harbor, where brilliant lights—something like a portal, but a thousand times brighter—are flashing off the building walls. I can't see the portal itself, but it must be simply enormous.

Harold, next to me, leaps with glee. "Let's get moving!"

He explodes with fire, some of which singes my pants, and flashes up into the air. With that, he flies off toward the light, but I stay put.

[ViperQueen: Come on, Jason! Get to it!]

[ShadowDancer: Yeah, you don't want him getting to the prize first, do you?]

I shake my head. "He won't. He might get to the entrance first, but . . ." I start ambling toward the gate of Central Park. Another Awakened, a man wearing a bearskin cloak, rushes past me and clears the wall in a single leap. "The race isn't won by the person who passes the midpoint first. In fact, that person usually tires themselves out." I come up to the gate and pause for a moment, just watching that flickering reflection. "Look at the facts. The System Administrators are closing all dungeons outside this Rift. That means that it's going to be tough, and it's going to take a long time. Given the unknown, I'd rather let other people go charging in first to scope things out, you know?"

[LunarEclipse: Ahh, that's smart!]

[GoldenShield: And cold, Jason! Sacrificing others for your own gain!]

"Not sacrifice," I answer. "I'm just trying to benefit from other people being stupid, and to avoid being stupid myself."

The chat seems to explode. Some people continue to urge me onward; other people comment on how I'm doing the right thing. At the end of the day, I have to make my own decisions. I open my portal and allow Bjorn to step out. The Frost Wolf tilts his head back and sniffs the air, and I scratch him behind his ears.

"What do you think, buddy?" I ask softly. "Do you know anything about this?"

Only a little. All the dungeons are more or less interconnected on the back end, if you know what you're doing. The Rifts are worlds in and of themselves. None of us have ever been in one, and that's by design. The sculptors don't want anyone spoiling their secrets.

"And what little *do* you know?"

About the same as you. They're big, they're dangerous, and they'll take a long time to clear.

"Alright, then." I puff out my cheeks and glance around. A flash of black flickers in my vision, and I find myself facing Father Brown, slowly ambling up in his flowing cassock. I dip my head in respect, and he returns the gesture. "Father? Something I can do for you?"

"No." Father Brown shakes his head, staring out at the flickering lights. "I simply came to see what was causing all the hubbub. Your presence here is merely coincidental."

He stands there for a moment longer, then reaches over and scratches behind the ears of Bjorn. The wolf seems to love the attention, and lets his tongue loll out of his mouth.

"You're okay touching that thing?" I raise an eyebrow. "It

was once a slobbering monster that only wanted to eat every-thing and everyone."

The priest simply shrugs. "The illustrious Francis de Sales once spoke concerning the natural world. In nature, every-thing that has been created contains both good and evil. It seems that you have a particular talent for dispelling that evil and bringing out the good, and for that, I can hardly find any fault with you or your pets." He pauses for a moment then slowly gestures toward the portal. "These holes that have been torn through our reality . . . Perhaps I am not so con-cerned about them because *prior* to all of this, I fought *daily* against portals of a far more malicious variety—the types that vomited forth monsters intent on devouring *souls*, not simply these mortal bodies."

"What are you trying to say?" I ask him, confused.

"I'm simply trying to provide a warning." Father Brown shrugs. "I know not what these things are, and I don't know what you'll find inside. The physical side of things I'm sure you can handle—you certainly seem skilled enough with a blade, so I offer no particular advice there. On the mental side of things, though, I simply warn you to *be careful.* These Administrators, as much as they seem to be on our side of things . . . there are few options that I can see regarding their involvement, and none of them really paint them as being truly on our side. If they've opened this Rift, it's with the intent of killing people inside. Do not trust anything that seems to be fair or good, unless you have first tamed it. Even then . . ." Father Brown gives the wolf another scratch. "Just be careful."

"And here I thought clerics were all about trusting

everyone!" I laugh as I step over the salt ring and start walking down the street. Bjorn follows, and I draw out my dagger. I miss my sword, but such is life.

"We speak of loving everyone, protecting them." Father Brown's voice has a light, almost joking tone. "Because of that very fact, we trust *no one*."

I laugh back at him, though I can't really tell how serious he's being. What I do know is that I need to get down to that portal, need to get inside, and need to stay cautious—as I've been doing—but destroy everything that I find inside. I reckon that enough time has gone by for the jump scares of the Rift to be revealed, so I start to move a bit faster.

Whatever this thing is, it must be destroyed . . . and in that duty, I shall not slack.

CHAPTER THIRTEEN

GoldenShield: WHOA!!!!!!!!!!!!!!!]

[ShadowDancer: Is there any form of punctuation that's stronger than an exclamation point? Because if there were, I would use it!]

[ViperQueen: It's awful!]

[Originalgoth: It's beautiful!]

[GrendleH8tr: Stay safe, kid.]

I let out a long breath as I stand in Times Square, looking up at the Rift. It seems to have replaced the gargoyle dungeon from earlier, or perhaps someone else closed it. In any event, the portal is massive: a rippling tear in space-time that stretches from the street all the way up to the peaks of the skyscrapers, wide enough to drive three busses through side-by-side. Lightning flickers around the edges, while the open interior is a mass of shadows. As I approach, a message appears.

[Warning: You are approaching a Rift. Level: F. This area

is extremely dangerous. Only proceed if you are willing to risk your life.]

I wave my hand to dismiss the warning, and I slowly stride forward. As I reach the edge and step through, energy surges through my body. Entering a portal is always kind of funny, as if your body is being pulled across multiple dimensions, twisted and distorted and sucked through a fourth-dimensional tube—but this one is even worse. As I pop out on the other side, I find a bit of smoke rising from my clothes, and I pat it away as I take in the situation.

All around me, combat reigns. The portal now stands just behind me, marking the exit of an extraordinarily large cave. I mean, this cavern is huge—hundreds of feet across—though, conveniently, there are almost no stalagmites across the floor, which makes the terrain easy for combat. Bodies of several Awakened lay strewn about amidst the corpses of monsters, but largely, the Awakened seem to be holding their own.

Across from the portal are large, gaping mouths that lead deeper into the cave system. Spewing from said caves are hordes of monsters of all shapes and sizes. I see goblins and slimes, kobolds and lizard-folk, and a great deal more. I brace myself and twirl my dagger then charge forward into battle.

There's really only one field of battle that isn't being covered by Awakened already, so I go there. Kobolds, each standing about three feet tall, scream and come scampering toward me. Their little claws skitter across the floor, and as they reach me, they jump upward, lashing out with tiny swords—or their very own claws.

"Right back atcha!" I slash my dagger through the neck of the first one, beheading it cleanly, then step forward into the midst of combat. I draw out my shield and use it to cover my left side, while hacking away with my right. It proves to be a useful tactic, and I soon cut down half a dozen of the monsters.

"SCREEEEEE!"

One of the kobolds jumps up and grabs onto my shield then starts trying to climb over the top. I grit my teeth and heft the shield upward then bring it crashing down onto the ground. The kobold is bashed against the granite, and it goes limp. Standing up, I swing the shield and bash another of the monsters in the face then follow up with the dagger to relieve it of its head. With that, I charge forward right into their midst, spinning around and lashing out at all that I can see.

I don't really succeed in killing many of them in this way, at least not immediately, but I deal an immense amount of damage, cutting off arms and limbs and landing long cuts through chests and bellies. Meanwhile, Bjorn—who has mostly stood back and watched—springs into action. His teeth latch down on the monsters, and he whips them around and shakes them about like rag dolls. I smile grimly at the destruction, and we press onward.

Quite suddenly, the last of the kobolds disappear. I slowly look around. Blood stains the stone, and I take a deep breath and try to size up the situation. The other Awakened are all standing there, four in total, and I give them a nod.

"Good to meet all of you." After a moment, I glance at Harold. "Mostly."

The five of us slowly walk to the middle of the room. Harold crosses his arms and won't look at me. The man in the bearskin cloak tucks a bone dagger into his belt and holds out his hand.

"Name's John. John Dartmouth."

"Good to meet you." I shake his hand then glance at the other two. There's a girl with bright red hair, wearing robes that almost look regal. I didn't get a chance to see what her powers were earlier, but I suspect that they're rather extraordinary. Meanwhile, the last individual is a rather short man, only about four feet tall, with a bald head. He carries a shield and a mace tipped with a spike-covered ball. I can tell that he's no one to mess with, despite his diminutive height. Neither of those two speak, nor do they offer to introduce themselves.

"Well? Which way should we go?" John asks after a moment. He turns and nods toward the different tunnels. "One of these ought to lead to the boss, right?"

I shrug. "I don't know that it will, at least not right away. I have a suspicion that the Rifts are going to take time to clear. We're probably going to be walking into a maze."

"Then we ought to stick together." John is adamant. "We don't know what we'll be walking into, and if we run into any rooms like this by ourselves, we're going to struggle."

"I'm not traveling with him," Harold snorts at me. He turns and walks over to the cave entrances then lets flames roll down off his hands. After a moment, he throws a fireball down one of them then down a second. "Come on! This one has gemstones. That means riches, not just more monsters to carve through."

The short man nods and trots off after him. The girl seems hesitant, though I can see her looking after the group. John's face twitches, but he nods to me.

"And what do you think?"

A roar suddenly echoes up out of one of the caverns—the tunnel on the far left. It's a deep, piercing sort of cry, one that makes the stones of the cave shake and shudder. John seems to grip his daggers a bit tighter.

"We're not going *that* way." The girl sounds determined. She starts to walk over to join Harold. "We should go this way, become more powerful, and then face it."

John shrugs. "It's not bad advice, really. You coming?"

"No!" Harold shouts back. "No, he's not coming with us! He can leave, or he can die!"

John's face twitches. I still haven't given my opinion, and he knows it. After a few moments, Harold starts into the cave with his two followers close behind. When he's out of sight, I nod at the tunnel that the roar came from.

"I'm no expert, but my suspicion is that the noise was intentional. It knows that we'll be taking this slow and purposefully, so it's trying to drive us somewhere."

"You sound awfully confident in that." John's eyes narrow.

"Call it an educated guess." I start off in that direction. "That way is most likely a trap. Gemstones? A mysterious roar coming from the opposite direction? There's something waiting there, and it isn't going to be good."

"Then why didn't you say something?"

"Because that'll only make Harold more reckless than before, which means he'll get into trouble, and I'll have to come rescue him. *Again.*" I reach the mouth of the cave and open the portal to my pocket dimension. Bjorn is joined by my gargoyle, who snarls and takes a pose. "You coming with us, or are you going to follow them?"

John chuckles. "I'll follow them. You look like a loner, and someone's going to have to spring them out of the trap when it comes."

"Fair enough." I start down the tunnel, and it closes behind me. Garg opens his mouth, allowing tongues of fire to flicker out and light the way, and we go on downward. Behind me, I hear some distant screams and shouts of battle, but I ignore them.

It isn't long before the tunnel stops leading downward and simply levels out. As I reach that point, I can sense something in the air. Something foul. Something smelly. Something . . .

[RazorEdge: SLIMES!]

[ShadowDancer: EEW!!!]

I frown as I walk into a smaller cave entrance covered in large, greenish blobs. Truth be told, it looks to me like a giant sneezed all over the location and didn't bother to clean up. It's not menacing in the slightest, and I certainly don't see the mysterious source of the roar. Still, as the slimes all start to ooze across the floor toward me, I take a tighter grip on my dagger.

"Garg? Light them up."

Garg roars and stomps forward, unleashing a gout of flame that explodes across the floor. Slimes wither and explode under the flames as the water inside of them begins to boil, before their membranes can be burned away. In an instant, a path is cleared, and Garg lets up on the attack. I start forward, smiling at the other slimes, which are now drawing back from the flame.

"There we go! That wasn't so—"

"*RRRRARGGGGGG!!!!!!!*"

There is that noise again, although it's now a great deal louder and more painful. The rocks around me all shudder, and I try to keep from clapping my hands over my ears. Whatever this is, I need to stay focused and ready to strike the moment that something presents itself.

[LunarEclipse: Whoa! What could be making this noise?]

[DarkCynic: I bet it's a dragon!]

[IceQueen: I bet it's a mimic!]

[ShadowDancer: Mimics don't roar.]

[IceQueen: Says you. Have you ever met one before?]

[ShadowDancer: Have *you*?]

I try to stay focused. Suddenly, a rock hits me from above, and I slowly look up. The slimes there are starting to merge, forming a large, dangling blob of . . . well . . . This one looks rather like a loogie, except with teeth.

A lot of teeth.

I dive forward as the thing falls from the ceiling, remaining connected only by a slender strand of thin snot. It snaps down on the place where I was standing then withdraws back to the ceiling. Carefully, it starts to slide across the ceiling to cover me, and I scowl. I prepare to dodge once it gets overhead, but before it actually reaches that point, it lunges down once again. I dodge the same way I was anticipating having to . . . and run smack into the thing!

It can predict my movements!

This is rather annoying. Now, thankfully, it was a smidge off, so I slam into its side rather than actually getting gobbled up. I stand and manage to get a single strike in with my dagger as it retreats, and I cause a good deal of oozing goop to erupt from the wound, but that's all I manage to accomplish. As I get my footing, it lunges once more, and I dodge again, this time away from the thing.

This time, though, I dodge right into the wall, where a nice, slimy bed is waiting for me.

Not only can it anticipate my actions, but it can also drive me places.

Instantly, the slime sticks to me, oozing around my arms and legs as it tries to hold me still. Overhead, the loogie brings itself into position, and I fight desperately to escape. This isn't looking good, that's for sure. I think through my options, desperately trying to come up with a course of action.

"Garg!" I shout. "Garg, I could really use you!"

A blast of fire rolls up from the side, slamming into the slime on the ceiling. It knocks the thing sideways for a moment, but I quickly see that it seems to have developed an immunity of sorts to fire. *More problems.* Slowly, the thing opens its gaping maw, and I look deep into its gullet.

And that's when I notice something.

The teeth are simply stones: bits and pieces of the cave that the slimes decided to make use of. That means that the creature really can't do much other than use what it has on hand, which has a handful of implications, at least in my mind. In any event, I see the smallest possibility of getting out alive, and I decide to take it.

I draw my dagger, and I stay perfectly still.

An instant passes, and the slime comes crashing down. The thick folds of slime engulf me, and I feel stones biting into me all around. I ignore it all, though, and simply start slashing around with my dagger.

That gets results.

The blade carves through the delicate membrane of the slime, even carving through some of the stones themselves. The loogie spits me back out and retreats, but I give it no chance. I stab backward into the slime holding me, carving it up as fast as I can, then lunge upward, grabbing hold of the thing and cutting it to bits.

I can see now how the slimes work. They can heal from wounds almost instantly but, by that same token, they can be damaged quite easily. I decide to not give it a chance to heal, and I redouble my efforts. The great blob falls to the floor with a *splat*, and I alternate bashing it with the shield and stabbing it with the dagger. A few moments later, it lies still and slowly dissolves into a large, greenish, oozing puddle.

[ChaosRider: Go Jason! You showed that thing!]

[DarkCynic: You went HAM on that slime! Never seen anything like it from you before!]

"Let's hope it doesn't happen again." I shrug, taking up a stance as my gargoyle and I walk through the room and down into another tunnel. "Not my most refined kill, by any means." A moment later, a thought strikes my mind. We're winding tightly downward, like a corkscrew, which gives me some time to think. "Does anyone know what's happening with the other guys?"

[FireStorm: They're getting their butts kicked! You were right!]

"I hope John's okay, at least," I mutter as I reach the bottom. There, I find a stone door, and I place my hands against it. "He seemed nice, at least. They should have seen the warnings, though, and—"

My voice trails off as I push against the door. It won't

move, and I grunt in frustration. I push again then look for a doorknob. I can't find anything, except for a small keyhole off to one side. I bend down and peer through the little lock, but I can't see anything but darkness.

"Great." I scowl. "Any idea where the key is located? I didn't see anything up there."

[ViperQueen: There's a big chest up in the trap room! I bet that's where it is!]

[LunarEclipse: Yeah, Jason! Go save everyone!]

I grit my teeth. I really didn't want to have to do that, but if that's the only way to move forward, I suppose I have no choice. Slowly, I turn around and make my way back up the tunnel.

Soon, I come to the room where the trap was set up. As I step inside, I must admit that the location is quite beautiful. Crystals cover nearly every surface, wrapping around a lake of fire—well, lava, but you get the idea. Narrow paths wind through the crystals, leading to a series of stepping stones that mark the way across the lake to an island at the exact center.

The other Awakened, at that moment, are on the far side fighting against a number of creatures rising up from the lava. I can see snakes and worms, along with something vaguely humanoid, though I can't tell exactly what it is. Bjorn pads up next to me, and I give him the nod.

"Cool it down."

Bjorn tilts his head back and howls, and a blast of freezing air sweeps through the room. The lava itself loses a bit of its shine, and all the Awakened turn and look at me. I smile and give a wave—more of a salute, really—to John, then stride forward.

Almost instantly, a large serpent erupts from the fire. I lash out, cutting through its neck. I don't sever the head—not quite, anyway—but the knife does its job, and the serpent falls backward with a fiery splash. Immediately after, several of the humanoid forms appear, crawling up onto the floor of sharp crystals, dripping liquid fire as they do so.

[Fire Sprite, Level 5]

"Well, 'Fire Sprite, level five,' prepare to become a corpse, level zero!"

It's not the best line, but it's the best thing I can come up with in that moment. I cut the head off the first one, and the thing falls backward. Bjorn howls directly at the second, and it simply cools into a statue, frozen as it struggles to stand up.

With that, more and more of the monsters rise up, pulling themselves onto the crystals, but I just forge my way through them. As they collapse and cool, their bodies are transformed into more of the crystals, which I appreciate. I scoop up a few of them, though I'm not exactly sure why. Good keepsakes, maybe?

Ahead of me, the short man makes a go at jumping across the stepping stones. He leaps to the first stone and catches himself then prepares his mace. A serpent explodes up in front of him, and he bashes it over the head. It completely explodes into lava, showering his armor. Some of it seems to find its way between the chinks, and he yelps in pain. Suddenly, a long, fiery tentacle explodes upward and wraps itself around his torso. He screams, and in the blink of an eye, he's gone, sucked under the surface of the fire.

Harold utters words that would make a sailor blush then rises up into the air. "I'm going next!"

I'm honestly not sure in this moment if his scheme will work, though I suspect not. As it turns out, I'm right. He flashes over the lava, trying to outpace the monsters beneath the waves, but a tentacle explodes upward and snags him, yanking *him* under as well.

"Alright, poll!" I shout as I try to figure out my options. "Who thinks he's going to come out alive because he has fire powers, and who thinks he's a goner?"

[A: Alive: 89%]

[B: Dead: 10%]

[C: Alive, but just barely: 1%]

"I guess we'll see." I think for a moment then nod at Bjorn. "Alright, boy! I need the biggest, best howl you've ever howled."

Bjorn bows his head then inhales deeply. For a moment, the cool wind he had been generating comes to a pause . . . and then he lets out an exhalation unlike any other.

My whole body feels as though a coat of ice has grown across my skin, and snowflakes float down from the ceiling in contrast to the fire. Slowly, painfully so, the surface of the lava begins to blacken. The moment it looks solid, I bolt forward, racing across the hardening surface for the island at the center.

The stone is still blazing hot under my feet, and I feel my shoes melt and catch fire, but I have no other choice. The stone cracks all around, allowing light to shine through, as fiery hands shoot up to try and stop me. All of it falls short, though, forced to move a great deal slower from the extreme cold. As I reach the island, I leap upward and onto the shore where the chest lies.

"Alright!" I hear John cry out. "That's the way to do it!"

The air around me starts to swell with heat, and I can hear that distant, rumbling roar from earlier. Quickly, I bend down to the treasure chest and flip it open. There's a flash of light, and the key appears in my hands. I jump back to my feet, turn, and bolt for the entrance.

Even as I do so, I hear a mighty *crack* from behind me, and I feel a great blast of heat. Bjorn turns and runs, allowing heat to once more blast upward from the lava as well. Stone melts under my feet, and I throw myself forward. Stone cracks, the whole cave seems to shudder . . . and a massive shockwave picks me up and flings me out through the mouth of the cave.

As I climb back to my feet, I glance over my shoulder and find only dust and rubble. The cave has collapsed. I don't know what to make of it, frankly. I have the key now, but . . . what happened?

"Does anyone have eyes on the others?" I ask softly, hardly daring to hear the answer. "Are they alive or dead?"

[ShadowDancer: Don't know. Their feeds all went dark, but I don't see anything that says they were defeated.]

[ViperQueen: Except for the short guy. His feed had a [You are dead] message appear just a few seconds after he was pulled under.]

"Does that mean that Harold is still alive?"

[ChaosRider: Yes . . .]

[LunarEclipse: Is that okay?]

"On this day, I'd rather have allies than enemies, but . . ." I shrug and start walking back toward the entrance with the locked door. "Any human still left standing, particularly an Awakened, is another blade fighting against the darkness enclosing our world."

[IceQueen: Well said!]

I don't respond any more, and just lower my head and press onward down the cave. I have a feeling that I'll be seeing them all again, likely sooner than I'd like to. For now, all I can do is press forward, deeper and darker, until this Rift is cleared.

CHAPTER FOURTEEN

Alright, poll time." I'm trying to keep spirits in the chat brighter as I come up to the door. "What do you think we're going to find behind here? I'll let you insert your own answers."

[A: MONSTERS!!!!: 51%]

[B: Lots of loot!: 30%]

[C: Just a dark tunnel: 15%]

[D: Something useless: 3%]

[E: The boss chamber!: 1%]

"We're way too early for the boss chamber." I shake my head. I hold up the key and slowly stick it into the keyhole. "And I really hope it's not something useless."

There's a flash of light and the door dissolves, revealing a darkened interior. As I step forward, torches blaze to life, and I find myself in a long, drawn-out cave that rather reminds me of a straw. I don't know why that's the sense I have, but it distinctly feels like something will try to suck me down inside.

The sense is reinforced by the fact that it slopes downward, down to another door, this one made of wood. I shrug and start forward, keeping my dagger and shield at the ready.

A low rumble rolls through the ground, and I freeze. A skittering noise rises up through the air, and Bjorn and Garg both start to growl. Suddenly, I notice holes all along the walls. Lots of them. Eyes start to glitter inside of them, and I smile.

"I think 'monsters' is going to win. I'd give you all a shout-out, but . . . it looks like a couple thousand of you voted, and I don't have time right now to go through them all!"

I can't say any more, as the holes in the walls suddenly come alive. Spiders scamper forth—hundreds, maybe thousands, of them. Each stands about a foot tall and has a leg span of perhaps two feet. Not large, but I can see green venom dripping from thousands of fangs, and I know we're in for quite a fight.

[GoldenShield: Don't let them bite you!]

[LunarEclipse: On your left! On your right! Behind you!]

[IceQueen: Call the exterminator!]

"I am the exterminator!" I laugh and charge forward. I jump up and over the first wave, allowing Garg to blast them with a ball of fire, and I come crashing down on several more. They're flattened under my impact, and I lash out with my blade as fast as I can.

My dagger moves with lightning speed—of that there's no doubt—but it hardly seems to make a difference; there are just so many of them! With every cut, I'm either sending splatters of green bug gunk across the wall or hacking off fangs and legs and all sorts of other body parts. But no sooner do I kill ten than another twenty replace them. There are so many that they're starting to pile up on top of each other, and I take a deep breath and step back.

"Garg! Light them up!"

Garg takes a deep breath and exhales a great gout of cleansing fire. Now, if you've never smelled spiders being roasted by a gargoyle's flame . . . let's just say that it's far from the most pleasant thing I've ever experienced. In fact, I'm pretty sure that the smell alone could be bottled and marketed as a weapon in and of itself, but I digress.

Regardless, Garg lets out a long blast of flame until he runs out, then he wades into the battle, stomping and smashing all the bugs he can manage.

[System Notification: Lesser Gargoyle has exhausted all flame attacks. They will recharge in 60:00]

"Bjorn!" I shout. "You're up, then!"

[System Notification: Frost Wolf has exhausted all ice attacks. They will recharge in 54:26]

"Not helpful!" I growl. I can see Garg taking a number of bites, even with his thick skin, and I know I need to do something quickly. "You two, back inside! I'll have to go through this myself!"

Bjorn and Garg both vanish as they dive into the portal, and I take a few steps back, fighting the spiders just enough to keep them at bay. As I reach the doorway once more, I take a deep breath then toss my shield onto the ground, rush forward, and leap onto it like a sled.

In all fairness, if we hadn't already killed quite a few of the spiders, I don't think anything would have happened, except maybe me slipping and falling on my head. As it is, though, the ground is plenty lubricated by all the spider guts, and I skim forward with ease. Spiders all around me blur by as I rush down and into the tunnel, and I crouch down.

Suddenly, my idea of the tunnel being a straw seems a lot clearer. All around me, bugs teem—countless thousands of them, and more by the second. The ones underneath are all blasted apart by my growing speed, leaving a trail of greenish slime behind me. A few moments is all it takes to reach the bottom, where I crash into the door with enough force to splinter, though not break, the wood.

"Come on." I look up at the teeming mass of spiders. I have the distinct feeling that this particular tunnel is an infinite spawn point. They cropped up every now and again in my old video games: locations where you could stay and fight for as long as you wanted, until you grew old, and things would just continue to appear. Now, while the prospect of leveling up for an infinite amount of time certainly sounds appealing, I know I need to keep moving. So instead of facing the horde, I turn and slam a fist into the door.

Already weakened under my impact, it yields *just* a bit. I snarl and punch it again. By now, it's weakening quite a bit, and I grit my teeth and throw one final punch.

Wham!

The door's lock snaps, and the whole thing flies inward. I step through just as the horde of spiders leaps onto my back, biting and snapping desperately at me. I feel sting after sting after sting, and darkness begins to flicker across my eyes almost instantly.

[System Notification: You are now Poisoned. You will begin experiencing adverse effects.]

[Strength: -5]

[Dexterity: -3]

[. . .]

The list goes on, but I don't have the time or energy to look at it. The only thing I see is a clock.

[Death: 0:29]

Thankfully, as spiders continue to bite me, the clock doesn't go down any faster than before. I snarl and take a deep breath, allowing all my elementary school training to come back.

"Stop."

I freeze in my tracks, allowing more of the creatures to swarm up over me.

"Drop."

The impact as I fall forward smashes quite a number of them into goop.

"Roll!"

This squashes the rest of the spiders quite nicely. As I feel the stings diminish and cease, I glance upward. My vision is darkening, but it doesn't look like they're following me.

"Guys . . ." I slowly sit upright, my head spinning. I try to open my inventory for healing items, but I only succeed in making the list whirl around in front of me. "If any of you has a Pumped! I could drink, I'd sure appreciate it."

With a flash, one of them appears in my hand. I don't even bother to take the lid off; I just put it into my mouth, bite down to crush the plastic, and then chug it as fast as I can. When I finish, I find that the death timer has frozen at [0:05], but it is still there.

"Thanks." I take a deep breath and slowly climb to my feet, turning to face the doorway. It's dark, but I can still see the spiders teeming just behind the invisible barricade, which they seem to be forced to adhere to. Slowly, I open up my inventory for healing items and, parsing through things *very* carefully, I select a few tablets of antivenom. Once I down those, my vision starts to clear, and I'm able to take a look around.

I seem to be in some sort of small crypt with cobblestone floors, with several coffins along the side of the room, all made of stone and sealed shut. They're marked with the image of a hammer, though I don't have the faintest idea what that might mean. As my health bar rises, I stand back away from them, knowing that if I get too close, I'll likely have to battle whatever's inside.

"Alright, Garg. Come on back out."

There's a flicker of light, and my gargoyle staggers back out into view. He looks all but dead, that's for sure. His scales are turning black, his eyes are watery and glazed, and . . . well . . . it just doesn't look like a good situation, that's for sure. He looks at me, sad, and lets loose a soft whimper.

"Skill: Rapid Heal."

A flash of green light shines around the gargoyle, and suddenly he begins to perk up. It isn't quite as rapid as I might have hoped, but that could be because the venom is still in his system. In any event, he's soon able to draw himself up a bit more, and I give him a nod.

"Stay close by, just in case I need you."

Garg gives a nod and steps back slightly. I bring out Bjorn and give him a look-over, but he seems to have come through the spiders without much harm. That's good, if nothing else. I give him a pat and a scratch then order him back inside.

"Alright, then. Let's get this over with." I walk to the first of the caskets and place my hands on the lid. I half expect it to fly open at my touch, but nothing happens, and I give it a shove. It slides off and crashes nearby with a massive thud, and I lift my dagger.

Except . . . there's nothing inside. Nothing at all. I mean, a bit of bone dust, but that's it.

"That's odd." I frown then walk to the next one. The lid crashes loudly as it hits the ground, once again revealing nothing at all. "Twenty bucks says that they're waiting for me just around the corner."

[ChaosRider: Totally agree! Stay safe!]

[Originalgoth: Nah, they're not in hiding anywhere, they're just . . . Maybe this was a decoy!]

I don't really pay any attention to Originalgoth, and just slowly walk forward, keeping my hand on my dagger. The soft thumps of Garg echo behind me, and I look along the path. Ahead, moving past the caskets, the path opens up into a soft, gentle-looking cave system and slowly turns off to the right. I keep my eyes peeled as I round the corner, and . . .

A loud rattle shakes the ground, and I find myself staring at a dozen skeleton warriors. They're standing before a gate, behind which seems to be a much more open room, though I can't tell exactly what's there. The skeletons all start to beat their swords against their shields, and I take my stance.

"You don't want to do this. Trust me."

The skeletons don't answer, but one of them charges forward, lifting its sword up above its head to bring down on me. I step up to meet it, lifting my own shield. The sword and shield meet with a mighty crash—which, of course, leaves its body exposed. I step forward and slash my dagger through its neck, crushing the dry bones, and its head falls to the ground with a clatter. With that, I kick the monster in the chest, smashing its ribs, which causes its two arms to detach and fall to the floor.

The other skeletons seem to take this as a signal, and they rush forward to meet me. Now, one of them was about as hard to defeat as a piece of paper. Eleven of them all at the same time? Still not *hard,* but . . .

I charge forward with Garg at my side. I hold my shield in front of me, but he just spreads his wings and throws himself into their midst. Bones crumble under the impact, but I have no time to watch him. Instead, I turn in the opposite direction and wade into the fight.

Two swords jab at me from the right, and I'm forced to block them. Another skeleton tries to shield-bash me from the left. That one I have to take. It hurts, but it makes me stagger into the two skeletons trying to stab me—which, frankly, helps. I'm now within striking range, and I slash my weapon through them as fast as I can. Bone dust explodes through the air, and they both crumble.

Rather on a whim, and wanting something a bit longer, I scoop up one of the swords and spin around. A skeleton lunges at me, and I throw my shield into its face with all my might. The head explodes under the impact, and the shield clatters to the ground not far behind. The body sways and takes a stance again, but I've had enough. I drop my dagger back into my inventory, then rush forward, draw my new sword back over my shoulder, and swing it.

Steel meets steel, and my sword explodes into slivers.

Apparently, it wasn't designed for someone stronger than a child. That said, it works well enough, and the shards take down both my target *and* one standing just behind. Left with only a hilt, I throw it at yet another of the monsters. It hits a shield, doing no damage except to jar the wrist of the monster so badly that the shield drops to the ground, still clutched by the hand. I follow up with a sweeping kick that finishes the job, and I stand there breathing heavily.

Only one skeleton is left. It rattles its teeth; I can't tell if it's afraid or trying to scare us. Both, perhaps. In any case, the thing charges forward after a moment, and Garg lets out a roar. It's not even a terribly powerful roar, but the mere sound of it blasts the skeleton into smithereens, and the pieces clatter to the ground.

"Perfect." I nod at the carnage then turn to face the gate. "Let's keep moving, unless you need to heal."

The gargoyle only gives a shake of his head, and we walk forward. Just next to the gate is a lever, which I yank firmly. There's a metallic rumble within the stone— the sound of chains being pulled over rocks—and the gate slowly slides upward. We step through, and torches blaze to life all across the area.

With that, my eyes open wider, and the gate behind us slowly slides back down again. We're in an arena. It's perfectly circular, with seats for spectators set about twenty feet above the rim of the pit where we find ourselves. At the other end of the arena is another gate, covering a dark, gaping hole. High above that particular hole is a booth decorated with tattered tapestries, where a skeleton in a jarl's outfit sits on a throne. He slowly lifts his hands and gives a soft clap, the faintest whisper of a noise that echoes throughout the arena, over and over again.

"Let the fight begin!"

The words are in a different language, but I understand them, nonetheless. Slowly, the gate at the other end begins to open, and I take my stance.

"No chance to rest, I see," I mutter. "That's alright. Bring it on, and we'll kill it, whatever we face!"

CHAPTER FIFTEEN

The gate slowly opens—painfully so—and the chat begins to fill out a poll even without my prompting.

[A: Cave troll!: 25%]

[B: Legion of skeletons!: 22%]

[C: Wargs!: 32.5%]

[D: Slimes!: 0.5%]

[E: Other: 20%]

When the gate finishes opening, I see dark figures striding forth. I start forward to meet them, only for—

"Jason Lee! Is that you?"

I draw up short then laugh. "John? You're alive!"

"Sure seems like it!"

John strides forward, grinning broadly. His cloak is a bit more tattered than before, but it's still there nonetheless, and his jovial nature doesn't seem to have changed a bit. Behind him comes Harold, a bit more furious than usual, which is really saying something. I don't see anyone behind them, though, and I frown.

"What happened to the girl?"

John sighs and runs his hand through his hair. "She got bitten by a snake. We did all we could, but we didn't have any antivenom, and . . . she died."

I grimace and look down at the ground. "I'm sorry to hear that."

"Her name was Astrid. She told us right before she zeroed out." John shrugs then looks back at me. "We're in a dangerous line of work."

"And it's about to get a whole lot more dangerous!" Harold comes stomping forward. "You're going to pay for what you did!"

"*Yes . . .*" the voice from the jarl hisses through the room. "*Fight, all of you! The winner will be given a crown of glory!*"

"Yeah, I don't think so." I shrug and turn away from Harold. "Not buying it. Come on, guys, let's keep moving."

I start toward the dark cave, but they stop me.

"There's nothing there. Nothing except a bunch of passageways back to a room filled with cooled lava." John shakes his head. "Wherever we go from here, it's in this room."

I look around. The only way I see out is up in the jarl's booth, and it's a long way up. Still . . . I do have a creature that can fly.

"Garg, go get that guy down from there and see if there's a way we can escape."

Garg nods and spreads his wings then explodes upward. As he does, a fireball hits him from the side, and he slews into the stands, where he comes crashing down onto the benches. Stone explodes up into the air from beneath him, and I see his health rapidly heading toward zero.

"Skill: Rapid Heal."

[System Notification: Remember, using the Rapid Heal skill too often can result in unpleasant consequences.]

"I'll take it." I wave away the message then turn to stare at Harold, who's smirking at me. Fire is blazing in his hands, and he slowly starts to rise into the air.

"You heard what he said," Harold snaps. "I have people watching, so I don't *want* to kill you in cold blood, but I will! If we don't fight, we'll be killed! That's the order of things! Now fight me or die!"

I sigh and glance at John. "Ready to teach this guy a lesson?"

"Ready enough."

Harold snarls then unleashes a blast of flame down at me. I dodge to the side then come up and throw my dagger. He simply waves his hands and forms a shield of fire in front of himself, and the dagger is batted to the side and falls to the floor. As the fire dies away, he laughs.

"You're both melee builds! You can't harm—"

Garg shoots through the air and hits him firmly in the torso, blasting him out of the sky and into the wall. Stone cracks behind him, and I pull out my shield and charge forward. A column of fire hits Garg in the chest and knocks him backward. Harold emerges from the dust of his impact to stare at me, his body brimming with hatred.

"You'll regret that!"

I throw my shield at his face, trying to show him quite positively that I don't expect to regret it in the slightest. He's able to bat the shield away, but a moment later, John hits him too.

That's when I realize just what John's special power is. He's *strong*. Like . . . *really* strong. The single punch lifts Harold off his feet and smashes him back against the wall. He rolls to the side, and John punches once more. His fist actually smashes through the outer layer of stone and, as John pulls his hand back, a section of the wall is ripped away, clinging to his hand. He simply flexes his fingers, smashing away the rock, and I whistle.

Harold, by now, is reacting a bit faster. He snarls and claps his hands, unleashing a concussive blast that knocks me over backward. As I hit the ground, I catch a glimpse of him creating a long, fiery sword in his hands, which he then plunges down toward my heart.

"I will have that crown!"

I have no other option but to bat the sword aside with my hands. Flames sear my arms and the blade drives into my shoulder. It's *beyond* painful, and I scream. Harold grins and leans down closer, and I kick him with all my might. While I'm not as strong as John, I'm still Awakened, and he's tossed up into the air just enough.

John grabs the man as he's still falling, spins, and slings him off against the far wall. The flame sword dissolves, and I slowly climb to my feet and let out a long breath. Garg is just staggering to his feet as well, and I notice that his health has fallen again. I need him alive, but I also need him in this fight.

"Skill: Rapid Heal."

There's a flash around Garg sand, suddenly, a red light around me. My own stats suddenly begin to drain, and I feel as though I'm too weak to stand. I drop to my knees, gasping in pain. Harold, off to one side, laughs as he recovers from John's attack.

"You're weak, boy! Even two against one, I'm still winning!"

I look up as he rises into the air, fire blazing in his hands. Garg snarls and flaps up to meet him, but Harold bats the gargoyle away with a wave of his hand. I allow Garg to go back into the portal, and a moment later, a terrible gout of flame comes pouring down from Harold.

I brace myself against the heat but John throws himself in front of me, holding up his bearskin cloak like a shield. Flames war against the leather, not doing a lick of damage. John looks down at me, his face beginning to sweat.

"Do you have a plan?"

I give a nod.

"Then I'll trust your lead."

"Good. When this lets up, fall down."

A moment later, the flames die down, and John obediently falls to the ground. Smoke rises up from the backside of his cloak, which makes the action that much more impressive. Overhead, Harold cackles then forms a blazing sword in his hands.

"And now it's time to end this scourge! Attack!"

He screeches, wild with rage, and dives down to strike me. As he comes shooting down and races along the floor, I send a mental command.

Now, boy.

Bjorn, who had slipped out of the portal when Garg went inside, suddenly leaps from behind me and howls. The air chills, and all of Harold's flames die out. Now, if he had been given time to brace for it, or if he had simply known that it was coming, he likely could have worked up a defense. As it stands, he simply gasps as his flames go cold, and I stand back up and punch him in the jaw.

I know a few tricks about street fighting, so when my punch connects, it does well. Harold's eyes roll closed, and he falls to the ground and rolls several times before coming to rest against the wall. John stands up next to me, and we regard the unconscious Awakened.

"How'd you know that would happen?" John glances at me, confused.

"Just a hunch. He created a sword earlier, and that's usually done by mages who want to get up close and personal for once with the things they're trying to destroy," I answer. "I didn't think the penalties for healing the gargoyle would be *too* intense, but I did need them to be triggered, in order for me falling weak to be believable. Thus . . . here we are."

"It certainly seems to have worked." John slowly turns and looks up at the skeleton jarl, who rises and looks down upon us. "What do we do with Harold? Kill him?"

"Nah." I shake my head. "Just leave him here. If he wakes up, there's a chance he'll still manage to do something good in the world."

"There's also a chance he'll just come and try to kill us again."

"Not without the offering of a reward. He's too practical for that." I start walking toward the booth, where the jarl is still watching us. "Speaking of which . . ."

"You will have to fight one another. There can only be one victor!"

"We're going to pass on that." I give a shake of my head. "How about *you* come down here, and we'll fight you?"

The jarl watches a moment longer then turns and runs through the open door behind him. John glances at me, and a strange light flickers in his eyes.

"Want to bet that he's the final boss?"

"No, but I'll bet that we have to go through him before getting there." I call Garg back out then climb onto his back. "Want to come, or are you going to jump up or something?"

"I'll find a way." John starts running toward the wall. He springs upward, bounces nimbly off a foothold so small I can't see it, and lands on top. Garg then flaps his wings and rises up, flying over to the booth.

As we land, I look at the dark, gaping mouth where the skeleton jarl went. I can hear things moving around, rumbling loudly. The easy part of the dungeon is over, that much I'm certain of. Now we face the true test: the final gauntlet down to the boss chamber.

CHAPTER SIXTEEN

As it turns out, another power of John's is that he can basically scale sheer walls. He can't actually, but his fingernails have grown in longer and thicker since he Awoke, which lets him use them like claws in order to climb things. When he gets up there, I order Garg back into the portal, and the two of us start forward into the darkness.

It's starting to seem commonplace, but I still get a shiver as torches blaze to life to mark our entry into a room. This time, we find ourselves in a short, cobblestone hallway with a handful of rooms branching off in all directions.

John walks up to the first door, which is wooden and locked tightly. He draws his hand back and essentially high-fives it, smashing it into splinters. Slowly, the two of us peer inside and find a royal bedroom, complete with a canopied bed, mirrors, and a large variety of Norse-themed items, such as horns, axes, and shields.

"Interesting," John muses as he walks inside and starts

rifling through things. "You wouldn't expect to find something like this inside a Rift, you know?"

"Does that mean you're experienced with Rifts?" I remark dryly. "Frankly, I'm still a little confused about this all."

"Fair point," John chuckles. He bends down, grabs the bed frame, and flips the thing onto its side. A mighty crash resounds through the room, and he lets out a long breath when we find nothing but dust bunnies. "I'm just putting the pieces together. Dungeons seem to be fairly small—at least the low-level ones I've been through so far. This Rift looks more like a collection of dungeons, a whole bunch of things all squished together."

"True," I muse. I turn and walk out of the room while John starts rifling through drawers and a few small chests. "What are you doing now?"

"Looting!" John beams as he comes walking out with a few handfuls of silver jewelry. "I figure that if you aren't considered encumbered, you're not playing the game right. I know this isn't a game, but . . ."

He laughs and dumps the gold into his inventory then flexes his muscles. I follow along behind him and raise an eyebrow.

"Is that why you're so strong?"

"Yup. My special skill is that my strength increases in proportion to the amount of stuff in my inventory. There are a few limitations on it, but that's the general idea."

"Fascinating." I shake my head. We walk up to the next door, and I slide my dagger in between the wood and the stone, then slash downward, cutting through the lock. Inside, we find another room, and John starts looting things once more. "I always had a particular affinity for animals prior to this. I know it's considered childish, but I would go to the zoo—any zoo—at least once a month."

"Makes you wonder if the System Administrators have profiles on us, or if the system itself can just scan that sort of thing." John flips over a bed then yelps. Underneath is a skeleton, which starts to rise, bearing a dagger in its hand. John stomps on its head, crushing the thing, and we both glance at each other.

Now as we move forward, we're a bit more cautious. We continue to open each door, but when we find them empty of enemies, we move onward. There's no sense in walking past a door full of warriors only to get ambushed, but there's also no sense wasting time when we still don't know what we're walking into.

When we reach the end of the hall, we come to yet another doorway. I'm getting sick of doors, but that's how dungeons are, I suppose. If you just put everything out there without any challenges, it would get boring. I draw my dagger and try to cut through, but I get a message instead.

[System Notification: This door cannot be broken, picked, or damaged.]

Almost instantly, a flurry of comments comes roaring through the feed.

[GoldenShield: What? That's ridiculous!]

[LunarEclipse: Has anyone seen a key?]

[ShadowDancer: I did, I did! Back in the third room!]

I glance at John then turn and walk back to the indicated room. He waits for me but doesn't ask any questions. I can only assume that his chat is telling him the same thing. I find the key sitting on a table, pick it up, and slowly walk back to join John.

"Thanks, guys," I answer as I unlock the door and step through. Truth be told, amid the battle against Harold, I had sort of forgotten that I was being watched. "Big shoutout to ShadowDancer, and your sharp eagle eye . . ."

My voice trails off as John and I step through into a treasure room. Maybe more like a dragon hoard; I don't know, it's . . . it's hard to describe. The walls and structure of the place are all made of carved stone without any mortar to indicate that it was built above ground. Great columns and archways mark immense alcoves in the walls—dozens of them, that stretch down the hundreds of feet that this great hall seems to fill. At the far end, I see two golden doors that lead onward—doors that seem to be made of solid gold and that stand a hundred feet tall, perfectly matching the height of the hall itself. Of course, in front of the doors is a pile of gold composed of coins, goblets, chains, armor, and more. Each of the alcoves is also filled to overflowing. Gemstones are mixed among the gold. It's truly a sight to behold, and I slowly let my gaze wander about, unable to believe it all.

"Wow," John whispers. "This will fill up my inventory a good bit."

I chuckle, but then pause as I get a message.

[Private Message from ShadowDancer: Look up.]

I blink in surprise, but then slowly let my head tilt backward. As I do so, my blood turns to ice. The ceiling is domed and arched, like any good example of Dwarven architecture, but . . . well . . . across the ceiling is a painting.

It's a painting of a great dragon: a fiery wyrm facing off

against a dozen armies scattered across the different arches. Toward the far doorway, the armies lie crushed and defeated, bleeding out across the ceiling under the coils of the beast. Toward us, the armies still stand, though . . . Even as I watch, the bulk of the dragon slides forward, plowing into a grand army clad in red and blue cloaks. All of them perish beneath the image of the beast, and soon, the dragon slides onward toward the next army, this one green.

[ViperQueen: WHOA!!! What is that?]

[DarkCynic: That's so cool!]

[ChaosRider: No . . . that's terrifying.]

"I'm afraid I have to agree with ChaosRider here," I murmur. "This is a dragon hoard, and that's . . . that's presumably the guardian."

"What do you think it means?" John whispers right next to me.

"Not a clue, but I think we need to get moving." I start walking forward. "Dragon hoards are cursed. Only the original owner can claim the goods therein, and even then, you ought to be careful."

"And how do you know that?" John chuckles as he strides along behind me.

"Everyone knows that," I answer. John doesn't seem convinced and starts wandering toward the piles of gold with more than a bit of curiosity in his eyes.

Up above, I find that I can't tear my gaze away from that horrid painting. It's hard to describe exactly what makes it so bad; there is just a sense of pure and utter *evil* that rains down from it. I hold my breath . . . and then, suddenly, the dragon's eyes dart away from the army and lock onto me.

With that, the roar that I've been hearing shakes the cavern. It's impossible to describe how loud it is. I hear it in my chest; my teeth rattle from the noise. There's a sharp clatter from off to the side, and I glance over to see John stumble and fall headlong into the dragon's treasure. Suddenly, a great hush falls over the room, and I have the distinct feeling that things are about to get very, very bad.

The pile at the end of the room suddenly starts to rattle and clank about, until the din is so loud that it hurts almost as much as the dragon's roar. Then, with a snap, a suit of armor comes tumbling out and lands on the floor.

The helmet's visor is open, allowing me to see a desiccated corpse inside. The armor . . . the armor is that of the red and blue army that I watched fall in defeat just a few moments ago, with the distinct difference that the steel itself is golden instead of silver. It starts clomping toward me, and John leaps to his feet.

"Alright, then! If that's the way it's going to be, that's how it will be!"

He rushes forward. I slowly lift my hand and, with a crackle, Garg steps out of my pocket dimension and joins me. Bjorn joins me on the other side, and we wait for a moment. John races up to meet the lone soldier. The soldier raises its sword, and John balls his hands into a fist and goes for the kill . . .

And with that, the pile *erupts* behind the lead soldier. Suits of armor snap together around the mass of bodies that had been piled up there, and an entire army begins to pour forth. I recognize all of them, legions that were crushed as depicted on the ceiling. Their armor and weapons have all been changed to gold, and some of them show dents and claw marks, but . . . that's who they are. John cries out in fright, but nonetheless slams a fist into the chest of the first soldier, blasting him backward into his companions, and then dives headlong into battle.

"Time to join the fray." I rush forward, feeling a great exhilaration as I pound across the floor. "Garg! You're up!"

Garg flies up into the air, then unleashes a massive gout of flame that pours down through the ranks of soldiers. Gold, which has a notoriously low melting point, dissolves into rivers of molten metal. The skeleton soldiers shriek and collapse, but soon, the gargoyle's flame attack dies away, and he drops back down to join me. Together, Bjorn, Garg, and I fly into the fray.

With that, utter chaos seems to erupt around me. Soldiers press in on all sides. I see Bjorn grabbing soldiers by the leg and slamming them to the ground. I see Garg lashing out with his wings and claws, but I'm quickly separated from them both. All I can do is attack and keep fighting, cutting down everything that comes my way. Blades jab me here and there, gauntlets crash down onto my back and upon my chest, but I stand strong through it all. Suddenly, I find John, and the two of us go back-to-back as the horde presses in around us.

My dagger flashes like lightning as I lop off limbs and heads and hands and feet and just about everything else I can manage. The bodies start to pile up around us, making a defensive ring of sorts, which helps momentarily; as the pile grows higher, we suddenly find ourselves struggling to reach over the top. Now, what had started as a defensive ring becomes something quite the opposite, and the soldiers begin flinging themselves over the top of the pile to simply squash us underneath.

"Jason!" John calls out. "Whatever you do, keep yourself loose! It'll hurt way less!"

"What w—"

John grabs hold of the back of my neck, flexes, and flings me up and out of the pile of bodies. I suddenly find myself arcing near the ceiling, which allows me to glimpse the battle. It seems to be going well, with Garg and Bjorn smashing steadily through things, though they also appear to be doing a good deal of damage. I know this can't continue and, as I come down, I see soldiers turning their heads to look up at me.

I know John said to stay limp, but I tense up, body-slamming several of the monsters as I land. It hurts quite a bit, actually, but it succeeds in knocking them flat. I jump back to my feet and continue to hack and slash. A moment later, John comes crashing down next to me as well.

Regardless, we fight on and on, pushing steadily through the crowd of monsters until my arms are so exhausted that I can hardly feel them. How many I cut through, I don't know, but when we finally find only one soldier left, which Bjorn takes down with a flying leap, both of us sigh in relief, exhaustion, and joy.

"That was . . . something else." John slowly turns and walks to the wall, where he slumps down and leans against the stone. "But we're alive, at least."

"Yes," I agree, sitting down next to him. I have to use my left hand to peel my fingers away from the dagger's handle, as they've seemingly frozen in place. It hurts worse than any of my wounds, and I gasp as I drop my dagger back into my inventory. "I don't know about you, but I need a rest before we go any farther."

"Agreed." John nods his head. "I don't know what's through that big door, but doors of that size rarely open into empty rooms."

We both seem to be on the same page. I lean my head back, but I only find myself staring up at the painting of that dragon, which has now devoured all the armies facing off against it. I have the distinct feeling that it desperately wants to devour me as well, if only it could find a way to peel itself off the ceiling.

[IceQueen: You should take some of the treasure now that you're safe!]

[ChaosRider: Uh . . . Objectively, that's a terrible idea. You don't want a dragon curse following you around, you know.]

"I have to agree with that." I slowly stand up then walk over to one of the alcoves. My fingers can barely unroll my sleeping bag, but I make it work. Slowly, I slip inside then order Bjorn and Garg to stand guard over me. I know the effect of the sleeping bag prevents me from being harmed by anything, but I also don't trust the dragon to adhere to the rules of the system. My pets will wake me up if anything happens, hopefully with enough time to avoid being eaten.

I don't know what time it is, but the moment my head hits the stone, I find myself falling fast asleep as the darkness closes around me. In my dreams, though, I still hear the dragon's roar . . . mingled with Harold's enraged cry. They swirl together, blending into one, taking the form of a hideous beast: half-human, half-monster, utterly evil. I don't know what it means . . . but I do know that, should I have the opportunity, I should destroy it before it has the chance to do the same to me.

CHAPTER SEVENTEEN

Riftwatch: Welcome to Day 5 of the Apocalypse Protocol!]
Today, as I open my eyes, I don't find myself looking up at a pack of wargs. That much, at least, is a bonus. That said, I *do* find myself looking up at the painted dragon, which snarls and hisses down at me. I hiss back at it for a moment, knowing it's a little childish, but . . . I can't exactly *attack* the ceiling, and it makes me feel a little better.

In any event, as I climb to my feet and roll up the sleeping bag, I find John lying down on the floor in front of the door, seemingly unconcerned by the whole course of events. I order Bjorn and Garg back into the pocket dimension, then slowly start walking around the room, taking things in.

It takes about twenty more minutes before John wakes up. When he does, he yawns and stretches then climbs to his feet and opens his inventory.

"Hungry?"

I shrug. "Wouldn't turn something down."

"Here." He pulls out two bags of fast food and tosses one to me. I catch it and tear it open, finding a hamburger, exceptionally greasy fries, some ketchup and secret sauce packets, and a bottle of Pumped! We sit down by the door and tuck in, and I glance at the name on the bag.

"Pumped! Drive-Through?" I raise an eyebrow. "Where'd you get this?"

"There was a dungeon in an old drive-in," John answers. "I got a whole slew of these things, along with *so* many bottles of that energy drink. If you want some, you're more than welcome to them."

I take a quick glance at my inventory. I don't have any food, excepting things like uncooked rat steaks and other things from monster drops, along with three more Pumped! bottles. "I'd appreciate it."

John quickly passes the food and bottles across, giving me about ten meals' worth. After I pocket them, we finish up our meals, then slowly climb back to our feet and turn to face the enormous doors.

"What do you think we'll find through here?" I ask as we push the doors open.

"Right now, my audience says there's a fifty percent chance that it's a throne room." John chuckles. "What about yours?"

I glance at the chat, which doesn't really seem to have warmed up for the day. I wait for answers to start rolling in, but nothing comes, so I shrug.

"Doesn't seem like they're awake yet. Either that, or watching us eat breakfast was boring, so they switched to someone else."

John laughs. We both give the doors one final push, and they lumber open to reveal a . . . throne room!

Now, I do have to admit that it's an incredibly impressive throne room. It's even larger and longer than the treasure room, with enormous archways framing stained-glass windows depicting sea serpents, dragons, and other such monsters. It certainly doesn't seem like a tremendously welcoming place, though I don't see any soldiers waiting to cut us into bits and pieces. Overhead, the painted dragon slides from the treasure room into the throne room, continuing to follow us.

At this point, it's still too far away to see who it is, but I can definitely tell that someone is seated on the throne. They're surrounded by immense paintings and statues of stone foliage and beasts—set with gold and jewels and all the trappings. Together, John and I start walking forward, and I draw out my dagger. My hands feel far better than the night before, and most of my wounds seem to have healed. There's a flash of lightning, and Garg comes out to stand next to me, spreading his wings to try and make himself look more intimidating.

[DarkCynic: Watch out, guys!]

[ViperQueen: Yeah, be careful!]

[ChaosRider: You're in danger!]

I glance over at John. "Are you getting these messages?"

"Yeah," he mutters. "They're not saying what the matter is, though."

I keep my dagger at the ready. I glance left and right, but I still don't see anything. What are they all talking about? On the bright side, though, my viewer count is steadily rising, which means that more people are tuning in. The only question is, where were they before?

"*Welcome!*" The voice of the jarl echoes, soft and serpentlike, through the hall. "*It's a pleasure to meet with you again!*"

"Is it, or are you just going to run away like a child again?" I ask, trying to pull myself up a bit taller. I don't know for sure if an undead skeleton is likely to be afraid of things, but . . . well . . . it's worth a shot. In all fairness, running away from a fight can be either because you're afraid or simply because you're trying to lead your opponent into a trap.

"*You know not of what you speak.*" The jarl chuckles softly. He rises from his throne and starts walking down to the floor, though he stops as he reaches the base of the stairs leading up to the chair. We both stop about thirty feet away from him, trying to maintain a respectful distance. "*I brought you here. I have watched your progress. Now, I wish to reward you for your perseverance.*"

"We've heard that line from you before," I answer. "Well, a similar line, in any case. We're not accepting any rewards from you."

Beside me, John's muscles tense. He doesn't say a word, and I can't tell if that's because he agrees, or because he thinks I'm crazy for turning down what would almost certainly be a power boost. Power, yes, but . . . well . . . the guy I'm talking to is an undead puppet controlled by a painted dragon. I don't care if it makes me strong enough to move mountains; if I'm not the one in control of my body, I might as well be as weak as a wet noodle. Frankly, I really want to lunge forward and teach this guy a lesson, but something tells me that here, in this grand throne room, he has at least a couple tricks up his sleeve, and I don't want to blunder into any of them.

"*So be it.*" The Jarl folds his hands. "*If you will not submit, then I shall call forth someone who will. He can teach you a lesson, I think.*"

There's a low rumble, and the dragon overhead opens its mouth wide. Fire blossoms on the paint and, with a flash of flame, Harold is spat out of the beast's gullet. He comes crashing down onto the floor in between us, and the jarl then groans and slowly hauls himself to his feet.

"You left me to die!" he spits at the two of us.

"Not exactly." I hold up a finger. "As I recall, you were promised a reward then tried to kill us, despite there being no proof that anything would actually come of it."

"I . . ." Harold snarled. "You're a problem! You need to be removed, and if he allies with you, so does he!"

"All I've ever done is ignore you. If that's a capital offense, consider me guilty." I hold up my dagger. "Come up and try to execute the sentence."

Harold's face twitches. Suddenly, I notice something: a ring. Not a large one—I can hardly see any of the details—but I can see a red gemstone. It glimmers a bit on Harold's hand, and I can't tell if it's producing its own light or if it's just catching the light of the torches.

"What's going on?" I ask slowly. "What have they done to you?"

Harold doesn't answer.

"Anyone?"

[DarkCynic: When he woke up, the dragon offered him power in exchange for tracking you down.]

[GoldenShield: Yeah . . . You might want to run.]

"Any particular idea how to stop him?" I nod toward the man, who seems to become angrier with every passing moment. "Just cut the ring off his finger?"

[RazorEdge: That would probably work.]

[FireStorm: Try it! Try it!]

[GrendleH8tr: That's going to be a whole lot easier said than done . . .]

I grit my teeth then charge forward. Somehow, I get the feeling that there's not really going to be any reasoning with him until I get rid of that ring. Next to me, John runs forward as well. We've fought Harold before. Yeah, he's likely a bit more powerful, but he won't be that—

Whoooooooooooosh!

Fire explodes from Harold's palms—a blistering inferno that crackles and roars across the floor of the throne room. I throw myself up into the air, flipping over the blaze, and I come down next to him. I'm not in a good position to strike with my dagger, so I just punch him as hard as I can. It's like punching concrete, and I'm fairly certain that I feel bones break in my hand.

Harold grins then adjusts his hands and lets loose another blast of fire. I dodge backward, and the flame scorches my front, but doesn't seem to do any real harm. Desperately, I grab my dagger and throw it as hard as I can, but he reacts like lightning, reaching up and snatching it from the air in the blink of an eye.

I'm quite certain that Bjorn isn't going to be of any help here, not the way he was last time. John throws himself into the midst of the battle, charging headlong through the flames. Fire trails off his cloak, and he slams a fist into Harold's jaw. Harold's head *does* turn slightly, but not nearly as much as it should have. In response, Harold headbutts John in the face, which sends the strongman reeling backward.

"Alright." I let out a long breath then open my portal. "Rat . . . Ratta . . . Squirrel!"

There's a flicker, and my large squirrel darts out.

[Ratatoskr]

"Right." I nod down at him. "I need you to get that ring. Can you do it?"

Of course I can, Master! Just watch me! Or rather, don't!

With a pop, he vanishes, and I have to blink a few times to confirm that he's no longer standing there. I can hear his little feet skittering across the floor, but I can't tell where he is in the slightest, and even that soon fades amid the noise.

"Jason!"

The noise comes from Harold, and I glance over just in time to see a massive fireball hitting me in the chest. It lifts me off the ground and throws me far backward across the floor, and I land and skid for a few long moments before coming to a halt. I groan and climb back to my feet, but by that time, Harold is already charging toward me. I know I don't have much time, and I snarl.

[ChaosRider: Don't give up, Jason!]

"I'm not giving up. Trust me."

I stand up and brace my feet right as Harold hits me. Our hands lock together, and fire blazes down my arms. It hurts like you wouldn't believe, but . . . well . . . one of the nice things about this world is the fact that, as long as I survive, I'll be able to heal. I grit my teeth and try to avoid screaming, and Harold opens his mouth to scream in anger.

"Hey, Harold, your fire is as weak as one of those fold-over matchbooks!"

The voice isn't a voice that I recognize. Harold freezes, and the fire dies out around my arms. He shoves me down, apparently deciding that I'm not worth the trouble, and spins around.

"Who said that?"

I catch a glimpse of John lying on the ground not far from the jarl. He seems to be unconscious—though, of course, that's hard to verify.

"I did!" The voice seems to echo out of nowhere, and I suddenly remember that Ratatoskr has the Taunt ability. Is he a bard or something? "You'd be able to see me, but your perception stat is weaker than my grandma's, and she has to wear quad-focal glasses just to find her way from the kitchen to the living room."

Harold's teeth grind together so loudly that I can hear it. "Your grandma would perish before me."

"Don't you dare talk about my grandma!" Something flickers in the air just next to Harold's body, though it seems like the noise is still coming from somewhere else. "She's the most beautiful woman you've ever seen! Well, if you're a squirrel. I suppose you humans wouldn't find her terribly—"

A loud *chomp* interrupts the dialogue, and Harold screams in pain. Distracted by the rambling noise, he hadn't noticed Ratatoskr moving into position. Now visible, Ratatoskr scampers desperately back toward me, Harold's finger dripping blood from between his large incisor teeth.

"*Pleh!*" He spits the finger into my hand then dives back into the portal. "He's all yours!"

I nod and face Harold; he suddenly seems a lot smaller. Overhead, the dragon lets out a *roar* like none other. I'm fairly certain that it'll take at least two Pumped! drinks just to heal my ears and, as it fades away, Harold sways on his feet and turns toward me. His finger drips blood onto the floor, but he hardly seems to notice.

"You good now?" I ask, walking past him.

He gives the smallest of nods.

"Good. Because we have a jarl to kill."

The jarl, down at the base of the throne, suddenly turns and runs upward. He leaps onto the throne and slams his hand down onto the carving of a wolf, and the throne suddenly falls backward through a hole in the wall. I go jogging up, but I only find a deep, black pit. Lights flicker at the bottom, but I can't tell for sure what they are.

"Hey." Harold walks up slowly. He's breathing hard as he holds up his injured hand. Fire flickers from his other hand to cauterize the wound, and he winces in pain. "Sorry."

"Don't do it again." I slowly pull the ring off his finger then toss the appendage back to him. "In case you want a keepsake."

Harold catches it then snorts and lets it fall. Meanwhile, I look down at the ring itself. The band is silver and shaped like a serpent, with the ruby set in a fitting shaped like the beast's mouth. It almost looks as if the snake is offering the ruby—which, in a way, is exactly what happened. I look up to see the dragon, high overhead, snarling and snapping. Without another word, I drop the ring into my inventory, then walk down to John.

It takes me a moment to get John to wake up. When he does, though, he inhales sharply and looks around then slowly rises and nods at Harold. Harold nods back, and that seems to be the end of it. I still don't trust him in the slightest, but at least he's confident now that we can beat him, which makes him much less of a problem. With that, the three of us approach the pit.

"Ready to go catch us a jarl?" I glance at the other two. "No more tricks. No more games. We find him, we kill him, and then we find whatever else is lurking in this dungeon."

"Agreed!"

Harold seems less convinced than John, but he gives a nod. With that, we lunge forward . . . onward and downward, to whatever we can find.

CHAPTER EIGHTEEN

The drop down the long shaft isn't one of the more pleasant moments of my life. It's pitch black, except for the distant lights at the very bottom. I can't see the edges of the pit; I don't know if there are blades ready to slice us to bits, or rocks that we'll be dashed against, or anything else particularly deadly. In any event, while it feels like an eternity, I soon enough come crashing down to the ground below, and I stand up to find myself on a pile of debris that was once the throne of the jarl.

Thankfully, the landing doesn't hurt, though the shockwave that erupts from John's landing isn't the most pleasant. Harold comes drifting down slowly in flight and lands just next to the two of us. Leading off from this landing point is a rough, unhewn cave, lit only by a few scattered torches on the walls. The ground rumbles again as we start walking forward, and I keep a close watch.

"I . . . Thank you," Harold speaks up after a moment.

"When I woke up, the thing swallowed me, and . . . the horrors it showed me . . . I shouldn't have given in—I know that now—but at the time, it seemed the only way out. Once I put it on . . ."

"Were you even in control of your actions?" John asks softly.

"Technically, yes, but only in the barest sense of the word," Harold whispers. "There was so much rage, raw and utter, and . . . you two seemed just as monstrous as the dragon—more so. I had to destroy you for the good of humanity."

"Well, I'm happy to have you feeling better," I remark, half-sarcastically. I am happy that he's no longer a murder machine, but I'm somewhat skeptical of his story.

[RazorEdge: I don't believe him! Quick, run a poll! Who thinks he's telling the truth?]

[A: Yes: 0.5%]

[B: No: 99.5%]

"Glad we're in agreement," I mutter softly. Moving down the tunnel, it's almost perfectly quiet. The ground shakes every now and again, but the noise isn't there the way it was overhead. Only the soft shaking sound remains. I'm sure that we're about to run into more trouble, but I can't place exactly what I think is going to happen. The only question is, where is that jarl? What's his plan? I don't know if we'll come to another room where we face him, or if we're just going to keep chasing him endlessly, or if he's the final boss, or what. If he isn't the final boss, this sure is a lot of lead-up for someone else to be the last person we fight.

In any case, we press onward. The tunnel continues to slope steadily downward, forward, and onward, until we come to an opening. Here, we peer out into a wide, dark area. I can see little flickers of bluish light, which seem to come up from underneath some sort of water, but it's tremendously hard to know for sure. I take a step out, but there are no more torches to come to life and light the way, which makes me nervous.

"What do you make of this?" John whispers softly.

"I don't know." I give a small shake of my head. "Harold? Why don't you light it up?"

Harold gives a brief nod then steps forward and throws a fireball out into the room. For a few brief moments, it's lit up just enough to reveal a massive chandelier, seemingly made of wood and bone, hanging over a wide, smooth cave. Scattered around the edges of the cave are pools of water, where the aforementioned light seems to be coming from. There's no sign of the jarl, but there are loads of areas where he could be hiding. The light fades away before I can see if there are any exits.

[ViperQueen: Watch those pools of water!!!]

[ShadowDancer: Yeah, there's going to be something gnarly in there!!]

[ChaosRider: We're rooting for you, Jason!]

"Try to light that chandelier on fire." I gesture upward. "That'll be a good start."

"Sure, make me do everything," Harold grumbles, apparently instinctively, and then throws a ball of fire upward. His annoyance at the action makes me suspect even more that his reformation is a bit shaky, but, again, I'll cross that bridge later. In any event, his shot is dead-on, and the whole thing bursts into flame.

As the flames lap away at the wood and bone, seemingly without burning it up, we walk into the room to wait for whatever will come next. Suddenly, I notice that the walls are covered in paintings. Not elegant paintings like those above, but simpler ones, like what might be seen in a cave or the inside of a tent made of hide. And, strangely, they all depict armies. A rumble shakes the stone, and I have a feeling I know what's coming long before it arrives.

The dragon, now detailed in cave paintings, rises up along the edge of the cave. It snarls and snaps its jaws, then begins systematically attacking and devouring all the assorted armies, just as it did high above. I shudder as I watch it all, then turn my attention to the pools. Slowly, grotesque and waterlogged forms begin to pull themselves up and out of the waters, and the three of us fight to keep from vomiting.

A corpse that's been dried out and reduced to a skeleton is one thing. A corpse that's been allowed to decompose underwater is something different entirely. On the bright side, they don't seem to have any armor. On the less bright side, well . . . they're bloated, lumbering blobs of flesh held together by what little remains of their bodies, with long, grotesque features. A few of them hold weapons loosely in their hands, but most of them just scream unearthly calls of horror and race toward us, desperately fighting to devour us where we stand.

"Stop!" Harold holds out his hands and lets loose a blast of fire. Now, I'll admit, I expected something like what happened with the slimes, but quite the opposite is true. The water inside the corpses seems to give them total immunity. Harold shrieks and flies up into the air, leaving John and me to deal with the creatures ourselves.

"It seems like there's a theme with this Rift!" John races forward and slams a fist into the first of the ghouls. His strike goes straight through it, and he frowns before grabbing hold of the attacking corpse's head and smashing it to the side. He then resorts to yanking out his two bone daggers and spinning like a top, slashing through the creatures like cheese.

I take a somewhat more tactile approach, wading into the midst of the monsters with my dagger. I attack as swiftly as I can, depriving the old warriors of whatever body parts happen to come within range of my weapons. That said, in some ways they're way easier to kill than the soldiers above: no armor, so my knife doesn't feel like it meets resistance at all—it's as easy as cutting air. By the same token, though, it makes it terribly easy to overextend attacks. Frankly, makes it a great deal harder to block attacks that they make. One of them throws itself forward, trying to body-slam me. I bring up an arm to knock it backward, but I only succeed in accidentally knocking off its arms. The rest of its body hits me firmly, smashing me back into the ground, and I groan as I hit the stone floor.

That proves a problem as, almost instantly, all the monsters begin leaping on me. Now, I'll make a quick note that there's a reason I'm calling them "monsters," and not simply "warriors." While the ones with weapons do still behave like warriors, and the ones higher up in the dungeon still acted like people, these act more like mindless beasts or like zombies from those horror shows on television. As they begin trying to gnaw me apart, this resemblance only grows. Thankfully, all their teeth are rotten to the core from so long underwater, so the chewing doesn't cause a great deal of damage, *but* they also continue to stomp, punch, and perform other sorts of attacks, which all combined together *do* start to lower my health bar. Rapidly.

"Bjorn! I need you!"

There's a flicker of lightning, but I can't really see where. Suddenly, a howl splits the air, and a pure and complete *chill* flows through me. The waterlogged zombies freeze solid. At this point, I can hardly move, but I muster up just enough strength to smash my way free and slowly stand up.

[LunarEclipse: Great job, Jason! I never would have thought to use something like that!]

[RazorEdge: Smash them into splinters! Show no mercy!]

[IceQueen: Go, go, go!]

I need no encouragement. I spin around, smashing the frozen zombies apart. You know how they use liquid nitrogen in high school to do stuff like that? Freeze a flower, like a tulip, and then smash it to bits? Yeah, that's exactly what I wind up doing, which I find to be an immense amount of fun. Off to one side, John seems to be buried underneath a large pile of the creatures. Given his strength, however, I'm not too worried. He still seems to be moving, and that's the important bit.

Harold, high above, is still just watching and waiting. I scowl up at him then slowly start working my way through the hordes. Bjorn briefly turns his attention to John, freezing the pile around him, allowing the muscleman to smash his way out of confinement. From that point on, we systematically work our way through the rest of the room, freezing each of the pools of water in turn. Soon, there's not a single zombie left, and Harold comes drifting back down to the floor.

"Some help you were," John mutters as we start toward the opposite side of the room, passing beneath the fiery chandelier. "Thanks, really."

"I'm doing the best I can!" Harold whines. "You could kill them! I couldn't. What was I supposed to do?"

"Something useful," I retort. I catch a glimpse of a small entrance at the rear of the cave, and I head toward it. "Now come on, both of you. I think this is our way out."

"What makes you so sure?" John comes striding up behind me.

"Because of the painting." I point upward at the space over the door. There, instead of an army, is a crude drawing of a king. A jarl. The dragon, upon reaching that one, instead of devouring or crushing it, slowly wraps itself around and around the jarl, until the mighty ruler is little more than a speck amidst the coils of the terrible creature. Then, after the jarl has been completely encircled, the dragon gobbles him up, only to shrink down and become the image of the jarl once more. This time, though, while essentially identical to how it had looked before, there's something different about the image. I can't tell exactly *what's* different, but I know something is, and that's the problem. It seems darker, more menacing.

The image of that jarl watches us closely as we walk through the entrance of the cave. Harold and John go first, so I'm the last one to see it. Right as I look away, I catch the barest flicker of red upon the jarl's finger, and my mind is drawn back to that ring. My hands ball into fists, and I let out a long breath.

"Not today," I whisper. "Today, *we* slay *you*."

The jarl doesn't answer, but I feel the cave rumble again. It's time to go forth, to put an end to all of this.

Either that . . . or we'll die trying.

CHAPTER NINETEEN

As we walk farther into the cave, it seems to grow increasingly rougher. The walls become more and more uneven, covered with bumps that look more like organic growths than cave trappings. I'm more than a little uneasy, but I square my shoulders and push forward. Harold takes the lead, using his fire to light the way, seeming to gain a wave of confidence after his earlier cowardice. I glance at John, then give a nod forward. He slides up next to Harold, and I fall back just a bit.

In the chat, my viewers are discussing a handful of assorted matters, mostly summing up the last several battles and contemplating what we'll find at the end. I send a mental command to Riftwatch, hoping it will work.

Change live feed.

The reason for this is simple: I've already been informed multiple times by my viewers about things that are happening elsewhere. While most of my viewers seem to be sympathetic to me and not Harold, I can only imagine that I have a few lurkers who will send Harold any indication that I might be looking to make a move against him. I'd really rather that not happen. There's a pause, and I get a notification.

[Riftwatch: Livestream is no longer transmitting from your eyes. You are out of the picture.]

A small, almost invisible box phases out of my head and moves forward, about two feet in front of me, and hovers there, keeping pace with my steps. Perfect. No one will be the wiser, as long as John and Harold don't turn around. Slowly, I open my inventory and pull out the ring.

It stares up at me as I turn it over in my fingers, full of malice, full of dread. I can't explain it properly, but . . . this thing is *full* of evil. The hairs on the back of my neck prickle, and the whole tunnel seems to grow darker—the ring feels cold and clammy against my fingers. And yet, I have the almost irresistible urge to put it on. It sounds cliche, I know, but . . . this thing, this epicenter of evil, so terrifying that I want to throw it down the passage and be rid of it forever—I *long* to put it on, to embrace the power that Harold was experiencing. I would be stronger than John! My beasts would become dragons in their own rights! Nothing would stand before me! I could stalk through this Rift, tear down everything in my way, come back to New York, and single-handedly destroy everything trying to take over the world! For that matter, this Apocalypse Protocol is supposed to be irreversible, but . . . what if it's not? What if I can take this power, march right up to the System Administrators, and destroy them with the very same system that they tried to use to destroy our world? It seems too good to be true . . .

And a little voice at the back of my mind tells me that it is.

I find my hands shaking, and I desperately have to snap my mind out of this. I'm locked in a mental battle against the dragon, and I didn't even realize it. Slowly, I lift the ring up to my eyes, staring down into the depths of that red jewel and the intricately carved serpent.

I don't know exactly what I'm trying to find in those depths. No, that's not true. I do. I need to know what influence, exactly, it had on Harold. It controlled him, at least to a degree. That much was evidenced by the fact that the dragon became so angry when it got taken away. Without the ring, that control is gone, but . . . exactly how much influence does the dragon still exert upon him? He didn't help fight against the monsters at all. Was that truly because he's a coward, and because his magic doesn't work, or was it because he *couldn't* fight against the minions of his dark master?

I don't have the answer, and the more I stare at that ring, the more confused I become. Finally, I sigh and slip it back into my inventory then close it down. The floating box seems to respond to my unsent command, and slides back into my head, restoring everything back to my sense, my eyesight. Once more, people can see what I'm seeing.

Whether that's good or bad, I suppose we'll see.

Up ahead, I hear a startled gasp, and I move forward, joining up with John once more. He gives me a little sideways glance. I don't know what look to send him back, whether to tell him I've succeeded or failed, so I just give a little shake of my head. If anything, I hope it tells him not to trust Harold. I can barely pull my mind away from the ring after only a moment of looking at it. He actually wore it, was actually in contact with the thing. I can't even begin to imagine what that must have done to his brain.

The gasp is in reference to the final door that we come to. I don't know how I know that it's the final one, but I'm very confident of that fact. It's made entirely out of bones, large ones, that are overlaid in a crisscross pattern. Harold steps up and sends a ball of fire through, and a moment later, light seems to explode outward from inside.

Flames rise up from an immense trench all around the interior of a domed room, firelight rising up the walls in a wondrous, almost mesmeric display. At the exact center of the room stands the jarl. Otherwise, the room has no distinct features. No thrones, no obstacles—just a battle platform about fifty feet wide, ringed by fire. The door of bones rumbles aside without any effort on our part, and we slowly walk inside.

That, of course, is when I see the dragon. This time, it appears amidst the flames, taking up the patterns of light, of smoke, of ash, of fire. I cannot describe how utterly horrifying this is. It swirls around and around, faster and faster, circling and snarling at us again and again.

"*I will give you one final chance,*" the jarl speaks slowly and softly. His voice is almost painful to listen to, as strange as that sounds. "*Give yourselves over to us, and you will be rewarded. Refuse, and you will suffer the consequences.*"

John snarls and draws both of his bone daggers. "Here's what I have to say about that!"

He charges forward, springing across the stone in great leaps and bounds. The jarl simply raises a hand and gives a flick of his finger. Lightning explodes through the air, and a portal appears just in front of him. John staggers through the portal, unable to stop, and it closes an instant later.

"*Your friend has just been sent back to the streets. He can return here, technically, but it will take him some time. As I was speaking to the two of you, I thought it appropriate.*" The jarl continues to address us, "*Give yourselves to me. Now.*"

Harold glances at me. I can see his face wavering, and I grit my teeth. I know what I must do. Slowly, I open my inventory then let the ring drop into my hands.

"*Yes. You've seen its power!*" The jarl sounds excited. "*Give yourself to me! Give yourself to—*"

"How about I just give this back?"

With all my might, I draw back my arm and fling the ring into the flames. I doubt the fire is hot enough to destroy it or anything, but my intuition is that it'll be hot enough to insta-kill a person, which removes it from Harold's reach. Harold, the moment the ring leaves my hands, shoots off into the air after it.

"No!"

He flashes just behind the ring, and I hear a startled roar from the dragon. As the ring passes through the outer barrier of the fire, another portal appears, flinging Harold out of the dungeon as well. Now only the jarl and I remain, and I draw out my dagger.

"Couldn't stand to allow one of your best minions to be destroyed?" I take my stance and prepare for battle.

The jarl, quite unfortunately, doesn't speak. Instead, he simply bolts forward, racing pell-mell across the floor to meet me. A battle axe appears in his hands, and I come forward to take up the challenge.

My dagger gleams in the light of the flames. As we come together, the jarl sweeps out with the axe, desperately trying to cleave me in half. I flip over the attack and slam an elbow into his head, knocking him backward. I slash my dagger through his decaying neck. Dust explodes through the air, and I kick him in the stomach with all my might.

[GoldenShield: Go Jason! Good hit!]

[IceQueen: You're taking on a Rift boss all by yourself? That takes guts! Best of luck!!!]

[ChaosRider: I hope this isn't the end of you!]

I can't answer the chat as the jarl returns with another sweeping blow. I dodge it again then rush forward to stab him through the chest. To my surprise, though, he drops the axe and grabs my wrist, moving fast as lightning. I stagger, and his free hand strikes me in both the neck and the chest. I go down hard, and he twists my wrist quite painfully.

This is no ordinary undead soldier. This is someone who fully and willingly gave himself over to the service of this dragon. He's fast, he's strong, and at that moment, I don't see any way to beat him.

Which just means that I need to find another angle.

I hear metal scrape against stone and know I have mere seconds. With my wrist twisted the way it is, I can't move . . . at least, not much. Desperately, I kick my legs up into the air, striking the jarl on the leg. It's not much, but it makes him stumble a bit, and I push away with all my might. My wrist twists impossibly—I feel bones rubbing against one another and tendons stretching—but it works.

The axe comes crashing down where I had just been lying. Thankfully, this makes the grip on my arm loosen, and I leap back to my feet. My dagger has fallen, so I grab hold of the handle of the axe, and for a moment, the two of us struggle against one another in an epic battle for supremacy.

"*You are nothing more than a weakling!*" the jarl hisses softly. "*A lowly human, meant only to serve me.*"

"If that were true, you'd have killed me by now." I head-butt the jarl as hard as I can. He's wearing a helmet, so it hurts as though I had slammed my head into a brick wall, but it does the job. His fingers lose their purchase on the axe, and I swing it around and bring it crashing into his side.

The axe bites through his armor and lodges about halfway into his body. The monster doesn't seem to feel any pain but, as I disengage and step back, it seems to throw him off balance. After a moment, the jarl takes notice of my dagger and slowly bends down to pick it up.

"*What a coincidence. You took my weapon, and now I take—*"

I call the dagger to my left hand. Not expecting the motion, the jarl staggers forward, and I follow up with a punch. My fist slams directly into his face, right below the helmet, and before he can get away, I hook my fingers on the bottom of the helmet and pull with all my might. It comes off, leaving him exposed. Just what I wanted.

Before the jarl can react, I bash him over the head with the helmet, smashing in part of his skull and then kicking him again. Once more, bone dust explodes through the area, and I sneeze rather forcefully after inhaling some of it. As I watch, though, the part of his head where I caved in his skull begins to heal. Dust simply comes back together from the air, rebuilding the crushed portion.

"*This body cannot be harmed in the same way that yours can.*

Foolish boy! Nor is there any ring or other talisman that you could simply remove for the same effect. No, boy, this body was given to me, and given to me fully!"

"Let me guess, then." I decide to placate the dragon's desire for chitchat. I suppose that when you're a dragon stuck in a Rift—even if you hate everyone who shows up and regularly try to kill or enslave them—good conversation is hard to come by. "You gave him the ring, and when he accepted it, it transferred part of his mind to your control. Over time, you gained more and more control, until you no longer needed the ring."

"Correct."

The implications of this revelation are numerous. What I'm concerned with is getting rid of this jarl. I need to destroy him before I can close the Rift, and that's a rather difficult thing to do when the boss is indestructible.

Or, at the very least, has a nigh-infinite healing ability.

Which means all I need to do to defeat him is find some way to deal damage faster than he can heal it.

Several ideas pop into my head. Dozens more come from the chat, but I don't have time to read them as the jarl pulls the axe out of his body and charges forward. I come up to meet him, and once more, the battle begins.

The next several minutes are filled with frenzied attacks. He strikes; I block. Trust me—it's very, *very* hard to block an axe with a dagger. I strike; he blocks. I land a few hits here and there, crumbling his aging body, only for him to heal. He lands a few hits on me. Those hurt, badly, and don't heal as instantly. I'm losing this fight, and that means that I need to find a solution—quickly.

Suddenly, though, the solution comes to me, and I nod.

"Alright, then. Mister Jarl, I'll give you one chance to surrender. Refuse, and I'll destroy this body, leaving you as nothing more than a painting on the wall."

"*You couldn't even if you wanted to.*"

"I do want to, and I will." I take a deep breath, steeling myself for what's to come. The jarl seems to sense this, and he tries to figure out what I'm doing. Then . . . I move. I draw back my dagger and throw it. The jarl dodges out of the way, and it clatters into the flames, where it stays. The jarl laughs then charges forward.

I dodge several attacks, mostly playing for time while trying to position myself. Finally, the time presents itself, and I hold up my hand. Right on cue, the dagger leaps out of the flames and comes flashing back through the air, red hot from a fire of impossible proportions.

The jarl senses the incoming weapon and turns. I, of course, have positioned myself so that he's directly between me and the dagger. He tries to dodge out of the way, but he isn't fast enough, and the weapon melts straight through his armor. As smoke and fire belch up out of his chest cavity, I stop calling the weapon and let it be, and the jarl tilts his head back and screams.

I'm not really certain why the jarl seems in pain. After all, he's long dead—the body is only a nerveless puppet controlled by the dragon. Perhaps the flames are a prison for the beast, some sort of mystical power, and now, as they destroy its only physical body, it can feel them in a way it never could before. In any event, the jarl freezes up, giving me the chance I need. I rush forward, grab hold of the thing, and sling it into the flames with all my might.

The moment the body hits the fire, it explodes into thick clouds of smoke and ash. The room goes dark, and I'm plunged into pitch blackness. At least . . . for a moment. Slowly, almost imperceptibly so, a light begins to flicker to life just above me.

[System Notification: Congratulations! You have conquered a Rift!]

[Please accept from the following rewards:]

[. . .]

The list of rewards is really quite long, but I don't bother to glance at them just yet. Instead, I keep my eyes fixated on the light, which resolves into a portal. Unlike the other portals, though, it doesn't flicker. It doesn't rage with electricity or lightning. It's ringed by a soft border of light, and it exudes a sense of peace. I take a deep breath then slowly step through.

My feet hit solid ground, and I blink in surprise to find myself back in Times Square. Harold and John are both there too. Around us is a crowd of people, several of whom I recognize from the Central Park settlement. The three of us look at each other, and then, as the massive Rift portal slowly closes behind us, a loud cheer shakes the skyscrapers.

Almost instantly, a procession forms back toward Central Park. The people around me start clapping and cheering, singing and hollering, but I can hardly focus on any of it. All around us, I can hear the telltale zapping of portals—the very ones that had closed during our foray into the dungeon— opening once more. I can sense a dark and foreboding presence watching us, and I can feel the weight of the fact that, soon, another Rift will be opening.

I can also feel, deep within my pocket, the very ring that I had cast into the flames. Harold glances sideways at me, and I see a hunger in his eyes. He knows that I still have it; somehow, he's drawn to it. All of it spells trouble . . .

Trouble and an upcoming fight of greater proportions than ever.

CHAPTER TWENTY

The trip back to Central Park is a joyous one, for the most part. Like I said earlier, all around me are the rumbles of thunder and monsters—but thankfully, I also hear a good deal of fighting. Explosions echo through the streets. I look around for some sort of an explanation.

"There are more Awakened who came into New York when the last Rift opened," John explains, apparently noticing my confusion. "Riftwatch called them, since it's assumed that the next Rift will open soon, and they want enough people on site to be able to handle all the other dungeons while the Rift is being cleared."

"Interesting." I frown in thought. "What happens to the areas they were guarding?"

"They're being covered by others," John answers. "One person is taking the territory of two, and so on. Jersey doesn't have nearly the same concentration of dungeons we have here, you know, and it gets even lower farther out. I've heard of some small towns in the Central Plains that aren't even sure if they believe anything's changed in the world."

[ChaosRider: That's me! Middle of Kansas, bro! If I hadn't found this livestream, I'd still be going to school like normal!]

[DarkCynic: I'm way down south, out in the country. I can hear a lot of chaos in the nearby city, but it's a long ways away.]

[IceQueen: Can't decide if you all are lucky or missing out. I'm in a high-rise apartment right here in New York. I've actually been able to watch a couple of these fights with my own eyes!]

"Interesting," I muse. It's all so interesting, and so *not* what I expected an apocalyptic, end-of-the-world scenario to be like. In any case, I'm itching to get back out and get into battle, but the people seem intent on celebrating, and it seems like John, Harold, and I are the focal points of this celebration. Though it may be the hardest thing I've done yet, I know that they need the release of tension, so I allow them to have their fun.

When we arrive at Central Park, a band begins to play, and an impromptu parade takes place, wrapping around the pond there, through some of the buildings and back to where we started. There, a cake is brought out from a local bakery, and . . . well . . . we eat it.

It sounds so strange, I know, but that's what we do. Dozens of people come up and congratulate me. I shake their hands and I nod in thanks but, through it all, I can't tear my mind away from that thing in my pocket. I have no idea why it's there, what it's trying to do, what Harold will do, nor if he even knows I have it. All I know is that it exists, and as long as it does, it's a liability. A great portion of me wants to just chuck it into the river, but I have a feeling that such a thing would be a short-term solution at best. Harold seems able to sense its power, which means that the only way to keep it away from him is to keep it on my person. Thankfully, my audience doesn't have a clue about the ring, which I think is a good thing.

The celebration lasts several hours, until the sun has set and bonfires crackle joyfully across the rolling landscape. I settle down next to one of them, enjoying the heat, and take a long, deep breath.

[ViperQueen: Hey, Jason! Are you going to check out all the loot you got from that dungeon before you go to sleep?]

[ShadowDancer: YEAH!!!! DO IT!!!]

[FireStorm: Please? I have school in the morning, and I won't be able to log on until after noon!]

"Alright, alright. You've convinced me." I smile and nod. "First off, I'm pretty sure I leveled up a few times. Let's check and see what level I am now, and if I get any rewards from that."

[You are now Level 17!]

[Please accept from the following rewards: (3)]

[Level E Weapon]

[Level E Monster]

[Monster Trainer Skill]

"Alright, folks. Let's think about this." I purse my lips for a moment. A great deal of advice comes from the chat, most of which I ignore. "I could really use a new weapon. Something with a bit more reach. This dagger is incredible—it can cut through almost anything—but it has such a short range."

There's a flash of light, and something materializes in

my hands. It's . . . another dagger. This one, unlike the dark, smooth metal of the Shadow Dagger's blade, has a shining white steel that almost glows in the darkness. I hold it in the palm of my hand, feeling as though I have a proper sword in my palm. It's heavy—in a good way. This thing can deal some damage.

[Weapon Acquired: Photonic Dagger]

[Level: E]

[RazorEdge: WHOA!!! Now you can dual-wield!!!]

I'm not so sure that'll be a good idea, but to placate the audience, I take out my Shadow Dagger in my right hand, hold the Photonic Dagger in my left, and strike a stance—at least as much of one as I can manage while sitting on the ground. My audience seems to love it.

[ShadowDancer: Can't wait to see this in actual combat!!!]

[ChaosRider: Go, Jason!!!]

I smile and make a couple simple attacks at the air then put my daggers away. For my next two rewards, I think for a moment then ask the system a question.

"Instead of getting a new weapon or monster, can I just upgrade one of the ones I have?"

[System Notification: That is acceptable.]

"Good." I nod. "In that case, I'd like an upgrade for Bjorn, as well as for Garg."

A soft twinkle of light floats through the air, letting me know that it's been done, but all the action takes place inside the pocket dimension. I suppose I'll find out what sorts of upgrades they got when they come up, but I don't want to risk it right now. They're tame, but it's dark, and I would hate for someone to mistake the monsters for a hostile mob and attack them. I lean back against my tree trunk, satisfied, and then check my last reward.

With a flash of light, a loot box appears on the ground in front of me. It's not a large box—really nothing more than an ornate jewelry box—but it has a golden clasp and is studded with dozens of gemstones. I slowly reach out and place my finger on the latch then give it a flick.

Light shoots up into the sky. When it fades away, I look down at the ground and find myself in possession of . . . a bag. I frown in confusion then slowly reach down and pick it up.

[Bottomless Bag of Shadows]

There are no indicated effects. I slowly open the bag up and peer inside, but I find only a swirling mass of darkness that likely indicates some sort of great void. I'm not really sure what it is, to be frank, and I close it up after a moment. In any case, the thing is quite small, with a mouth only a few inches across. I tuck the bag into my inventory after a moment, and my chat explodes.

[RazorEdge: WHAT? No cool weapon? You should complain!!!]

[IceQueen: Yeah!!! You cleared a Rift. That should be worth something!!!]

"I'm sure it is worth something; I just have to figure out what that use is." I chuckle and slowly stand up. "Besides, let's keep in mind that it *was* just an F-Ranked Rift. My guess is that the next one will be a whole lot more enticing, but . . . if they give out everything right at the beginning, it doesn't really give you much incentive to keep going, you know?"

My chat seems to agree with this assessment, though begrudgingly so. I smile at them then move a bit closer to the dying fire and pull out my sleeping bag. As I start to crawl inside, I hear footsteps, and I look over to see John approaching. His face is warped with worry, and I straighten up.

"What's the matter?" I ask softly. "Everything okay?"

"That depends," John murmurs. "I just got word . . . I think the next Rift is opening tonight."

"Tonight?" I hiss back to him. "That's insane! Are you sure?"

"That's what the word on the street is." John gives a small nod. "There's an Awakened who just came into town—his name is Elijah, I think. He can't see the future per se, but his special skill gives him insight into what the System Administrators are thinking and planning. Apparently, he made an offhand comment that they're planning on opening it soon—a whole lot sooner than they had originally intended."

"Why?" I ask softly. "What changed their minds?"

"According to him. . ." John pauses then nods at me. "You."

[LunarEclipse: WHOA! Jason, you're so powerful that you actually changed the minds of the System Admins? That's incredible!]

[FireStorm: He's even more powerful than we thought!]

I frown in concern. I have a distinct feeling that I know what he's talking about, but I can't say anything in front of my chat, in a place where it could get back to Harold. "Did he elaborate?"

"He said a few things, but nothing that was understood by the people who heard the message. I'm not sure I understand it myself, but I think I have an idea." His eyes narrow slightly, and I suddenly have the feeling that he's not coming to me because he trusts me. He's eyeing me with suspicion because he knows I have the ring, or at least suspects it, and thinks that it might have something to do with what the System Administrators are doing. I hold his gaze and try to signal to him that everything's going to be okay, but I can't tell if my message is getting through.

Regardless, I refuse to let the conversation stall. "Did he say where the next Rift will be opening?"

"Statue of Liberty, break of dawn."

"Great." I cross my arms and try to think. "Are you heading that way?"

"That's my plan. I wanted to see if you wanted to come along."

I give a brief shake of my head. "I need to catch a few hours of sleep first. I'm utterly exhausted and not in any shape to take on a full Rift. I'll stay here then take off in a little bit."

John gives a small nod of his head and claps me on the shoulder. I don't return the gesture—partly because I'm not really a physical touch sort of guy, and partly because John's so strong that the parting pat *hurts*—and it takes me a moment to recover. As he strides away into the darkness, I sigh, then lie down on the ground and crawl into my sleeping bag.

As usual, the moment I pull myself inside, my eyelids drift shut. My feed goes dark, and I quickly begin to fall into slumber. I think it must be an effect of the bag, which I appreciate. I've always been a bit of an insomniac, and it's nice to be able to fall asleep as soon as you lie down. That said . . .

Tonight, I just want a few moments to collect my thoughts, and to ponder everything that went on in the dungeon. Thankfully, after I fight the sleep for a few moments, it goes away, and I'm left to stare up at the stars—just me and my thoughts. I hear the soft crackling of the bonfire, and the harsh crackling of Harold's fire off in the distance. He seems to be amusing himself by performing for a small crowd. I snort in derision; though, on the other hand, if he wears himself out before the next Rift opens, it means that I won't have to worry about seeing him on the inside.

I don't know exactly how long I lay there, but it's so peaceful that I can't bear to pull myself away from the serenity. Finally, though, as the stars turn lazily over me, I allow my eyelids to flicker closed and yield to the sweet slumber of sleep.

CHAPTER TWENTY-ONE

Riftwatch: Welcome to Day 6 of the Apocalypse Protocol!]

Crack-peeeeeeeeeeeeeeeeeew!!!!!

Lightning explodes across the sky, startling me out of sleep, and I jump to my feet as quickly as I can. A great beam of purplish energy streaks through the great blue dome, crackling and hissing, and arcs off toward the harbor. It vanishes behind the rows of buildings after a few moments, and I shake my head in amazement.

[ShadowDancer: WHOA! That's really cool!!!]

[GoldenShield: Yeah! Go clear it, Jason!]

"Patience." I hold up a hand. "I haven't gotten this far by being hasty. Let's get moving, and we'll get there when we get there."

I bend down and roll up the sleeping bag then slowly start heading toward the gates of Central Park. All around me, Awakened are getting around much faster than me. Several take flight and start flashing off in that direction, while others start running. Suddenly, though, a message flickers across my vision.

[Riftwatch: Attention, Awakened! Due to the larger nature of this Rift, and the necessity of protecting our fair city, all Awakened will be assigned to either enter the Rift and clear it or to continue to protect our city outside. Disobeying will have consequences.]

At that, a tingle of electricity shoots through my body. It rather hurts, and I get the feeling that the people behind the message aren't joking. If you try to enter that portal and aren't authorized to do so, you're going to pay the price for it.

[Riftwatch: You will be assigned to . . .]

[. . . Calculating . . .]

[Enter the Rift!]

"What a shocker." I roll my eyes. I have a very good feeling that the selection was far from the most random thing in the world. I stride up to the gates of the park and pause, watching several Awakened grumbling about having to stay and watch the city. A large scorpion boss comes charging out of a portal a few streets down, though, which gives them something to do.

"Alright, Lightfax." I open the portal and allow my noble steed to come out and join me. "Let's get moving."

Lightfax snorts, and I climb up onto her back. The great horse takes off, lightly dashing across the city streets just as smooth as a lazy river, though a good bit faster. It's not long at all before we come up to the harbor, where the great Statue of Liberty stands high above the waters, looking out to sea.

It's amazing, really, but . . . somehow the structure doesn't seem to have suffered any damage from all the chaos. Prior to this, no dungeons seem to have opened on the island, and nothing has touched it from this side of the universe. It's still standing as a pillar of freedom, a beacon of hope . . . albeit one that's currently ringed with lightning and dark energy and all sorts of other chaos.

In any event, Lightfax trots up to the docks, then pauses. A large boat—I think it's the usual Ellis Island tour boat—is chugging slowly over the choppy waters. I can see the decks crowded with Awakened, several dozen at least, while more watch from the shoreline. One of them dives into the water and starts to swim, only to get struck by a bolt of lightning from above. He swims back to shore, screaming in pain, and I grimace. They weren't kidding. They want the fighters to go and the protectors to stay. Overhead, a few flight-based Awakened zoom off toward the island, Harold chief among them. He leaves a long trail of brilliant flame, and I scowl. Of course he is one of the chosen ones. I mean, *maybe* it's because Riftwatch recognizes that he's a danger and is hoping he gets pasted against the walls, but I sort of doubt it. Most likely, they want another showdown between us.

I continue to sit there on Lightfax for a moment longer then tap my heels against her flanks. She leaps forward with gusto, flashing across the water as if she had wings. Her hooves dance lightly across the waves, barely seeming to touch them, and I find myself breathless. We quickly catch up with the boat and go racing past, eliciting gasps of awe. I must admit, I'm in awe myself. Lightfax is a magnificent creature, and her white mane streams out behind her; she looks like something out of a great mythic tale.

We come racing up to the shore and canter onto the beach there. By now, a handful of Awakened are standing before the

Rift but aren't entering. I ride up to meet them then swing down. John is already there, soaking wet from apparently having swum the distance. Harold lands as far away from us as he can, though I can see fire in his eyes as he looks at me. Soon the barge comes up, and the rest join us. There are about twenty of us all told.

[System Notification: This is a C-Ranked Rift. If warriors do not enter, it will begin discharging ferocious monsters that will devour your planet. If all warriors inside are killed, it will begin discharging ferocious monsters that will devour your planet. There are several other conditions that may cause this outcome as well.]

[ChaosRider: C-Ranked!!! That's insane!]

[FireStorm: Just got in! Way earlier than I thou— WHOA!!!!!!!!!!!!!]

[ViperQueen: I don't know if even our Jason can handle this.]

[Originalgoth: I'm pretty sure he can't.]

I notice Originalgoth's presence, but I don't say a word. Her absence was a pleasant high point of the previous Rift. Now that she's apparently come back, I have a distinct feeling that it doesn't bode well for me. I swallow that, though, and try to stay focused.

"Well?" A girl with long, dark hair slowly nods at the thing. "Who's going to go first?"

Everyone looks at one another. I sense my chance, and I step forward and square my shoulders.

"I will."

[RazorEdge: Yeah, that's our Jason!]

[ShadowDancer: Good luck!]

[IceQueen: He doesn't need luck, he's got skills!]

"Don't wait too long to come after me." I pull out my twin daggers then spin them around in either hand. "I'd hate to kill everything and leave you guys without anything to fight."

A smattering of laughter echoes from behind, defusing some of the tension. I stride forward, stretch out my hands, and step through the portal.

It's just as bad as last time. Maybe even a bit worse, really. Lightning erupts up and down my arms, making my limbs twitch as I come out into a large, cold area. I take a moment to catch my breath, and I look around as quickly as I can.

Immediately, several things come to my attention. First, I'm in a cave again. Second, the cave is being lit by a small hole in the center, high above my head, where a few pale beams of light shine down onto the gray slate. Third, a great deal of snow is scattered through the cave, and long icicles hang from the ceiling instead of stalactites. Not technically how things would work in the wild, I don't think, but it does look cool. This, of course, means that Bjorn likely won't be a great deal of use here since his attacks work best on fire-type creatures. At the end of this cave, two dark openings stretch outward, though I can see light in both of them as well.

Of course, I observe all of this in the blink of an eye. Charging headlong at me is a great snowy beast—I can't tell exactly what it's supposed to be. It has the body of a bear, but with long, white hair. The head looks something like a cat, and it has long claws like a cat as well, but it has a tail that . . . well . . . *maybe* looks more like a dog's tail with a sharp barb at the end? Whatever the case, it looks rather hungry, and to its eyes, I'm sure I look like a nice dinner.

I decide that I'm not in the mood to be eaten.

[LunarEclipse: That's cool! What are we looking at? Let's name it!]

[ShadowDancer: How about the frost-bear?]

[ViperQueen: No . . . frost-cat!]

[RazorEdge: Frost-cat-bear!]

The debate over the monster's name continues, but as the thing jumps at me, I quit paying attention. Long claws slash down at me, and I narrowly dodge and roll out of the way. As I stand up, though, it follows me, and rakes me across the front of my chest. Let me tell you, those claws *sting*, though they don't carve me terribly deep. I'm picked up and thrown backward against the cave wall, landing in a pile of snow. My blood drips down into the white powder, and the monster roars and comes racing at me pell-mell.

I grit my teeth, take a stronger hold on my daggers, then push off the ground and leap at the thing. Its slanted eyes grow wide, and I lash out with my right arm, slicing my Shadow Dagger across its nose and back down across its face. It howls and spins, and I turn with it, slamming my Photonic Dagger into its right shoulder. The pain-filled scream of the creature echoes through the cave, rattling the icicles and making a good bit of snow drift down from the ceiling. I pull as hard as I can, drawing my dagger back from its shoulder to its hindquarters. It springs away, limping and bleeding, and we size each other up once again.

For a long moment, neither of us moves, and then, suddenly, I charge at it. It takes a step back, and I know I have it on the ropes. I spring upward quickly, driving my daggers down between its eyes. Bone cracks, and the thing howls.

Suddenly, though, it rears up, catches my legs on its claws, and slams me back down to the ground.

The stone shudders under my impact, and claws bite deep into my flesh. The pain is impossible to describe, and before I can move, the creature bites my torso, sinking long teeth into my gut. I can see fury, pain, and desperation in its eyes. I decide to remove that desperation by slamming one of my daggers *into* its left eye.

It drops me almost instantly, and I stand up and throw both of my daggers into its chest. The monster staggers backward, and I race to the side, putting myself in its blind spot. It tries to follow me, turning slowly, dripping more and more blood into the snow. With that, I send out a mental command, and Garg comes stomping out from the portal.

The cat-thing spins to face Garg, who launches a fireball at the monster. It leaps to avoid it, but now its single eye is focused upon the gargoyle, not me. I hold up my hand and call my Shadow Dagger back to my palm, which causes the monster to yelp in pain. It starts backing up, trying to keep both of us in its vision, and I know my time to strike is waning.

"Get him!"

Garg obeys my command and starts making his way off to the side, leading the cat-thing away from me. Quickly, I throw the Shadow Dagger up at the ceiling. There's a sharp crack, and a massive icicle—five feet long—comes crashing down to land in front of me. I pick it up, take a deep breath, and charge forward, leaping across the ground as fast as I can. Behind me, I hear the crackle of the portal, and I throw the improvised spear with as much force as I can.

The sharpened ice pierces the side of the monster and

drives all the way into its heart. This makes the monster let out one final howl of pain, freezing it in place. Garg follows up with a barrage of fire and, overwhelmed, the monster collapses. When it hits the ground, a loud *thud* rings through the room, and a few more small icicles fall to shatter on the stone below. I retrieve both of my daggers, and I turn to find John looking at me with a small smirk on his face.

"When you said you'd kill everything without us, I didn't really think you'd take it so literally." John starts walking toward the back of the cave. "What is that thing, anyway?"

"My viewers have decided that it's a . . ." I glance at the chat. "Frost- bear- cat- dog- scorpion- mammoth."

"Mammoth?"

"I dunno. Long hair?" I flash a thumbs-up. "You guys are great! Keep up the commentary!"

John just laughs. "And that's why your viewership is almost twice as high as mine. Alright, what seems to be the deal with this dungeon?"

I glance over my shoulder as more of the Awakened start to come through the portal. Harold comes near the rear, fury written across his face.

"I think I'd rather ask what took you so long." I shrug as John and I walk to the rightmost of the tunnels. I keep my daggers at hand as we slip along quietly through a short, dark tunnel, angling toward that soft shimmer of light I had seen earlier.

"Problems with a certain fire-type," John answers. "He tried to blockade the portal so you'd die. A few of us took issue with that. You can probably find a recording of the fight online when we take a breather."

"I'd like that." I hold my breath as we reach the next section of the dungeon and slowly step out into . . . well . . . a very similar room as before.

It's a lot smaller than the entry cave, but the basic principle is the same: light coming down from a small opening, snow everywhere. There are four exits: one leads back to the entry; one off to the left, which seems to lead to the *other* patch of light I had seen (this is confirmed a moment later when we see some other Awakened showing up there to look at us curiously); one that leads deeper into the stone (I don't see any light in *that* direction); and a hole in the exact center that goes straight down.

"It's a maze," John murmurs. "What do you think?"

"I think we're going to have to go down," I answer. "That's the only thing that makes sense to me. After you?"

John laughs. "I suppose it's only fair!"

He jumps down into the hole, ignoring the ladder carved into the side of the stone. There's a brief whistle as he falls, followed by a resounding *thump* when he hits the bottom. I pause then hear a powerful roar.

"And that's my cue." I jump in after him, also ignoring the ladder. Most likely the ladder is primarily for getting back up, anyway. I'm plunged into darkness, and a moment later, I hit the stone in a chamber illuminated only by a few small torches.

John is standing there, arms spread wide, his bone daggers in either hand. Facing him are large bats—bats that are using their wings as legs, hobbling across the ground toward us. Each is the size of a Great Dane, though far less cute. One of them already lies dead nearby, and I lunge forward.

The bats lunge as well, slashing and biting at the two of us. John cuts the head off the first one that attacks. I hit the second, cutting off one of its wings with my own two daggers. The bat screams and falls to the side, and I ignore it while the next one hits me. It's a lot faster than I anticipated, and it sinks long fangs into my right arm. I scream in pain, then stab it with my Photonic Dagger held in my left hand. It sinks in up to the hilt, carving straight through the bone, and the bat goes limp and collapses in a heap. I kick it away, then stagger backward as several more detach from the ceiling, which I hadn't noticed up until that point. They roar and charge forward, and I brace myself . . . only for one particularly large one to land directly on top of me.

It's like being hit by a ton of bricks. Now, in fairness, as an Awakened, I sincerely doubt that getting hit by said ton of bricks would hurt nearly as much as before this whole process began. That said, it's still not terribly *pleasant*, and I'm knocked flat on my back. The bat begins snarling and chomping at my face, and I only narrowly manage to beat it away. Thankfully, all my daggers are still in my hands, and I'm able to cut through its neck. I don't quite sever the spinal cord, so the whole thing collapses on me, and I slowly climb back to my feet, shoving the giant corpse off my body as I do so.

As I stand up, John grabs two bats and dashes them together, then throws them to the back of the room. By this point, I'm bleeding pretty badly, but I know I can't give up. Several more bats drop down, and I look up to see how many are left. There are quite a few, and I get the feeling that they're just going to keep coming down until they're all dead.

"Garg! I need you!"

Garg appears with a flicker of portal energy then spreads his wings and launches into the sky. Rather than using fire in such a tight space, he simply sweeps along the ceiling, tearing the bats into bits and casting the remains to the ground. I look up and nod slowly and, after a moment, Garg comes crashing down, fluttering his wings before folding them behind his back.

"Efficient." John gives me a nod. "You should heal before we go any farther."

I raise an eyebrow. "You're not looking so great yourself."

John glances down at his arms, which are covered in dozens of bites and scratches. He chuckles after a moment. "Yeah, but I didn't go toe-to-toe with a frost-bear-cat-dog-scorpion-mammoth, level twenty-one and a half."

"Fair." I open up my inventory and pull out a Pumped! drink. As the healing liquid begins to flow through my body, I sigh deeply then give him a nod. "Well, now, do you think we should—"

A low rumble shakes the ground, cutting me off. I feel the floor begin to shake, and suddenly a crack explodes across the stone. John dives for the wall and manages to catch hold of several small cracks, but I have no such luck. A powerful roar shakes the Rift, and I suddenly find a void opening up underneath my feet. I feel myself sliding, getting sucked downward . . . and then I'm gone, vanishing into the depths of the Rift.

CHAPTER TWENTY-TWO

Stone whirls around me as I fall, and I find the cold air slowly being replaced by a much warmer air. No . . . a much *harsher* air. I can smell sulfur gas; I can hear the soft burbling of a thick liquid. Suddenly, I come crashing down onto solid stone, and I stand up to find myself on a lone island amidst a large, bubbling pool of lava.

"What is this?" I murmur, turning to look around at my surroundings. At a glance, I don't see any way out of this room. It can't be as simple as a trap, or it would have just dropped me into lava and been done with it. No . . . there's something else going on here. I just have to figure out what it is.

[ChaosRider: WHOA!!! Jason, where are you?]

[DarkCynic: Is this like some secret boss room?]

[ViperQueen: I bet it's a—]

A roar shakes the room—a roar I know well. The ring in my pocket begins to tremble, and I'm overcome with the urge to pull it out and look at it. My hand actually slides into my pocket and grabs hold of the thing, as, all around me, lava bubbles and explodes. A dark form begins to materialize in the air over the lava, and I grit my teeth.

"Everyone?" I speak softly, not wanting to make the dragon any angrier than it already is. "I need you to contact John. Let him know what I'm seeing, and tell me anything important that pertains to . . . this."

There's a long pause before anyone answers.

[LunarEclipse: We told him! He's currently trying to get down to you, but the floor resealed after you fell. Now it just keeps telling him that it's an immortal object.]

"I was afraid of that." I desperately try to think of a way out. "Tell him to ignore me for now, then. Have him keep going through the dungeon. I'll find a way back to him."

[LunarEclipse: We've got your back, Jason!]

I flash a smile in their direction, then slowly let out a long breath and nod toward the dragon.

"You really, really want me to put this thing on, don't you?"

It doesn't answer, but it does begin to take on a clearer shape. Scales form, wrapping around my little island entirely. Its eyes . . . They're like two tiny points of fire, burning holes through the air itself.

"You can't talk right now, can you?"

A roar is my only answer. Gravel dribbles down from above, and I nod slowly.

"Alright, then. I think I see how this goes. In the last Rift, your plan was to sacrifice your last puppet. Your plan was to give one of us the ring—Harold was the one who wound up with it—and that person would defeat your last minion. They would then march out of the dungeon, taking your mind along with them. It was a chance for you to escape your own Rift."

The dragon still doesn't answer, but he seems to be growing more and more agitated.

"When I took the ring from Harold and cast it away, your last-ditch effort was to send it with me. Well, now I'm here." I slowly pull out the ring, and the dragon begins to move a bit more. It's excited. "Let me see . . . You'd like me to put it on? Or would it be better if I were to throw it into the fire and try to destroy it?"

The dragon continues moving and, if anything, seems to become even more excited. Until this moment, I haven't been sure if destroying it is the best thing or not. Perhaps the ring is an extension of the dragon's power, and destroying it would break that power. On the other hand, perhaps the ring is a prison of some sort and destroying it would *release* said dragon. It's hard to know for sure. Now I'm fairly certain I know the answer.

"Either way, I'm pretty sure that you're not really supposed to be here and that the boss of this dungeon doesn't know you've infiltrated his little lair. Should we alert him?"

I hold the ring high above my head. To be honest, if the roaring hasn't alerted the boss of this Rift to the fact that we're here, I don't really think anything will. That said, the bosses of the Rifts aren't the most powerful beings in this new order.

"Command: Send messages to System Administrators."

Quite suddenly, lava explodes around me, rising as if to wash over me and destroy me and the ring all at once. Fire swirls on all sides; I feel an intense heat around me. . .

Only for it to be replaced by a biting cold. I blink then

slowly straighten up. I'm in another room, one I don't recognize. It's on the top layer—that much I can tell—with a small hole letting in equal parts light and cold, and letting *out* just about as much heat as you could imagine. I shiver, stunned by the stark difference, then try to get my bearings. There's a small table carved out of stone near the back of the small cave, where but a single exit leads back down into the ground. I look around for a moment then slowly walk over to inspect the table.

[DarkCynic: Jason! You're out of there! Good to see you safe and sound!]

[ViperQueen: YAY!!!!! I thought you were a goner!]

[RazorEdge: I TOLD you all that he would be fine.]

I ignore the chat, at least mostly. I don't know why I was put here in this room, but I imagine there's a reason. Slowly, I reach out and wipe away the snow from the table, finding a carving of some sort with dozens of lines drawn through the stone. I start to wipe all the snow away, then get a sudden idea. My hands grow cold, but working quickly, I pat down the snow firmly, pressing it all into the table, then carve away everything above the flat surface. This leaves snow in all the depressed lines, and it gives me a clear indication of what's there.

I finish quickly then take a step back. As I do, I let out a frosty breath of surprise.

It's a map.

The sketch is a mass of circles connected by lines. There are three distinct sets of these interconnected circles, which to me indicates three layers. Some of the circles—caves—have small dots, which I assume are the shafts going up and down. I wish I had some pens and paper, but alas, none of the assorted things I have in my inventory would work to make a copy.

"Let's see here," I murmur, looking at the map closely. "Here's the entrance . . . and . . . this must be the boss room."

The boss room, thankfully, is pretty easy to find. It's easily the largest room, on the second floor, and connected to a single room that has a single shaft as its exit. I start trying to figure out where that room connects to, though, and I suddenly see the issue. The maps don't exactly come with a grid to show how they all line up, and I cross my arms in thought.

[ChaosRider: Hey, Jason! We can take screenshots and analyze it ourselves!]

[DarkCynic: Yeah! And then you won't have to do anything except figure out how to kill everything in your path!]

"You make it sound so easy." I laugh a bit, but nod. "Much appreciated." I wait a moment for them to get screenshots then start looking things over more closely. I need to figure out which room I'm in right now, and unfortunately, there's no real indication of that. Soon, though, I find two rooms on the upper level only connected to the rest of the complex by a shaft, which tells me that I'm in one of two locations. My chat seems to realize it, too, and I walk up to the shaft.

"Alright, everyone. When I hit the bottom, I'll fight whatever's there, and you'll tell me where to go from there. Got it?"

I take a deep breath then leap down into the pit. Wind whirls around me, and a moment later, I hit the ground with a large *thump*, coming up in a wide room with a low ceiling. There are a few pools of water here and there—water that seems to be steaming, but nothing more. I let out a long breath as torches flicker to life then I slowly start to walk forward.

Hrnf!

The noise is an odd one, rather like a snort, and I freeze. I glance around, but I don't see anything. I take another step, and another similar noise echoes loudly. I draw out my daggers, but I still don't see anything . . . And then, slowly, something pulls itself up out of the water.

It's an ape of some sort—that much I can see at first glance. It has long arms and short legs, and a face as red as blood. It reminds me of a terrestrial animal I've seen in a zoo, but this one is quite obviously otherworldly. The limbs aren't the right proportions for a regular animal, and the fangs on the thing, as it opens its mouth and roars at me, aren't quite right. Monkeys can have some pretty long canine teeth, that's for sure, but these look a bit more pointed than I think most monkeys tend to have.

As the roar echoes across the room, I brace myself. More monkeys begin to pull themselves up out of the pools, and with that, half a dozen charge me all at once. I take a deep breath and run forward to meet them, throwing myself into battle.

Whack!

The monkeys, as it turns out, are a whole lot faster than I initially gave them credit for. Something cracks under the impact as two or three fists hit me in the chest, and I'm blasted back across the room, slamming into the wall underneath the shaft leading up to the map room. For a moment, I consider climbing up, but I shake my head.

No, I'm here to fight, not to run.

As the horde comes charging forward, I ready my daggers once again then step forward as they arrive. As fast as lightning, I lop off the hands of the closest monkey, who howls and falls backward. I duck under another strike then stab a knife deep into the chest of the closest. It falls backward and collapses with a gurgle, and I spin to face the next several.

"Garg! Bjorn!" I dive headlong into one, knocking it backward while stabbing it several times in the chest. I come out of the roll and stand up, leaving the bloodied corpse on the ground, then turn around and throw my Shadow Dagger through the neck of another. "I could use some help!"

With a flicker, both of my favorite pets emerge and immediately dive into the fray. Garg can simply gore the monkeys with his long claws, while Bjorn grabs them by their long limbs and shakes them about like rag dolls. I join in the fray with my daggers, and together, we're able to work our way, slowly and purposefully, through the room.

When the last of the monkeys falls, Bjorn and Garg head back into the portal, and I start to look around the room for loot. There's not really much to be seen, though there might be something golden at the bottom of the hot springs. I'm nervous to dive in to get it, though. Just like dragon gold, there are rules when dealing with treasure located at the bottom of deep pools of water. Usually, there's a reason why it's there, and it's not because it's easy to get out.

I'm still thinking it over when chats start coming through.

[RazorEdge: Alright, I think we've got you located. Turn to your right . . . Not that much . . . There! Go there!]

I follow the instructions, finding myself looking at yet another dark cave; this one seems to be hewn by hand, as if someone had carved it some long, indefinite time ago. I let out a long breath and start forward, and soon slip up to that entrance.

Yes . . . there are definite pickaxe marks here, and as torches flicker to life, it only becomes clearer. I start forward, making my way steadily onward, but . . . even as I do, I can hear a soft rumble shake the ground. That dragon, whatever his game happens to be, isn't gone yet.

He's just waiting for another chance to strike. I, in turn, must make sure I'm ready for him . . . or else—even if I find something that makes me the most powerful Awakened in existence—I know I won't stand a chance against his deceptions.

CHAPTER TWENTY-THREE

The hallway isn't long, and it soon comes to an end in an elaborately carved wooden door. I pause for a moment, looking over the symbols and markings. Most of the carvings are of plants— ivy, trees, and things—though tucked away amidst the greenery are little creatures. Elves, dwarves, and other such things. I nod after a moment, then slowly reach out and twist the knob.

Locked.

I frown, then rattle the doorknob, as if such a simple trick could work. It doesn't, obviously, and I take a step back.

"Alright, folks. Let's see if my lockpick still works."

[RazorEdge: What lockpick?]

[ViperQueen: I think I know . . .]

I draw out my two daggers and drive them into the lock. It takes me a moment, but I'm soon able to cut my way through the wood and metal, and I kick the door open. Splinters sprinkle down to the ground, and I step inside.

Now, I must admit that while I've hardly been dungeon delving for an extended portion of my life, this is the strangest dungeon I've ever seen. A chandelier, adorned with hundreds of candles, hangs over a neat little reading place. The walls are squared off and lined with bookshelves, all of which are piled high with hundreds of tomes. At the exact center, under the chandelier, is a series of chairs and some tables, where more books are piled. Several clay pipes lie scattered across the tables as well, ashes spilling out of the bowls and across the wooden surface.

"This is unusual," I murmur as I walk inside. The door falls shut behind me, though it obviously can't lock, given that I carved that portion of the door away. "Alright, folks. Any sign of an exit?"

[DarkCynic: Yeah! Go straight. There's supposed to be one on the back wall.]

I frown as I reach said wall. The only thing I see is shelf upon shelf of books. Thousands of books. The first thing that comes to mind is some sort of secret door, but I can't be certain.

"Is there another way?" I ask, taking a step back as I think.

[ShadowDancer: Yeah! But it's way longer. I think this is a shortcut, and the map room was an indication of it, if you knew what you were looking for.]

"Then that's just swhat we'll have to work with." I order Garg to come out of the portal. "Blast it open!"

It's almost sad to see Garg launch a massive fireball into the shelves of books. A resounding boom shakes the room from top to bottom, knocking books off shelves even from behind us. Smoke and fire belch out from the point of impact, and I slowly step forward as the debris fades away, revealing a small, dark corridor behind the shelf.

"Very good." I pat Garg on the nose then start to crawl forward. "Now, let's get—"

Skreeeeeeee!

It's a noise I've heard before; I've heard all sorts of variations. Some are higher pitched, some lower, but they're all the same, ultimately, and they indicate only one thing: small, fast-moving monsters that can take a hit and still keep biting.

"Light it up!"

Garg unleashes another fireball, which flashes down into the tunnel. To my dismay, it goes straight down the middle, illuminating—but not killing—hundreds of imps swarming forward along the walls. A moment later, they come scurrying out into the open—at least the first wave—and I suddenly find myself overwhelmed.

I rush forward into battle, my knives moving as fast as I can possibly swing them. Imps are so small and wiry that I hit with almost every swing, lopping off limbs and heads and legs and all sorts of other things. Still, it's not enough, as they just keep coming. Two of them manage to sneak around behind me, and they jump up to wrap their arms around my neck. Almost instantly, they tighten like a rope, and I find myself without an adequate way to breathe.

If you've ever been in a position like that, it's not . . . How to put it? You're not dead yet, but you're going to be soon. You don't have a timer, so you know it won't be long, but you don't know *how* long you have; you just have to fight with everything you've got. It's utterly terrifying, in every sense of the word, and that's all there is to it. I try to keep my head, and I throw myself backward against one of the tables. Books go crashing to the floor, and that knocks a couple of the imps away from my back just enough for me to gasp a bit of air. I stab around behind my back a bit—and manage to nick myself a few times—but I don't kill either imp. Growing desperate, I back up more, smashing myself against the bookshelf on the far wall. That dislodges them enough for me to spin around and deprive them of *their* preferred method of breathing, but it still leaves a lot more.

By now, imps are pouring out of the tunnel like ants out of a hill that you just poured water into. They're climbing up the bookshelves and swinging from the chandeliers; it's all quite awful. Bodies lie scattered across the ground, but more and more of them keep coming, and I know that it's only a matter of time before they overwhelm me. I need a new plan.

"Garg! Grab one of those tables!"

Garg spins around and grips one of the reading tables with his claws. He's a smart gargoyle, and he immediately picks it up to bring it smashing down on the imps near him. Dozens of them are crushed under the blow, and I grab hold of the bookcase behind me. As the monsters come pouring in from in front and behind, I yank it with all my might, and hundreds of books—along with an extremely sturdy frame—come crashing down, flattening what must have been almost fifty imps. I don't have time to count them in the chaos, and I jump up onto the back of the shelf and continue to fight.

Garg and I battle ever onward, carving our way through the monsters. Soon, they're growing so thick across the floor that I'm certain I'm not actually walking on the ground anymore.

It smells terrible, that's for sure, and I struggle to keep my footing. Finally, after what must be close to half an hour, the last one comes limping up out of the darkened tunnel, and I wearily throw my dagger through its torso. It falls backward, sliding down a now-empty tunnel, and I walk forward and let out a long, pained breath.

"We did it." I hold up a hand, which Garg high-fives. The force of the gesture almost knocks me over, and I laugh despite myself. "Alright, boy, let's get moving. Here, join me on my shoulder."

Garg nods and teleports up onto my shoulder, shrinking down to a height of about two feet. After a moment, he straddles my neck, rather like a toddler, and I chuckle and start down the tunnel, slowly and surely. I hold out my hand to call back my Shadow Dagger, then slide it into my inventory along with my Photonic Dagger.

"Hey! Jason!"

I pause, halfway down the darkened tunnel, and turn to see John appear at the top. He lets out a whistle then starts down to join me.

"Once more, I think you've taken your own words a little too literally." He laughs and shakes his head. "How many have you taken down?"

"I don't even know. I'll check my stats once we're out of here." I puff out my cheeks. "It's good to see you. How have things been on your end?"

"Fine, I think." John shrugs. "I'm just glad to see you alive. After two days, I didn't think we'd see you again."

I gape at him for a moment. "Two days? *Two days*?"

[FireStorm: Yeah! I just thought you knew.]

[ShadowDancer: We *said* we were glad to see you out of there!]

"Yeah, I just thought those were general congratulatory messages," I murmur. John just stares at me for a moment then bursts out laughing.

"You were gone for two days and still managed to do all of this? Remind me to never get on your bad side!"

I frown, thinking desperately. The time skip must have happened when I was teleported away, out of that fiery pit. The only question is *why*? So the System Administrators could hide me from the dragon? Or—and I shudder to even think about this—did something happen to me during those two days, something that was wiped from my memory?

I have no answers, but I'm not really given time to find them, as John steps past me and continues down the slope. "Come on. I assume your extraordinary ability to stumble into things let you find this shortcut. At least I assume it's a shortcut?"

"That's what I'm told." I nod in agreement, striding along behind him. "Once we get out into the next room, we'll . . ."

I pause for a moment, waiting for a reply.

[LunarEclipse: You'll go down a shaft!]

"We'll go down a shaft," I answer. "I found a map of sorts that ought to lead us to the boss room."

"Good to know." John flashes me a small smile. "We all talk about our DPS as Damage Per Second, but I sure wouldn't mind a good Dungeon Positioning System. 'Take a slight right at the drooling troll. Continue onward for seven hundred feet then fall into the blazing pit of lava. You have reached your destination!'"

I laugh despite myself. We soon reach the end of the tunnel and slowly emerge into a much rougher cave covered with large crystals, some as large as ten feet long. I whistle as I look them over and slowly walk up to one, placing my hand upon the smooth surface.

"It's beautiful," John whispers. He looks around then frowns. "I don't see any shaft that goes down, though."

I look around as well then nod. "There."

Near the center of the room there's a crystal, three feet across, sticking up out of the ground. We both approach it, and John reaches out and touches the thing. Garg spits a small ball of fire at it, but it only tarnishes the surface a bit.

"Stand back." John slowly pulls himself upright then takes out a pickaxe and raises it above his head. "I've got this."

I'm happy to let him take the lead, as my mind is still spinning a bit from the strange revelation. John swings downward, and the pickaxe slams into the peak of the structure, shattering a great deal of it and sending large cracks through the whole interior. He grunts, and pulls the axe out then swings again. This time, almost half of the crystal is broken away, and I think I glimpse the dark shaft underneath the thing.

At the same time, the crystals around us begin to crack. At first I don't think anything of it, but when John takes the third swing and shatters the crystal all the way down to the floor, a great blast erupts from the crystals all around us. Bits and pieces of the clear stone fall away, revealing forms that were previously hidden.

Forms that look entirely too much like monsters.

They're humanoid—that much is fairly obvious at a glance—but they're not quite fully human. I think they're shorter, and a good bit slimmer. They're also all folded in the fetal position. Slowly, I draw out my daggers, and I jab one of them as hard as I can. My blade simply skates off the surface, and I pause. It's possible that I can't harm them, but more likely it's something along the lines of not being able to harm them *until* they reanimate.

"Hmm. That's interesting." John looks up at the creatures then down at the crystal. "One more blow ought to do it. You ready for them?"

I puff out my cheeks and nod. "Let's do it."

"Alright, then." John takes one final swing, smashing the remainder of the crystal with one smooth blow. Crystal rains down into the open shaft, and, with that, all the crystal forms around us animate; if they haven't already fallen to the floor, they detach from the wall and jump down.

John is quick on the uptake, I'll give him that. He whips his pickaxe around like lightning. His strength smashes straight through half a dozen of them in a single blow, showering me in crystal shards. I stab the nearest one with my Photonic Dagger then a second one with my Shadow Dagger. Both crumble into rubble, and I smile.

That'll work well enough for me.

John and I quickly move through the room. There aren't many of the crystal creatures, and a lot of Awakened—Harold, particularly, comes to mind—would have struggled, but we don't seem to have any real issues. Soon, only one creature remains, which positions itself on the brink of the pit. I pause for a moment, and John gestures at the creature.

"Would you care to do the honors, or do you want me to take it?"

"I'll do it, if you don't mind." I slip both of my daggers into my inventory then slowly walk forward. The crystal creature crouches down, then jumps forward, rather like a frog or a cricket or something. I don't really care what it looks like; I just kick it in the chest as hard as I can. It's flung backward down into the pit, where it cracks loudly on the lip before falling into darkness. There's a long pause, followed by a crash, and John and I fist-bump.

"If I've been gone for two days, I suppose I should ask if there's been any drama with Harold." I nod at John as we approach the top of the shaft.

"Quite a lot." John chuckles. "I'll give it all to you—down at the bottom."

"Fair enough."

John jumps inside a moment later, and I follow once I hear him land. As I fall, I can't be certain, but I *think* I catch a flash of a person standing in the darkened tunnel—the one leading from the library down to this cave. I'm gone before I can confirm it, though, and I'm simply left to wonder.

Is someone following us?

If so, is it Harold?

If so, what does he know?

The questions have no answers, at least none that I have access to. I simply have to stay on my feet and stay ready . . . ready for whatever comes next.

CHAPTER TWENTY-FOUR

John and I land in a pit, the exact opposite of the caves on the very top level. Down here, instead of light coming in through small gaps in the ceiling, dark red light drifts up through cracks in the floor. I can feel the soft burble of magma from below, and I catch a few wisps of sulfur. John shudders a bit, but frankly, this is a whole lot better than what I was experiencing a few hours—or apparently days—ago, so I'm not complaining too much.

[LunarEclipse: Alright, you're going to head through this cavern and then take the passageway on the left. That'll take you to a small shaft that goes all the way up to the top floor, and then you'll be almost there.]

"This way." I point ahead, slowly striding forward across the cracked stone. My shadow flickers oddly on the ceiling, waxing and waning with the ebb and flow of the fire below. The ground shakes and quivers, though it isn't quite the same as the dragon rumble from the previous Rift—or even from earlier in *this* Rift. Something bumps against the underside of the floor, and I get the feeling that we're essentially walking above a great pool of magma.

"I don't like the look of this," John murmurs. There's another bump from under our feet. "I like knowing what's trying to eat me."

"On the bright side, it provides an extra layer of tension," I remark, somewhat sarcastically. "It keeps the viewers entertained."

"Very true!" John laughs. "Alright, then! Give us a quick poll, both sets of viewers! Which would you rather have? Would you rather see the two of us making our way through an easy dungeon, where you know your beloved heroes will be safe, or fighting our way through the darkness, where we never know which moment will be our last?"

[A: Safety: 11%]

[B: Danger!: 89%]

I laugh at the numbers and so does John. We glance at each other, share a knowing look, and continue onward.

"Well, in that case, here's a shoutout to all you viewers who actually care about my life and limbs, at the potential expense of your entertainment pleasure." I heft an imaginary wineglass. "To all those who—"

A loud *crack* splits the air from behind us, and we slowly turn to find a much larger patch of lava appearing near the shaft where we came down. Slowly, almost painfully so, a large chunk of the stone sinks into the lava, leaving behind only a few rising bubbles. I brace myself and wait as a hole forms, perhaps twenty feet across. Then, with a loud *splurch*, figures begin to emerge.

Well . . . Honestly, they're rather hard to describe. In the other Rift, creatures made of the lava itself had emerged from the pool. Now, lava bubbles upward, only to have flames shoot out with loud *hisses* and take on forms of their own. As the flames free themselves from the stone, rock cools and falls back down, and the figures step out and prepare themselves. They're humanoid, at least essentially—though, being made of fire, they obviously don't adhere to the exact proportions. Their eyes are as black as coal, as dark and as deep as the void between the stars, and I feel like I'm being sucked in simply by looking at them.

"Huh." I take a moment to size them up. "Any idea how to kill creatures made out of living fire?"

"Not a bit." John shakes his head. He turns to look in the direction we're traveling, likely trying to decide if we can make a run for it. Strictly speaking, the area is open, but I can see the light from beneath the floor beginning to flicker a bit more brilliantly. If we try to run, *something* will come bursting through and roast us to a crisp. I think for a moment then draw out my twin blades.

"Well, only one way to find out."

[FireStorm: That's our Jason! Not scared of anything at all!]

[DarkCynic: You can do it!!!]

[ViperQueen: Try hitting their eyes. They look like the only solid parts of the creatures.]

I'm not really given much of a chance to absorb the advice as the monsters come racing forward. Their limbs move, but they don't really walk across the ground so much as glide. Several in the lead advance with greater vigor, and I decide that I might as well meet them on my own terms. I jump forward with all my might, hoping to catch them off guard, and lash out with my twin weapons.

To my great surprise, the blades dig into the fire almost exactly the way they would ordinarily cut through . . . well . . . pretty much anything else. I can feel the resistance of the body, incorporeal as it may be. The two creatures I hit reel back in pain, and a blinding light escapes from their bodies for a moment, at least until the wound heals. That gives me hope, and I charge headlong at them.

"*Hi-yaw!*"

I dive into their midst, my blades flashing as fast as I can make them go. I land dozens of cuts up and down their bodies, carving them apart as fast as I can. As I reach the other side of the pack and turn back, though, I find that all of them are still intact. They seem injured but far from dead, and while about half of them race at John and fling themselves upon him, the other half come right at me. I brace myself, swinging madly into their midst as we come crashing together.

That . . . Well, it doesn't go as well as I'd hoped. Flames scorch up and down my arms and legs as the creatures pile drive me down to the ground. Several of them grab hold of me, and I feel my flesh starting to blacken and char under their touch. I gasp in pain, then wrench myself free and stab my blade through the neck of the closest one. It screams and jumps backward, but once again, the wound heals after only a moment. I groan then kick away the monsters as best I can, jump back to my feet, and fling myself headlong into their midst once again.

I can see my health bar draining slowly as I take more and more damage, but at the same time, I can see *them* slowly waning as well. Finally, as I see one stagger backward, I lunge at it, tackling the thing to the ground. I stab both blades into its back and hold them tight, ignoring the damage that I'm taking from pressing so close to the beast. It screams and tries to pull away, but I continue to press it tightly, not allowing the blades to leave its body, so it can't heal. A long moment passes, and the creature dies, vanishing and dissolving in a puff of smoke. I gasp as I fall to the ground, and there, I notice several small crystals lying on the stone where the monster had been.

I frown and pick up one of the crystals. As I do, the other monsters let out a scream and come charging at me with ever-greater vigor. I snarl and perform a roundhouse kick that is flawless, if I do say so myself, catching the leader in the side of the head and knocking him into several of the others. I then, rather by reflex, throw the crystal into the mass of fiery bodies charging at me.

Now, if I had been given time to think about that action, I doubt I would have done it. After all, these crystals are probably the essence of the monsters, so throwing one at another monster of the same type should, by all accounts, really do nothing except make that monster more powerful. Thankfully, that's the exact opposite of what happens. The crystal hits one of the monsters and, with a resounding *bang* and a flash of smoke, the monster dissolves, allowing a handful of similar such crystals to clatter across the floor. I blink in surprise then smile.

"John!"

"Got it!" he shouts out. I risk a glance in his direction, and I see him struggling to wrestle several to the ground. He looks even more burned than I feel, but still, we both fight onward. Desperately, I dive for the rest of the crystals, scooping up the three from beneath my feet.

The fire monsters are on me a moment later. They seem to sense their danger and throw themselves headlong upon me, raking their claws across my face, my torso, my arms and legs—anything they can touch. I stagger backward, trying to get my bearings, and then grip my hand tightly around the crystals. I hold one of them between my thumb and forefinger and throw it as hard as I can through the head of the one closest to me.

Bang!

The monster explodes into a thick cloud of smoke, sending out a small shockwave. Before anything else can happen, I spin and throw the last two crystals at two other nearby fire monsters. One of them dies; the other is simply wounded and thrown backward. I consider that fact to be acceptable, and I bend down to scoop up more of the crystals.

By now, the other fire monsters are starting to take notice. One of them bolts for the pool of lava, and I fling another of the crystals as hard as I can. It catches the creature in the back, and the thing vanishes in a puff of smoke. The crystals continue along their trajectory and fall into the lava, which makes a resounding *boom* that shakes the whole cavern.

Well . . . I should probably elaborate a bit more. The monster drops three crystals, all of which land in the lava. As a result, three great geysers of molten stone explode upward, showering the nearby area, while thick cracks spread across the rest of the floor. I scramble away from the closest crack, spinning my head left and right as I try to make sure I don't fall into anything. The few remaining monsters all dive back into the safety of their home, and I let out a long breath.

"And . . . there's to you!" John slams a fist through the head of a monster. It explodes around his fist, and he catches several of the crystals as they materialize where the creature was standing. One of them, though, rattles through a small crack next to his feet, and the resulting explosion throws him backward across the lava field. I can hear the *crack* of his head against the stone, while his leg falls into one of the wider gaps. Smoke and fire belch upward, and the smell of burning flesh fills the air.

I grit my teeth and race forward, bouncing across the shifting stone as quickly as possible. As I reach him, I jump over his body, grab hold of his shoulders, and pull him up and out of the lava as fast as I can. His health bar stabilizes just a few millimeters above empty, and I take a deep breath, bend down, and haul him up onto my shoulders. By now, all the fire monsters have escaped our wrath, having descended back into the flames below. I see several of them starting to swirl under the surface of the liquid, watching us, but afraid to actually engage.

I take a deep breath once more, trying to ready myself. John is *heavy*; his muscle mass must make him at least two-fifty, if I had to guess. In any case, I quickly trot forward, leaping over the small chasms that are still opening, and I soon make it to the next passageway. I find the one on the left, from which blows the faintest wisp of cool air, and I jump over the last patch of lava to safety in the hall. There, I set John down, then sit down next to him.

"We made it." I chuckle softly, taking a deep breath. A

great exhaustion overwhelms me. I don't know how long I've been awake, but it's been quite a while. I need a rest, and so does John. We'll move on when we're ready. . . Until then, we simply need to recover, if we're going to have a single hope of making it to the boss.

CHAPTER TWENTY-FIVE

Before I go to sleep, I make sure to take care of John and myself. First, I open my inventory and look for any healing items that I can apply to other people. Unfortunately, there isn't much, as most items are designed to be consumed.

[ChaosRider: Jason! I have a way you can do it! Take some of those healing tabs, crush them up, mix them with a bottle of Pumped!, and then use the syringe to inject it straight into his veins.]

I laugh at that suggestion. "That's the worst medical advice I've ever heard!"

[ShadowDancer: You yourself have literally drunk a bottle of soda to heal from gaping stab wounds, venom injections, and a whole lot more.]

[IceQueen: Yeah! Jul Lee used this method to heal her friend, Clum Si, a few days ago.]

"I'll give it a try, then." I shake my head in amazement, then open my inventory and get to work. Thankfully, I have everything I need. Healing tabs are a pretty common drop from monsters; they sort of just give you a general health boost and can heal topical wounds. Pumped! is a bit more comprehensive, healing more major wounds, which in my mind is sort of the opposite of what it *should* be, but . . . you know how it goes.

I find a small, flat rock along the side of the passage, place several of the healing tabs on it, use another rock to crush them up into powder, and then dump it all into a bottle of the energy drink. It fizzes quite strongly for a moment, then calms down, and I pull out a surgical syringe and proceed to start sucking up the liquid to inject into my friend.

He winces a little bit in his slumber as I insert the needle, but not too much, and the results are near instantaneous. I repeat the process several times, adding about half the bottle, then chuck the rest of it into the lava. There's another small explosion, and I sink down next to him. I take out my sleeping bag and prepare to crawl inside, then I pause. What kind of a friend would I be if I give myself monster protection and not John?

I sigh after a moment then nod. I unzip the bag and lay it over top of him, then sit down nearby, resting my head against the wall. I open my inventory and eat a bag of Pumped! fast food, then I sigh and try to keep myself awake to keep watch. I'm fairly certain that, here in the tunnel, we're safe—but I don't want to bank on that fact.

The hours slowly pass by. I ask my chat a few questions here and there, mostly about where the other Awakened are located, and they give me a few answers that I don't really understand—the "icechopper" room, for example, which was one of the locations I apparently bypassed. I keep an eye on the room we just passed through, but not a lot happens there. The rest of the floor sinks into the lava, leaving a single, open space—until, almost five hours after we left, it starts to cool and reform itself.

It's around that time that John stirs and wakes up. He gasps and rises, bringing up his fists, then pauses. I give him a weary nod, and he nods back. Slowly, I lie down, and he drapes the bag over me. Within seconds, I'm asleep, slumbering peacefully amid the dungeon's chaos.

[Riftwatch: Welcome to Day 9 of the Apocalypse Protocol!]

I blink as I slowly wake up and find John sitting nearby, looking out across the room. It's back to being a field of lava again, and I sit up and start to roll up the sleeping bag.

"How are things?" I ask softly. "See anyone else?"

"I think Harold is trailing us," he answers quietly. "The room reset, as you know, but it keeps activating. We're outside of the detection range of the monsters, but . . . the whole thing will crack and break apart, the monsters will come up, and they'll run around until lava covers the whole floor. And then they'll go away, and the room will cool. Only thing I can figure is that someone is standing *just* outside the radius of detection and every now and again accidentally lets a toe slip through, you know?"

"That does sound like we're being followed," I murmur. "Has the chat said anything?"

"They won't confirm or deny anything." John shrugs. "I think they're enjoying the whole 'dark-mysterious-dangerous' thing."

I chuckle then slowly stand up. John does as well, and I

notice that he's holding something in his hands. His right hand holds a steel dagger—not one of the ones he wields in combat, while his left holds a crudely carved wooden bear. For a moment, he leans against the wall and goes to work on it again, making several marks that sharpen the features around the legs, and then he tucks both items into his inventory.

"You carve things?" I ask as we turn and start down the hallway.

"Whittle, yeah." John gives a nod. "My grandfather taught it to me, years and years ago. I'm not any good at it, but it's a good stress reliever, you know?"

I chuckle softly. "I don't know if I really have a stress reliever, to be honest."

"Then when we get out of this dungeon, we'll have to find you one! Something that doesn't involve killing monsters."

The air in the tunnel continues to blow colder, and a few moments later, we come to a small chamber, only a few feet across, really. A shaft leads straight upward—a *long* shaft. At the very top, I can see a flicker of sunlight, and I know that this is what my viewers were telling me about.

The only problem is that the inside of the shaft is coated in icicles, long and pointed, directed *down* at us. I have little doubt that coming down the shaft would be incredibly easy, but getting back up it? I honestly don't know how we're going to manage.

"Well, no use standing around." John crouches down then jumps upward. His claw-like fingernails smash through the outer layer of one of the lowest rings of ice, and he starts pulling himself up. "Come on!"

I watch him for a moment. There's no way I'm going to be

able to do that. An idea crosses my mind, though, and I open my pocket dimension and bring Garg out.

"I need a ride, boy."

Garg nods, and I scramble onto his back, holding on tightly to the base of his wings. He waits until John is most of the way up, then folds his wings tightly against his back and jumps upward, smashing through the ice with his own claws.

Now, at this point, he's so large—and I'm so small—that I'm nearly smashed up against the far side of the shaft. Garg seems to realize this, though, and flattens himself as well as he can and wriggles his way along. Ice crashes and breaks around me. The noise and the scope of the process are truly astounding. Through it all, though, one single thought echoes through my mind.

Harold will have absolutely no issues following us.

He can fly over the lava, straight past those monsters, and then fly straight up this shaft. What's taken us hours to do will take him mere minutes. He doesn't *need* to follow us all that closely, because he can just bypass most of the same things that we're struggling with. Of course, there are all sorts of arguments that could be made about how fighting through adversity strengthens you—and I'd probably agree with the lion's share of them; however, it's also rather annoying when someone as utterly arrogant as Harold can just flicker around like a fairy and dodge everything that you've worked so hard to achieve.

I digress, though. The two of us, working together, soon manage to reach the top of the shaft. There, the ice has grown across most of the entrance, leaving only a small hole about six inches across. John does his best to break through, but he has a hard time getting a grip. After a few failed tries, I motion for him to stand back, at least as best he can. He presses himself to the side of the shaft, wedging himself between several icicles, and Garg lets out a mighty bellow.

Foooooom!

A blast of fire rolls upward, hurling straight through the layer of ice. The ice all around us melts into a slurry, of course, and John suddenly finds himself without anything to cling to. He falls, only to catch hold of Garg's wing on the way down. Garg howls in pain, but he grits his teeth and forces his way upward. We all tumble out into the fresh snow, and I lie there for a moment, gasping.

"John." I glance over at him for a moment, an idea coming into my mind. "You wouldn't by any chance have some sort of a trap tucked away in your inventory, would you?"

A grin comes across John's face. "What do you mean by a trap?"

"Nothing lethal, probably, just in case the person who comes along isn't Harold, but . . ." My eyes twinkle. "I don't know. Something that could give us a bit of a warning?"

Of course, any trap that we set up will be automatically flawed, knowing that anyone watching our feed could just switch over and alert Harold to the danger. That said, putting up something could still slow him down, especially if we do it well. Now, it takes us a few moments to come up with an appropriate trap but, after a bit, we settle upon a large assortment of fireworks that John had stored away from an overturned truck he found in Chinatown. After carefully arranging hundreds of screamers, smoke bombs, firebombs, sparklers, and—I don't know the name for them—the big ones that you see at firework displays, we set up a tripwire across the entrance, hooked up to a flint striker over the top of the wicks. If the string even gets a breath of wind that's too powerful, it'll set everything off. Harold will have a hard time coming through, that's for sure.

In any case, it's fun to set up. The moment it's ready, John and I stand up and start looking around. The room is small, almost as small as the one so far below, and hardly big enough for the two of us to fit inside at the same time—especially with all the fireworks. A small tunnel, really more of an extended archway, leads a few short feet to another, nigh-identical room. At the center, there's a raised ring of stone: a well with a ladder going down the inside. I pause at the top then slowly look down the long, darkened shaft.

"What do you think we'll find at the bottom?" I ask softly, not really wanting to startle anything lurking down below.

"One giant fight that will last all the way to the end of the boss battle itself," John answers. "Did you play many video games before everything exploded?"

"Hardly at all," I answer, laughing. "A few, here and there, but I was always too busy."

"Well, this just has that feeling about it. One final gauntlet." John puffs out his cheeks. "We go down that thing, and we'll be plunged into a chaotic rumble of chaos that will lead up to the door of the boss chamber. There will be a brief pause, mostly a chance to grab any healing items we need, and then . . . *Boom.*"

"Are you ready for it?"

"Ready as I'll ever be."

"Then let's go."

I swing my legs over the edge of the well, take a deep breath, and drop down, ignoring the ladder. The darkness closes in around me, and I brace myself for whatever I'll face below. I'm going to close this Rift and bring an end to this particular bit of tyranny.

. . . And, hopefully, get powerful enough that I can close the next one too.

CHAPTER TWENTY-SIX

When I land, I throw myself forward into a roll. John lands behind me a second later, his feet shaking the ground. Torches blaze to life all around us, and I hear a familiar roar.

As I climb back to my feet, I find a frost-bear-cat-dog-scorpion-mammoth coming straight at me. No . . . two of them. No . . . three. I hardly even have time to glance at our battle arena—it's a cave, and I think it only has one entrance—before they're upon me, and I throw myself headlong into the combat.

[ShadowDancer: Hey!!! This is cool! Closing out the dungeon just like it opened!]

[ViperQueen: But now there's three of them! We should work on the name more, since it's applicable again!]

[ChaosRider: What do you think about frost-bear-cat-dog-scorpion-mammoth-thing?]

[DarkCynic: No . . . more like frobecadoscomam!]

The first of the creatures, *whatever* it's called, leaps at me. It seems to be trying to direct me to roll underneath it, but I can see its claws at the ready. Instead, I jump upward, choosing to face the might of the thing's teeth and the brunt of its body weight.

A moment later, I honestly can't decide if that was a wise thing or a terrible thing.

Its head slams into my torso, *hard*, and flings me back against the stone wall. I groan and sink to the ground, and it opens its mouth wide to snap down on my gut. I stab it inside the mouth before it can, making it reel back. Without giving me a break, though, the next of the creatures darts forward, snarling and slashing at me with all its might. Several long claw marks trail down my arm and across my chest, and I grit my teeth, muscling through the pain as I stand back up.

It hurts, but I dare not show even the faintest bit of weakness.

As the second one lunges forward again, I step up to meet it and drive my Photonic Dagger into its nose. At the same time, I grab one of its ears and hold fast, digging into the monster as hard as I can. I know it won't kill the thing, but if I can wound it enough, it'll give me some wiggle room. I can see the first of them coming up at me again, and I know I have only moments. Quickly, I pull the dagger out of its nose and slash off the left whiskers, then kick the thing away and turn to face the first one again.

As it lunges at me, I spin to the side and slam my blade into its shoulder, then I draw a long line back to its haunches. It howls in pain then kicks out at me sideways. The attack hits me in the leg, and I scream as something breaks. I fall backward. A moment later, as the creature turns, its barbed tail slams into my side, biting deeply. It whirls away after a moment, but the wound immediately begins to burn. There was venom of some sort in that tail—that much I'm pretty sure of.

I groan and grit my teeth then sway and try to keep my balance. Suddenly, the world seems to tilt slightly, and I let out a long breath. I can handle this. One of the cat things comes charging at me again, and I brace myself.

This time when I jump, I jump backward, allowing myself to push against the wall. Before I start to fall, I push off again, launching myself into the air over the creature. It snarls and yelps, spinning, and I come down hard just behind its haunches. As quickly as I can, I reach out, grab hold of its tail, and slash my dagger clean through the bone. The tail, stinger and all, falls to the ground, and I whirl it around like a whip over my head.

The monster turns to snarl at me then howls as it realizes what's happened. Quickly, I step forward and land several long lashes across its shoulder, inflicting massive cuts. Blood drips down to the stone floor, and it howls and steps back, retreating into a corner. I can see it starting to sway, and I know I have it in the bag. I then glance at the monster whose whiskers I cut off. It's running in a circle, unable to get its bearings, which means I have some time.

[GoldenShield: Alright, guys! When it kicked him, it was sorta like a horse! Should we add *that* to the name?]

I snort at the chat, which apparently cares a great deal about the name of the monster, then open my inventory, pop an antivenom, and chug half a Pumped! drink. My health, which had started to drop, stabilizes, and it even starts to rise as the world stops spinning.

"I've got you now," I mutter. I charge headlong at the monster I poisoned, and it snarls and braces itself. The positions have been reversed. As I come up, I feint to the left and then roll to the right, slamming both of my daggers into its body, just behind the front legs, aiming for the heart. I can't tell if I actually hit the organ, but it only takes a few moments before the monster, which almost instantly begins to snarl and claw at me, tilts over to the side and hits the ground with a loud *thump*.

I take a long breath and step back. Suddenly, John is thrown through a small alcove on the side, slammed flat by his own monster. He punches it in the jaw in response, knocking it aside, then grabs a large rock and smashes it over the creature's head. I don't watch the rest of the fight, but John seems to have himself handled, so I charge forward to engage the disoriented monster.

That fight is quite a bit quicker, though it still isn't a cakewalk. I approach from the left side, since that seems to be where it's the blindest. It sees me and stops spinning, managing to just get its footing. I can tell, though, that it's still skewing a bit to the right, and with triumph in my eyes, I rush forward.

The monster jumps at me. Its body passes off to the right, the same direction it's been skewing, but . . . at the same time, it seems to compensate for this fact and lashes out with its tail.

That tail! I had forgotten about it entirely, and somehow, this beast seems to be intelligent enough to realize that if it can't hit me one way, it'll hit me another way. The barb flashes straight at my heart, and I bring up both daggers to block.

My intention had been to score a long strike along the unprotected side. Instead, I suddenly find myself slammed to the ground, the stinger only an inch away from my chest—the only things holding it away from my body are my daggers and my strength. I gasp in pain and exertion, and the beast slowly turns around and snarls, keeping me pinned in place. Drool and venom drip from its mouth as it approaches me.

"Alright," I gasp, trying to keep my focus. "I can do this. I just need to . . ."

A thought strikes my mind, and with all my might, I lay my Shadow Dagger flat against my chest, allowing the stinger to rest against it. My Photonic Dagger keeps the barb from slipping, while the pressure on my chest becomes so great that I'm not sure I can withstand it for more than a few seconds. An ordinary person would be crushed in mere instants, that much I'm sure of. Then, slowly, I reach up with my right hand and grab hold of the tail, though I don't apply any pressure.

Yet.

The mouth of the creature comes up just next to me. It seems to be savoring its victory, and it opens its mouth wide to bite down on my head and end me for good. That, of course, is when I use all my effort to lift the point of the tail and shove it into the mouth of the creature.

That makes it sound easy. In reality, I use my right arm to just *barely* lift the stinger away from the blade of my dagger, grab hold with my left hand as well, and shove it into the gaping maw of the beast. It chomps down in surprise, and I roll out of the way as it howls in pain and backs up. The tail flops around now, a stump where the pointer had once been.

I don't see the barb on the floor, which means that the beast must have swallowed it.

At least, that's my hope.

I scoop up my daggers from the floor then throw them both at the monster. It snarls and spins to its right as the weapons sink into its shoulder, deep into the muscle. That makes the thing howl even louder, and it starts to limp a bit. I rush forward, and it performs a similar move as before, but this time, I'm ready.

As it passes by, instinct making the creature forget that the barb is missing, I catch hold of the tail and pull with all my might. We're both drawn to a halt, and I spin around. The monster spins and charges back at me, now that it knows exactly where I am, and I kick it in the face. That makes it stagger a bit, and I lunge forward and catch hold of its other whiskers. I then reach up and yank out one of my daggers, cut the last of the whiskers free, and give it a solid kick to make it stumble away.

The creature sways, unsteady and weakening. After a moment, it sinks to the ground, and I approach slowly. I can see it whimpering, suffering as its own venom tears it apart from inside, and the wounds across its body do an equal amount of damage. For the briefest moment, I have a flash of pity, and I open my inventory, draw out my battle axe, and chop off its head.

The head rolls across the floor. An instant later, with one final heave, John slams down his own creature with one last *thud*. It groans and stays still, and John lets out one long breath. He, like me, is covered in cuts and bruises, but overall seems no worse for wear.

"That's done," I murmur. I gather up my daggers then chug the remainder of the Pumped! I drank earlier in the fight.

"You're just lucky I took the big one." John shrugs as we start to walk onward, deeper into the cave.

"Big one?" I snort. "I don't know what fight you were watching, but I had to take on two!"

"Yeah. Two little ones." John flashes me a smile, and I know he's joking. We finally have a chance to look around, and we find it to be quite small, consisting of little more than one central antechamber with a few smaller alcove-like things that really only serve to allow the fights to range a bit and not be quite so close. The final feature is an archway that opens into a much larger, well-lit room, and the two of us slowly approach it.

Inside, we find a massive, open room, almost the size of the entry area, with two golden doors at the far end. In between us and the doors is a small, flat area, then a set of stairs as wide as the whole cave that leads down to another small, flat expanse, which leads up to the door itself. All told, it more or less divides the room into thirds. It's a perfect battleground, that's for sure. Wide and open, so you can move around a lot, with the smallest bit of an obstacle to allow for some variation. The only thing I don't see are any monsters.

"What do you think we're fighting here?" I murmur as I step forward. "One last volley, so to speak?"

"Has to be," John nods. He chuckles and steps past me. "I'll go first. Wouldn't want a frail little one like you to get your clothes dirty, you know."

I draw myself up. "Frail little one? And *who* was the damsel in distress who was pulled from the lava?"

"Damsel in distress? Think of all the people who get pulled from lava in movies. They got momentarily beaten, but those are always the most epic, the—"

John steps through the archway and into the room, and his voice gets cut off as a giant millipede slams into him from behind, jumping on him from the wall—which, as we hadn't yet entered the room, we couldn't see. It coils around him within a split second, a thousand legs all scrambling to tear into him. I rush forward as well, but he throws himself on the ground and begins to roll, splattering bug guts across the floor.

As I enter the room, I spin around and look up at the wall. Now, I was fully expecting to see another millipede waiting for me—maybe even two or three. What I wasn't expecting to see was a whole wall of them, at least a hundred, all with beady eyes and countless legs. One of them jumps at me an instant later, and I bring up my dagger and lash out in instinct.

My weapon carves through the underside of the monster, and bug guts explode across me as the monster hits. I'm knocked backward by the sheer force of a two-hundred-pound arthropod landing on me, and I find myself whacking the ground with a great deal more force than I had expected. Almost instantly, the other millipedes on the wall react to the hit, and they come surging down and onto the floor to help their fallen companions.

At the same time, a buzzing fills the air, and I look up to see dozens of large locusts, almost identical to the mostly forgotten locust I have hiding away in my pocket dimension. They're swarming down out of several large holes in the ceiling, alongside giant wasps, centipedes, and other massive insects.

Now, I'll admit that, at this point, I'm rather shocked. The insects don't exactly fit with the other monsters I've been seeing in this dungeon, but I suppose that I'm not really in a position to critique the monsters charging at me. As such, I simply rush forward into the fray, trying to kill as many of them as I can before they take me down. My health is almost full, which is helpful, and I start lashing out at pretty much anything I can reach.

For a moment, it's easy. The millipedes are basically just bug gunk surrounded by a thin shell—a shell that my blades can easily peel apart. I land long cuts along several of them, only for two of them to rear up, blocking my path. Now, they're all about ten feet long, so as they pull themselves up to a height of about six feet . . . well, it's a lot of legs, and their pincers certainly look rather intimidating. Still, all this move ultimately does is expose their bellies, and I'm able to carve my way through them as well.

I've just taken down the two standers when a wasp hits me from behind. It drives its stinger clean through my shoulder, and I scream in pain. Without losing my cool, though, I reach up and grab the thing by the neck. Its long legs flail against my arms, and I'll admit that my initial reaction is to fling it away, but only because the sensation of legs from smaller insects and wasps is designed to elicit such fear. I grit my teeth, bear it, and pull as hard as I can. The wasp's neck snaps, and I pull the stinger out and slam it to the ground.

More of the monsters come buzzing down from the sky, though, wings fluttering wildly as they seek to tear me to bits. I brace myself, kick a handful of nearby millipedes away, and then throw myself into a defensive pattern. I dodge, striking at the insects as they pass by. Most of them I'm able to hit, and they go spiraling down to land against the stone far below. A few of them manage to get past me, and one or two are able to sting me. Soon, blood drips down my back and my chest from the wounds, but I grit my teeth and bear it. I will not fall to these beasts, no matter how hard they try.

Suddenly, a centipede bellows and charges through the midst of the millipedes. Now, I should probably explain that the centipedes here are a good bit larger than the millipedes. Perhaps not as long proportionally, but they are quite a bit thicker, and . . . Well, they can make a bellowing noise that sounds like an angry bull, which isn't exactly what you'd expect from a giant bug. They also have much larger pincers, like something you'd see on a beetle.

Anyway, the thing hits me square in the torso, and I'm knocked backward. I come down on the bug guts and slide right off the edge of the upper platform and down the stairs, which are also covered in bugs. Dozens of them snap at me as I pass, and I strike at as many of them as I can. When I come to the bottom, I climb back to my feet and brace myself. The centipede is still charging at me, and I throw my daggers as hard as I can.

The blades slam into its head among its many eyes, and the whole thing comes crashing down, sliding down the stairs as well. A millipede rises just next to me, and I hear a distinctive buzzing in the air. Quickly, I grab the millipede's legs and sling it around, causing the wasps to sting and kill *it* instead of me. I then throw the whole thing at a locust also trying to charge me, dive forward, and retrieve my daggers.

"Why don't you call out your pets?" John calls to me. He

slams his foot down onto the stairs, blasting a chunk of stone up into the air. Expertly, he grabs it, then throws it through the mass of insects, blasting dozens of them into goo.

"Because I want all their powers to still be active when we face the boss!" I answer.

"Won't be much use in that if we can't get *to* the boss."

That's a fair point. I open the portal and call out Bjorn and Garg, and with that, the four of us charge headlong into the bugs.

Even with Bjorn's frost and Garg's fire, it still takes us another half hour to clear out the last of the insects. By the time we're done, John and I are both exhausted, and Garg and Bjorn have used up all their attacks. The ground, the walls—pretty much every surface in the room is covered with a thick layer of bug guts, so much so that it makes it slippery and almost impossible to walk. I laugh and sit down on the steps, on the cleanest section I can find, and John does the same.

"Well, that was something else!" He chuckles softly. "We'll have to—"

Whoosh.

The sound comes from the entrance, and we both turn just in time to see a massive boulder crashing down over the tunnel leading out. With that, the golden doors rumble, and almost imperceptibly, they begin to open.

[System Notification: The doors to the boss chamber will now open. They will fully open in 10:00. You may, of course, enter before then. You may not leave this room again until the boss has been defeated, or until you have been.]

I shake my head. "You weren't kidding when you said it would be a brief pause."

"I guess not." John glanced at me. "Do you have any more Pumped!? I used up my last one, and I know I gave you a bunch of them."

"Here." I toss him one from my inventory then drink one myself. "What's the plan? Wait or engage?"

"My guess is that if we enter earlier, it'll be an easier fight, at least by some standards. And the longer we wait, while we have more time to heal, the harder it will be." John shrugs. "Heal for five minutes, and then . . . then we'll go take down whatever's lurking behind that door."

CHAPTER TWENTY-SEVEN

The doors are about halfway open when John and I stand up. The boulder is still blocking the entrance, making it impossible for us to leave. On the bright side, though, it makes it impossible for anyone to sneak through and snipe our boss battle, which is comforting. Together, a bit shaky on our feet but otherwise ready, we stride toward the growing hole in the darkness.

"What do you think we'll face?" John asks.

"I don't have the faintest idea," I answer. I glance at my chat, which is debating the different healing properties of a wide assortment of medicines and things. Apparently, someone else in the Rift got pinned down by a boulder that was constantly draining their health, and they managed to survive by hooking up a drip-fed IV out of a trash bag, some soda straws, and a ballpoint pen. A brief image of the setup rises in my mind, and I push it down as fast as I can. I can handle gross monsters, but some things . . .

Anyhow, John and I approach the threshold. Unlike some places, there's no warning. The moment my foot crosses that barrier, the doors fly open, and the darkness transforms into light. For a long moment, I look at the battlefield, hardly comprehending what I'm seeing.

In many ways, the boss chamber is a combination of everything we've been fighting thus far. The floor is largely gray slate, though in the middle sits a pool of lava perhaps fifty feet across. Radiating out from that pool are little rivulets of lava, stretching like tentacles across the floor and up to the walls. The walls, meanwhile, are uneven, with large steps and platforms rising up like stairs. Then, high above, large arches of stone stretch out across the expanse, meeting a great pillar that rises up from the pool of lava. Above that, there's a short stretch of sheer, unclimbable stone, topped by an immense, open space. Cold wind and snow drift down from the blue sky above, while hot air and sulfur rise up from below. The picture of snow above, fire below . . . It really sets quite the striking tone and lodges itself firmly in my memory. The only thing I don't see, of course, is the boss.

"Come out, come out, wherever you are," John murmurs as we look around. The golden doors don't close behind us, leading me to suspect that the bug-coated stairs are also counted as part of the boss arena. We walk forward, slowly and carefully, looking back and forth for anything that could indicate what we're actually supposed to be fighting.

Quite suddenly, a roar shakes the chamber. Not the roar of a monster from *this* Rift, but the impossible noise of the dragon from the last one. The very walls rumble, lava bursts and explodes up into the air, and snow is shaken down from the stones high above. I brace myself as the noise thunders and rages around me, and John crouches down on one knee.

"That thing again?" John frowns. "What's going on here?"

"I wish I knew," I answer. Suddenly, pain lances through my side, and I look down to find the ring blazing with light. Light and fire. The flames don't actually burn their way out of my pocket, but they do burn my skin beneath, and I gasp in pain.

"Take it out!" John orders.

"No!" I snap. "That's . . . that's what it wants." I grit my teeth, forcing myself to endure the agony. "Trust me. We need . . . we need to . . ."

Chuff hoot!

An odd, half-grunting, half-hooting noise echoes down from above, and I see a shadow appear on the lip of the battle arena. After a moment, a monkey leaps down, landing with a crash on the ground about twenty feet in front of us. It looks like the hot-spring monkeys, with the distinct exception that it's a good bit taller—almost ten feet—and a great deal more muscular. It opens its mouth and roars at us, and I take my stance and draw out both of my daggers. John does the same, and we stare up at the great beast.

"You'll not stop us!" I taunt the thing, knowing that it won't do any good.

"I think it understands punches a bit better than English," John suggests. He slowly crouches down, grabs hold of a small protrusion of stone, and breaks it off as he stands back up.

"Works for me." I draw back my hands to throw my daggers. "On three?"

Quite suddenly, the dragon's roar echoes once more, even louder. My ears ache under the assault, and my chest throbs painfully as my lungs are rattled about. The monkey draws itself up and begins to thump its chest mightily, roaring back at the unseen aggressor.

[FireStorm: Wait, are there *two* bosses in this Rift?]

[IceQueen: This is going to be the best boss fight EVER!!!]

[GoldenShield: I just hope Jason comes out of it alive.]

[Originalgoth: I don't.]

[GrendleH8tr: Just keep your head, kid. Use everything you've used so far, and you'll get along just fine.]

I glance at John, and we both throw our weapons at the same time. Two daggers, one stone; it all flashes through the air. My daggers both slam into the monkey's chest, sinking deep into its flesh, while John's rock hits the beast straight in the face. It falls backward into the lava, sending up a mighty splash of the molten metal, and the two of us high-five.

And then, of course, the creature comes right back out.

At this point, the dragon's roar is fading away. All pretenses are gone, and the monkey charges headlong at us. John races forward, jumps into the air, and punches it in the face. The monkey reels back a bit, then snaps back, grabs him, and flings him across the battle arena. He smashes against the stone on the far side and slumps to the ground. He's not out of the fight yet, but he's hurting.

I stretch out my hand and call my Shadow Dagger back to myself then rush forward to meet the beast. It snarls and raises its mighty fists, then brings them crashing down. I drop down to the ground and slide beneath its legs, then stand back up and leap onto its back, digging my dagger between its ribs. I pull myself up as best I can, and I wrap my arms around its back. The monkey begins to hoot and holler, rushing madly about, and I reach out to its chest and pull out my Photonic Dagger. I have every intention of stabbing the thing a great deal more than I've already done but, before I can manage it, it whirls rapidly and flings me away, and I come crashing down near the entrance.

As I climb back to my feet, I find the monkey rushing at me, and I know I have only seconds to live. Quickly, I stand up and fling my Shadow Dagger into its face. It only bounces off the bone and falls, though it does manage to land a long cut along its cheek. I call the weapon back to myself, then turn and throw it into the beast's belly. The beast rumbles and snarls, and I call the weapon back again. It lunges, throwing a massive punch. I only just manage to dodge it, and I try to slash its wrists on the way back, but it's too fast for me to land more than a superficial slice. The beast roars, then throws itself into a great body slam, trying to flatten me underneath. I barrel-roll off to one side, and I try to jump onto its back before it can stand up, but it whirls too quickly, grabs my leg, and slams me back against the ground.

Now, I should probably say that, at this point, the pain from the ring hasn't really gone away at all. In fact, it's only growing more intense, though it's not shining with quite as much light. Thankfully, it's also not diminishing my health bar. Frankly, I don't know exactly what's happening with the thing, but I know it's not good. All of this flashes through my mind in a moment as I'm lying there on the ground—largely because I notice, at that very moment, the fact that shadows are beginning to ripple along the walls of the structure. They haven't actually taken on form yet, but they will soon, and I grit my teeth.

"I have bigger problems than you, primate." I kick the monkey in the face as it tries to chomp down on me. It doesn't stagger backward, but it is prevented from devouring the lower half of my body, which is always a bonus. I jump back to my feet, and the monkey lunges, throwing its full body weight at me once more.

Wham!

A flash of gray blurs through my vision, and a massive boulder slams into the monkey, blasting it sideways. I glance over to see John, swaying a bit on his feet, flash me a thumbs-up. I nod back at him then point upward. He gives a nod and starts climbing up the walls of the battle arena, scaling toward the upper levels of the place.

The monkey has been blasted off into the entry arena, all the way to the bug-covered stairs. As I race after it, it shoves the boulder aside then slowly stands up. I throw my dagger as hard as I can, hitting it in the neck, then call my weapon back to me and throw it once again. As I come racing up to the monster, I pull out my Photonic Dagger. The monster roars and tries to stomp on me, but I use the bug gunk to my advantage and slide out of the way, landing a long cut just below one of the beast's knees. It howls in pain then punches me in the gut and races for the safety of the main battle arena.

I race along after it—after I pick myself up, of course. My health has dropped to around half, and I pop a few health tabs as I pass through the golden doors. Ahead, the monkey jumps across the pool of lava and grabs hold of the central pillar, which it begins to climb. I smile then open my pocket dimension and let Garg come out.

"I know your attacks aren't recharged yet, but I need a lift."

Garg spreads his wings, and I hop onto his back. With that, we launch upward, rising on the hot updrafts caused by the lava. As we rise, though, the air grows colder and colder, until we suddenly enter the frosty realm of that top layer. There, the monkey sits at the exact center of the transforming stone walkways, thumping its chest and snarling at us.

I don't see John, but I know that only means I'm not looking closely enough. "Get me above him, Garg."

Garg nods and flies closer. As he does, the monkey reaches down and breaks off a chunk of stone, which it flings through the air with deadly accuracy. Garg dodges to the left, only narrowly avoiding being crushed like a bug. I still feel the breath of air from the stone's passing, though. With that, he flaps his wings even harder, and we rise faster and faster.

The monkey continues to fling rocks, and we continue to dodge. Soon, the two of us are high above the monkey—so high that I can actually see out over the frozen landscape around us. I take a brief look, but I know I can't turn my attention away from the fight below.

[ViperQueen: Wow! It's . . . beautiful!]

[ShadowDancer: I never would have guessed.]

[LunarEclipse: Yeah . . .]

I must admit, I'm right there with them. The view is breathtaking. Stretching out on all sides is a vast expanse of snow, dotted with rolling hills, pillars of ice, evergreen trees, and more, all reaching out to snow-capped mountains that ring it on every side. I let out a great sigh . . . then get drawn back downward as the monkey roars and thumps its chest once again.

"Alright." I stretch then stand up. "Break's over, I guess. Back to work!"

With that, I jump off Garg's back and plummet through the air, feeling the freezing wind swirling all around me. The monkey, whose attention was turned away from me by the appearance of John, suddenly seems to hear me. It looks up and snarls, and I strike a moment later. I'm not going to say that I hit it like a missile or anything, but when I land on its back, it's blasted into the ground, sending up a massive plume of snow. I stab it multiple times with both of my daggers, then jump free, landing on a stone platform perpendicular to where John is standing.

The monkey stands back up, and John cuts loose. Stones flash through the air, straight and true, striking the beast up one side and down the other. He roars and stumbles backward, and I have an idea. "John! We need to make it fall!"

John gives a nod then rips up a particularly large boulder almost the size of his upper torso. He flings it, hard, and it tears through the air so fast I can hardly keep track of it. I throw my dagger at the same time, hitting the monster in the knee. The monkey roars and staggers, off-balance, and John's stone hits it a moment later. The great beast is picked up and thrown backward, clean off the pillar and down to the fire below. It slams into the shore just next to the flames, thankfully, and I see stone crack and break under its impact.

It doesn't move for a long moment, and John and I walk up to stand on the top of the pillar, looking down at it.

"The bigger they are . . ." John murmurs.

"Want to finish him together?" I flash a grin at him. "If we both jump together . . ."

"I wouldn't have it any other—"

At that very moment, the dragon chooses to roar once

more, shaking the arena so powerfully that even the rocks themselves crack under my feet. The column sways and shakes then crumbles; we find ourselves falling . . . not quite according to our plan. The lava flashes below me, and I know we only have seconds before we hit.

How high is my heat resistance? I have no idea, but unless I figure out something within the next several seconds, I'm going to find out firsthand.

CHAPTER TWENTY-EIGHT

My mind whirls. Thankfully, my gargoyle has been watching—and, unlike me, hasn't forgotten that he exists. He comes swooping down, grabbing both me and John, and throws us onto the ground. Stone comes raining down around us as we land and roll, coming up to our feet. We look at the monkey, which is now struggling back to *its* feet, and I groan.

"Oh, well." John shrugs. "More fighting. I don't know about you, but I can always use the exercise."

The monkey roars and starts thumping forward . . . only to be hit by a massive blast of flame, right in the chest. It's launched back into the pool of lava, and I see something streak overhead. My jaw sets, and I slowly look up as a familiar figure drifts down out of the sky and lands where the monkey was just standing.

"Harold." I grimace and prepare my weapons. Garg lands

just behind me, spreading his wings to appear more menacing. "And here I thought extra guests couldn't get inside."

"I sneaked in *right* before the door closed." Harold snorts. "I almost thought I'd been caught, but then the boulder fell, and you both just assumed that you'd heard *it* instead."

"What are you doing?" I slowly take out a bottle of Pumped! and take a quick swig. Harold likes to talk, and I won't turn down the opportunity to heal a bit.

"You know why I'm here," Harold snarls. "I'm removing a menace from the world."

"Coming from the person who's been sneaking around behind our backs? Of the two of us, which one has been fighting monsters?"

Harold snarls, "It's all just a clever ploy! I know what you have in your pocket. Hand it to me, and hand it to me now."

John looks over at me. "What's he talking about?"

"This." I take a deep breath then reach into my pocket and pull out the ring. It burns my fingers now, not my leg. It gleams in the light, and we all look down at the little symbols etched in metal: that serpent, coiled in a circle, devouring the small ruby. Devouring . . . or, perhaps, offering it to those who would take it.

"Give it to me," Harold snarls. "That ring holds true power. If you put it on, you'll become corrupted."

"And you won't?" I snort.

"I've seen the inside of the beast," Harold snaps back. "I've seen the horrors the dragon can hold. You haven't. I'm the one who can withstand its advances. I'm the one who won't succumb to its temptations. It calls to you, I know it. The dragon calls to you. One of these days, you'll put it on, and you'll become a mouthpiece for that monster. If *I* put it on, though . . . I'll be able to control it."

"You're insane if you think so," I answer him.

Harold only shakes his head. "I'm not the insane one. I—"

Now, I should say that, through all of this, John and I are communicating as best we can with our eyes. We both know he is crazy, and John isn't fooled for a moment by Harold's claims of my ineptitude. I don't know exactly what we are planning to do, but we realize that it doesn't matter as the monkey comes roaring up out of the lava.

Molten stone pours off its fur as it lunges forward, grabbing Harold from behind. Harold yelps and spins around, blasting it in the face with flame. That allows the monkey to let him go free, and he flies up into the air. The great beast snarls and slowly pulls itself up, and I take a bow.

"How about this? We form a temporary truce until this thing is dead, and *then* we beat each other up?"

"No deal." Harold laughs. "When that boss dies, the Rift will close. I'm not stupid. I think . . . Instead, I think I'm going to make a truce with the monkey. When *you* two are dead, I'll take the ring from your corpse, and then I'll be powerful enough to protect our world. Using the weapon of the enemy against the enemy!"

[DarkCynic: . . . I don't think that's how that works.]

[IceQueen: This is nuts!!!]

[GoldenShield: Who will win?]

Harold snarls, then falls to the ground, unleashing a blast of fire as he does so. John and I both charge toward him, even as the monkey thunders toward us as well. Now, at this point, I think the monkey is a little confused, but it can see Harold fighting us, so it ignores him for the moment. As we all come together, Harold opens his inventory, and I suddenly see a flash of sparks.

So, you remember those fireworks that John and I had been so proud of? Turns out Harold simply gathered them all up. Streaks of fire, multi-colored lights, smoke, flame, and a great deal more all come streaking out.

My eyes are dazzled as hundreds of explosions go off in front of my face. Sparks scorch my clothes and skin, but I largely just ignore them and push onward. Little stings from sparks, I can live with. As I come through the barrage of fireworks, though, I find that Harold isn't where he had once been. I've fallen for a trap that I myself have used countless times.

A blast of fire hits me from behind, and I'm thrown forward, sliding up toward the lava. The monkey jumps from the side, bringing both fists crashing down upon me. I only narrowly roll out of the way, though the shockwave still picks me up and flings me to the side. As I climb back to my feet, the dragon roars again, and the shadows on the wall begin to take on a familiar, serpent-like form. I grit my teeth and rush onward. This is *not* how I intended things to go. I jump up at the monkey, stabbing it several times, only for Harold to swoop through the air and catch hold of my arm. I'm launched high into the sky, where I whistle sharply.

Garg appears out of nowhere, hitting Harold firmly. The two of them zing down to the far side of the arena, where a great blast of rubble explodes up into the air as they land. I come crashing down on a snowy outcropping high above, and I stagger back to my feet as Harold and Garg both rise. They tussle briefly then step back. Flames flicker in Harold's hands, and Garg opens his mouth. With a mighty blast, fire erupts from both, meeting in the middle in a great display of fortitude.

I've seen this same display—dual energies raging against one another—countless times in movies and television, but this time . . . this time, it's personal. I can see Garg's narrowed eyes, his intense concentration, and I can see Harold's hate. I draw out my dagger to throw it, but I know I don't have the range.

[ChaosRider: Jason! Use your bow!]

That's right! I'd forgotten that I had a bow. Quickly, I pull it from my inventory, fit an arrow to the string, and draw it back. I've never shot a bow and arrow before—not since scouts back in elementary school, anyway—so I have to make do on the fly. Carefully, I sight down the shaft of the arrow then let it go.

My aim is horribly off. The arrow rises a bit as it passes over the lava, then dips to the side as it hits some sort of breeze, though it does manage to clatter to the ground next to Harold's feet, which makes him lose his concentration for the briefest moment.

Foooooom!

Garg's fire hits Harold firmly in the chest, blasting him back into the stone. Garg steps forward, pressing the attack, and I cheer. I put away the bow and begin to bound down the stones, desperately racing for my quarry. A moment later, though, I glance back to the entryway, where I see John tussling with the monkey. Sidenote: that monkey is a *tank*. I have no idea how much damage we've dealt to it, but I'm quite certain it should be dead by now. Suddenly, John punches it on the underside of its jaw, knocking it backward, and follows up with a roundhouse kick to the chest.

The monkey flies across the arena, where it smashes into the stone not far from Harold. As it shakes itself loose, it catches a glimpse of Garg, and I feel horror shoot through me. Before I can do anything, it springs forward, grabs Garg, picks him up, and brings him crashing down over its knee.

"Skill: Rapid Heal!"

[Error: Rapid Heal may only be used to target creatures that are still alive.]

No! How could it have happened so fast? Even after so much damage, the thing just . . . just insta-killed Garg? Rage fills my blood, and I bolt down to the ground as fast as I can.

John is circling from one side, I from the other. Harold, more than a bit charred but still standing, staggers away from the wall. He and the monkey face John and me as we charge headlong at them. And that's when I have an idea. It's probably a terrible idea. It might even verge on the realm of the absolutely horrible. It is, however, an idea—and at this point, I'm getting desperate. This fight needs to end, and it needs to end *now*.

"Hey, Harold!" I call out. "You want this ring?" I pull it out of my pocket and hold it up. It shines brilliantly in the light, and the dragon shadows take on form behind Harold. "Here! Take it!"

I fling the ring at him with all my might. The dragon roars once more and, just next to him, the monkey's eyes grow wide. Harold, so stunned he doesn't know what to do, reaches up and catches the ring with a scarred, charred hand. For a long moment, it rests in his hand, and behind him, the dragon roars.

"Alright, Harold!" I yell at him. "Use it! Do your worst! Save our world! Do everything that you claim you're going to do!"

Harold blinks in surprise then smiles. It's a dark, twisting, sinister sort of smile, and he holds the ring up.

"You just made the biggest, last mistake you'll ever—"

Thump.

[ChaosRider: WHOA!!!!]

[RazorEdge: I did NOT see that one coming!]

[IceQueen: Jason did, at least!]

[LunarEclipse: Very true! Go Jason!!!!]

Harold, rather as I had hoped, is flattened under the mighty fist of the monkey. Harold groans and staggers to his feet, but the monkey simply bends down, grabs the ring off the ground, and holds it up itself. Harold staggers forward and holds out a hand, and the monkey spins toward him. There's a sharp snort, and it suddenly folds the ring tightly into its palm.

"Give . . . give it to . . ."

The monkey draws itself up, thumps its chest, then sucker punches Harold in the face. His body is slammed to the ground with sickening force. I'm pretty sure that he's already dead, but if I needed more confirmation, the great beast grabs his legs—with the hand that doesn't hold the ring—lifts him up, and proceeds to dash Harold against the stone until he has been so disfigured that he's hardly even recognizable as human. It then, just to top things off, throws Harold into the pool of lava. Flames explode across his body, and not the type that come from him using his power. He sinks out of view, and . . . well . . . that's the last of him.

[Poll:]

[Will Harold be coming back from *that*?]

[A: Yes: 0.5%]

[B: No: 99%]

[C: Depends on whether or not someone needs his help a bit further down the line: 0.5%]

Now, though, the monkey holds the ring. It slowly unfolds its hand then takes it between a thumb and forefinger and lifts it up to the sky. The sunlight shimmers off the ring, catching the light of that red gem, and fire seems to flow from the object. Slowly, carefully, the monkey stretches out its second hand, and I notice the ring growing in size.

"No," I whisper. I had rather been hoping that the monkey would be unable to put it on. Behind the monster, shadows gather, and I see the wide-open mouth of the dragon, ready to devour the monkey. Slowly, the monkey slips its finger through, then roars in pain and thumps its chest.

It's hard to describe exactly what happens now. Fire explodes down the finger, up the monkey's arm, and through the rest of its body. The skin blackens, hair falls out, and magma begins to shine forth from inside the monster itself. I wince in pity, if it's possible to have pity for such a beast, and its eyes begin to glow with an infernal light.

Behind the creature, the dragon grows larger and larger, then suddenly plunges downward. Shadows pull themselves off the walls and flow into the monkey like smoke, as if they're being inhaled. In mere seconds, the process is complete, and the monkey shakes its head as if getting its bearings.

"Now what?" John gapes, jogging up to me.

"Now we finish the job once and for all," I answer. "Don't

ask me how I know, but . . . trust me, this fight is going to be a much shorter one than before."

"I'll take your word for it." John shrugs. "What do we do?"

"First, break out every single healing item you have," I order. "We're going for broke here. Secondly . . . well . . . I need a bit of help from my friends."

CHAPTER TWENTY-NINE

John nods, and as the monkey-dragon starts thumping toward us, he opens his inventory. I open my own and toss him my small, bottomless sack. "Here! Put it all in there! I'll keep this thing busy!"

John races away, doing what I've ordered, while I face off against the great monster. My portal opens, and Bjorn and Ratatoskr emerge. I give them a nod, sending my commands to them mentally, then rush forward to face the beast in single combat. I may need help, but I'm still going to have to do the bulk of the work myself.

The next few minutes are both the most terrifying and the most exhilarating of my life. The monkey-dragon is faster than ever, spinning and slashing and punching with extraordinary ferocity. I focus mostly on just staying out of its grasp—dodging between its legs, jumping around it, making it spin left and right. Its punches come faster and faster, blasting craters out of the stone around us with every strike. It's almost impossibly strong, that's for sure. When I manage to land a strike against it, the heat that pours out from inside is almost unbearable. Still, though, onward I push.

"Alright, Jason!" John calls from across the lake of fire. "I think I'm good to go!"

"Perfect!" I call back, then nod at my companions. "Do what you do best!"

Bjorn steps forward and howls a long and mournful call. The air chills, and the great monkey-dragon pauses for the briefest of moments.

[Warning: Undead Primate is resisting Frost.]

"Yeah, I kind of counted on that, but at least it slowed it down," I answer as I race away, mostly for the benefit of my viewers. "Ratatoskr, you're up!"

The squirrel, who had scampered up onto the snowy paths above, chitters. "Hey, dragon! I've seen level one wyrms that were scarier than you!"

The monkey-dragon snarls and spins, then jumps forward and smashes itself into the cliff just beneath Ratatoskr. The squirrel nimbly leaps to safety as his perch crumbles into nothingness and calls down once more.

"Is that the hardest you can hit? I was going to stay safely out of reach, but with a punch that weak, I might just come down and shake your hand! No . . . best not. I might hurt your wrist."

The monkey-dragon actually lets fire roll out of its mouth, and it jumps upward and starts scrambling up the side of the cliff face. Stone and rock explode all around it as it climbs, and Ratatoskr races away as fast as he can go. A moment later, I arrive at John, and he hands me the bag. "What should I do?"

"Just keep him busy." I nod. "That's all you can do. Stay out of his reach. He's dangerous."

"And just what are you going to do with all of our healing items?" John scowls at me. "Take them all? Turn yourself into some sort of super soldier to combat him?"

I give him a wink. "Just you watch."

John shrugs, then picks up a boulder and throws it at the monster. He moves to the side of Ratatoskr, and between the two of them, they start pulling the monkey-dragon back and forth, first taunting it one direction then the other. Meanwhile, I retreat to the open doors, sit down, and dump out all of John's healing items. They're mostly an assortment of medicine, which is what I would expect. I then dump out my own, which are also mostly pills, injections, and a handful of remaining Pumped! Quickly, I grab a flat stone and begin crushing up as many of the pills as I can, turning them all into a powder.

[GoldenShield: Jason, just what are you doing?]

[ShadowDancer: I'm really favoring the super soldier idea.]

[RazorEdge: Nah, I'm sure he has something *much* cooler than that!]

I don't answer. When I have everything crushed up, I scroll through my inventory until I find a bag; it's just a small plastic bag, like you'd get at a grocery store, but it'll have to work. Quickly, I dump in all the powder then add my last three Pumped! bottles. That done, I squirt in all the injections. It fizzes and boils then slowly solidifies.

[Bag of Healing. Contains a mixture capable of healing someone up to 1245159742 HP.]

"Wonderful." I nod then scroll through my inventory a bit

more. "Now . . . let's see . . . Straws!" I pull out the last two bags of Pumped! fast food, tear them open—regrettably spilling the burgers out across the ground—and pull out a handful of bendy straws. I thread a few of them together then get ready for my last act. "And finally, a ballpoint pen."

I'm not exactly sure where I picked up the ballpoint pen, but as I pull it out, I give it a few clicks for dramatic effect then twist off the end and pull out all the inky bits. Soon, I have a perfect, or at least passable, IV bag. Now all I have to do is use it.

"Alright, John! Last bit!" I run forward. "I need it to be held down, just long enough to administer all of this!"

John blinks in surprise, but he nods. He flexes his muscles and steps forward, challenging the monkey-dragon. It throws a massive fist, and he grabs hold. It takes all his effort, but he gives the wrist a sharp twist then pulls it to the ground. Bjorn bounds up and latches onto an ankle, and I quickly stab the ballpoint pen through the outer layer of skin.

Smoke explodes up from the point of impact as the healing liquid flows down into the body of the monster. It only takes a few moments to deliver, and as the bag empties, I nod to John and Bjorn. We all leap backward. The monkey-dragon roars and lurches back to its feet, snarling.

"Jason?" John glances at me. "I've been trying to trust you, but I think I liked the super soldier idea better. Why, after we've been fighting this thing for so long, would you *heal* it?"

"Because now it's undead." I take a deep breath, feeling my plan accelerating. "And everyone knows that healing items will kill undead."

The monkey-dragon roars and thumps its chest, and I wish

I knew whether it was working. Unfortunately, I have no way of knowing—not yet—so I charge into battle one last time.

I truly wish I could describe this one last fight to you. I dodge left and right, over and under, my blades landing long slices across the monkey-dragon. John punches, throws rocks, grabs its arms and legs to slam it down, and more. I mean, we're *pounding* this thing, but still it stays upright. Still it's not dying. The damage counter goes higher and higher and higher, and suddenly, I take a hit to the chest.

Oomph!

I'm blasted across the arena, slamming into the stone next to the golden doors. My health drops to a mere sliver. I see John charge the monster and jump up into the air, preparing to smash it over the head. Before he can, the monkey-dragon nabs him by the feet, spins, and throws him high into the sky. I don't see where he comes down, but I can hear the impact. I slowly rise back to my feet then sink back as my weary body starts to rebel. It's been a long fight.

You will die, Jason Lee, the voice echoes in my head. *All your effort, all your work, and it all comes down to this. You will perish. You will fall beneath my fists. You will—*

With one last burst of effort, I turn to the doors themselves. They're tall, fifty feet or more, and I throw my Shadow Dagger with all my might. It sticks in the upper portion of the door, right next to the hinge, and I stretch out my hand.

You are weak. You are nothing.

"Taunt me all you want." I take a deep breath. "Words don't work on me. If they did, I'd have given in and put that ring on a long time ago." I stare it down, and I feel a great sense of . . . something . . . swell up inside of me. "True power doesn't come from yourself, but that's the only power you have. I have thick skin. So go ahead, taunt me all you want."

You're bleeding. Your skin isn't that thick. The monkey-dragon steps right up to me.

"Thicker than yours." I call the blade back to my hand. It slices down, carving through the door hinges. There's a mighty crash as the solid-gold object falls forward, and the monkey-dragon is flattened underneath. Gold is immensely heavy, if you didn't know.

"Good . . . shot." John wearily starts to limp up from the side. "I almost thought it was going to—"

The gold suddenly melts, at least in the spot directly above the monkey-dragon, and the creature slowly rises. Molten gold drips from its body, its eyes glowing like twin suns, and it snarls. It doesn't say a word, but it slowly takes a single step forward and raises a burning hand.

[Bag of Healing has finished healing Undead Primate.]

[System Notification: Congratulations! You have defeated a Rift!]

The monkey-dragon sways then slowly falls backward with a resounding *bang*. Its body relaxes, then dissolves, turning into smoke that swirls up into the sky. A rumble flows through the ground, but it's not the rumble of the dragon. No . . . it's the rumble that indicates that the Rift has been defeated and will soon be crumbling into nothingness.

As the last of the monster fades away, John walks up and holds out his hand. I shake it firmly, and he lets out a whistle.

"You actually did it. I can't figure out how, but you actually did it."

I shrug as something lying at the door catches my eye. The

ring. I bend down to pick it up as a portal of light appears just a few feet away.

"You know." I shrug. "Bit of luck. Bit of teamwork."

"A whole lot of brains and a whole lot of brawn." John laughs and shakes his head. "You amaze me, Jason Lee. If you ever want to fight together again, please know that I'm here for you."

"I'll keep that in mind," I murmur. I can't take my eyes off the ring, though not for the same reason as before. It doesn't have the same pull that it once did.

"Do I need to beat *you* up and take that from you now?" John asks. His voice is light, but I can tell he's not joking.

"No." I chuckle and slowly lower the object. "I was just . . . just looking." I toss the ring to him with a sharp *ping*. "It's dead now. The dragon is gone, so the ring . . . it's just a ring now. A piece of metal. Nothing more."

"Huh." John frowns, turning it over and over in his fingers. "It's amazing to think that something so small could become so powerful a thing."

"I think that's sort of the point," I answer. "It never *did* have any power, not in itself. The dragon . . . the dragon wanted to control people. To do that, it needed to get people to consent to let it into their minds. It knew that if it just appeared in all its fury, a few people might accept it, but . . . it needed something more subtle. A ring is perfect: small, innocuous, and most people wouldn't blink twice when putting it on. And yet, in that small, insignificant action, it took control." I sigh after a moment. "And, more importantly, the people who wore it never had any power themselves, either. They felt like they did for a time, as the dragon slowly absorbed their minds, but . . . you saw what happened with the monkey. It was a mindless beast. It had no will of its own to subdue, allowing the shadow to absorb it almost instantly. The same thing happened to the undead warrior back in the original Rift. The same thing would have happened to Harold, or to me, or to you, or anyone."

"Huh." John looks down at the ring again. "Can we keep it then? As a memento?"

"No," I answer. "We're being watched by thousands of people. If the ring still exists, *someone* will take it up and use it as a symbol. Symbols, in a lot of ways, truly *do* have power, and that's not something we want getting loose. We leave it here in the dungeon and let it die."

"Then I'll yield to your expertise on the matter." With a practiced toss, John throws the ring into the pool of lava, where it sinks into the liquid fire. "Goodbye, ring."

"Shall we head back to the real world?" I gesture at the portal of light.

"I'd be honored to." John turns and makes a sweeping motion. "Ladies first."

"Age before beauty."

At that, John snorts. "You're like thirty years old. Doesn't take much to be older than you, so that's not exactly an insult."

"Well . . ." My brain is exhausted from all the fighting, so I just punch him on the shoulder. "Let's get out of here."

Across the Rift, portals flicker to life as the assorted Awakened are told that the dungeon has been cleared and that they can proceed back to the streets. I step through, followed by John . . . and with that, we return to the world of man.

CHAPTER THIRTY

Light flares around me, and I'm sucked across the inter-dimensional divide that separates the Rift from Earth. With a thud, I fall out the other side, staggering a bit. The weariness from the battle is starting to take its toll on me, that's for sure. All the other Awakened, at least those who have survived, appear around me. Then, with a crackle, the giant portal before the Statue of Liberty fades away, leaving us alone on the island amidst choppy waters.

This time there are no crowds to greet us. This time there's no welcome procession back to Central Park, and once we arrive, there's no party. I'm getting ahead of myself, though. The group of us slowly walks down to the boat, which has taken some light damage from sea monsters but is still floating. We all chug back to the mainland, battered, bruised, but victorious.

When we come chugging into the docks, the sounds of combat echo off the walls of the New York skyscrapers, but it's not as bad as when we left. As we walk up to the street, we even hear a horn, and a yellow taxicab comes rumbling around the corner. He pulls up, and the window rolls down to reveal a grizzled man with a stubbly beard.

"Sorry I'm late! We saw the portal vanish and figured you all could use a ride."

I blink in surprise, then gesture at the other Awakened. "Let's see . . . It looks like you can fit three, maybe four, and—"

"Don't worry about spacing! We've got more coming!"

More taxicabs roll around the corner, and soon a whole fleet has come. John and I step into one together. It's at that point that we realize how much we've grown physically as we leveled up, as the two of us can barely squeeze inside. The cab rocks on its shock absorbers but soon enough rumbles off, and we roll down the windows and look out.

Monsters are still running about, but the city is healing. People are walking down the sidewalk, going to stores, waving at one another, and calling in friendly voices. It almost feels like we're in a Midwest town instead of New York; everyone seems far happier than usual, even. Funny what the apocalypse will do.

When the cabs come rumbling back up to Central Park, John and I climb out, and the taxicab driver leans over.

"Let's see . . . That'll be fifteen dollars."

"What?" I scowl. "That seems expensive!"

"You know how inflation is." The driver shrugs. "Sorry, but I've got to pay the bills. I was hopeful all of that would go out the window with this apocalypse, but the Federal Reserve got back on its feet while you were in there, so . . . taxes are taxes, and rent's due, and everyone rejected my idea to use bottle caps for currency instead of money, so . . ."

"I'll pay." John opens his inventory, then takes out several solid gold goblets, which he tosses to the cab driver. "That ought to do it." I raise an eyebrow as the taxi pulls away, and he shrugs. "What? Yeah, dragon curses and all that, but the dragon's dead now! Besides, it just sort of accidentally fell into my inventory earlier."

"Uh huh." I roll my eyes. "Come on. I need some rest."

"You can go where you want." John pauses. "I'm going to head back to Jersey, at least for a bit. I have a sister who lives there, and now that things are starting to come back together, I'd really like to check on her. I'll be back in a few days."

I nod then hold out a hand. He clasps it, and we pull each other into a bro hug, thumping one another on the back. As we pull apart, he flashes a thumbs-up, and I puff out my cheeks and turn to the park.

There are fewer tents now than there were before. I stagger forward, looking for a good place to rest, but don't really see anything that looks quite right. Finally, I find myself at the makeshift museum where *The Starry Night* is being held. The guard recognizes me and lets me inside, and I sit down in a chair opposite it. That pretty much clears out the room, and I suddenly realize that I'm covered in bug guts, monkey blood, mud, dirt, snow, cooled lava, my own blood, and really, just about everything you could think of that might be considered gross or disgusting. A good bit of it starts to drip down onto the floor, and the guard shoots me a long, stern look.

"I'll clean it up, I'll clean it up." I sigh. "Ahh, what I wouldn't give for a Pumped! right now."

The guard looks at me for a long moment then shakes his head and steps away. A moment later, he returns and tosses me a bottle. I catch it firmly then blink in surprise at the label.

"Pumped! Cherry." I raise an eyebrow. "I didn't even know that existed, or that civilians could get their hands on it."

"I've got friends." The guard shrugs. "I also think the flavors are a new thing."

I nod, though I don't really have anything else to say about it. The *crack* of the bottle opening echoes through the room, and as I tilt back my head to drink it, I realize that it's almost awkwardly quiet. Once I'm finished chugging the drink and my health starts to rise, I lean back and close my eyes.

[ChaosRider: Jason! Wait! Don't go to sleep! You need to check out your prizes from the dungeon!]

[FireStorm: Rift, not dungeon. But yes, you should!]

[ShadowDancer: Yeah! GO!!!!!!!!!]

I open my eyes again and smile. "I forgot all about it, but you're right. Let's see here . . . First, what level am I now?"

[You are now Level 20!]

[Please accept from the following rewards: (3)]

[Level D Weapon]

[Level D Monster]

[Monster Trainer Skill]

"Choices, choices." I think for a moment then nod. "First, I need a new monster. No one will ever replace Garg in my heart, but I do need a new monster. Particularly a fire or a flight type."

There's a flash of light, and a small bird appears in front of me. It flutters up to land on my arm then gives a chirp and pecks at my cheek.

[Phoenix, Level 20]

[Abilities: Inferno, Flight+]

"Just what the doctor ordered," I whisper, stroking the back of its neck. The thing gives a soft coo, and I chuckle softly. "You're a good little bird. I think we're going to have some good times together, eh?"

The phoenix coos again then vanishes into my pocket dimension. I let out a long breath then nod. "Alright, let's move on. Next . . . next I think I need a new weapon."

There's a pause, and with a flash, a—well, it's hard to tell exactly what it is—appears in my hand; it looks like a sword, but it's spectral, almost incorporeal.

[Sword of Phasing. Please place a chosen weapon into this weapon.]

I frown but nod, slowly pulling out my Shadow Dagger. As I start to place it there, though, I pause. The Shadow Dagger is nice, but . . . I tuck it away after a moment and pull out my Photonic Dagger. The blade shines brilliantly in the small room, and I place it within the spectral sword. With a flicker of light, it suddenly grows to fill the space of the spectral sword, becoming a sword of light. I gasp, holding it up as it becomes a proper beacon, driving the shadows from every corner of the room. At a command, it shrinks back into a dagger then grows into a sword. I can now adapt my fighting style as needed! It's the answer to a great deal of the questions I've been facing. I tuck the dagger away then choose the last one.

"A skill."

[Skill Acquired!]

[Brief Acquisition: Gain temporary control over a hostile mob. The duration of this will depend on the strength of the monster, as well as your level compared to its level. You can tame higher level monsters with this skill than with your basic [Tame Monster] skill.]

[LunarEclipse: Now that's cool! How do you think you'll use it?]

[IceQueen: Do you think you'll go get your own undead legions?]

[DarkCynic: This will be epic!]

I laugh softly, then cross my arms and lean back in my chair. "It makes me a lot more powerful, that's for sure, but it doesn't mean that I'll suddenly be able to take on S-Ranked Rifts or anything. That will come with time, but for now . . ." I shrug. "Let me get a good night's sleep, and I'll go out and run some tests in the morning. How's that sound?"

[ChaosRider: I can't wait!!!]

[FireStorm: Don't do too much before I can log on!]

[Originalgoth: This will be . . . interesting.]

I laugh a bit at the replies, then sigh and look up at the intricate swirls of *The Starry Night*. I'm still looking at it when a black robe flickers in the doorway, and Father Brown pokes his head inside.

"Ahh! I was told that I could find you here."

I give him nod. "What can I do for you? Need me to make another run to your church?"

"Actually, that's been mostly taken care of." Father Brown shakes his head. He sits down next to me and crosses his arms, ignoring the mess and the stench. "I watched a good bit of your fight against the monster."

"It was your advice that got me through." I shrug. "You cautioned me to avoid . . . Well, you know what you told me to do. I appreciate it, in any case."

"I'm happy to have been some help and to have contributed, in some small way, to the saving of our fair city." Father Brown sits in silence for a moment then glances at me. "I wanted to ask you something. When I was watching you . . . That moment. That moment when you threw the ring to Harold. I saw the pain on your face, and I don't think it was the physical damage that the ring was causing. How did that feel, in that moment?"

I shudder as I think back over it. "It was the worst pain I've ever felt. Giving it away… The dragon wanted me more than it wanted anyone else. Harold would have been nice, but he was too willing to give himself. The same thing with John."

"How do you know that?"

"It's just . . . imprinted on my mind." I glance over at the man. "That beast, that *thing*, it was impossibly strong. Not physically, certainly, but . . . I've never seen something that could overwhelm a mind so intensely. It finally settled on the monkey because that was the only thing that would take it. It was almost impossible to beat in the physical realm, even given how weak it was. If Harold had taken it, I imagine that the effect would have been similar, perhaps a bit stronger."

"But if *you* had succumbed . . ." Father Brown smiles. "I thought as much. The dragon, much like John's strength, grew stronger the greater the resistance that was given. That, though, was his weakness. He desired strength beyond all else but, to get that, he had to seek out the people most willing to resist him. The moment they gave in—like the skeleton you fought down in the first Rift—he abandoned them, as in that act of submission, they gave up something he so ardently desired."

"Exactly." I nod. "When I cast the thing away, I felt like my entire mind was being ripped asunder, as if my soul were being torn from my body."

"And your ability to endure *that*, more so than your ability to endure any of the physical punishment you went through, is what shows your true strength. Maintain that, hone it, perfect it, and not a single beast in this world, not a single horror of the Rift, will be able to stand against you." Father Brown slowly starts to rise. "I have a distinct feeling that you're going to be facing off against a great many of them."

"And where are you going?" I ask, raising an eyebrow. "You just stopped in for a quick chat? That's it?"

"I simply wanted to confirm, from your lips, what I already knew." Father Brown pauses, a twinkle in his eyes. "To confirm what *you* already knew. I know you're not the type to stay in one place for long, and it wouldn't do for the lesson to be so quickly forgotten. *The serpent offered, and you rejected.* Just keep that handy."

With that, Father Brown leaves me in silence. I pause for a moment then shake my head. My health bar is almost all the way up, causing the great weariness I've been feeling to leave me. I do need to get moving, to get back out there. I'll rest when the sun goes down and I can no longer fight. Until then, I have work to do.

The guard seems thankful as I walk out of the museum, and I see him waving at a custodian. I turn to offer to help, but he only motions me along. I suppose there's nothing more for me to do, and I stride through Central Park, preparing for my next move.

First, I make my way to the lake. I dive into the water and

swim several laps, taking an impromptu bath that manages to get most of the gunk off me. As I come out the other side, I'm dripping wet, but that's a good deal better than everything before. I dry off as I walk forward up to the gates and step carefully across the salt ring to look out at the city.

Ahead of me, lightning flickers, and a new dungeon opens. Massive roars echo from within. A taxicab, which had been driving down the street, suddenly spins away, drifting around a corner as it fights to escape the horde of monsters pouring out.

[RazorEdge: Yeah! Go Jason! Save the world again!]

[IceQueen: Quick, they're after him!]

Pouring from the portal are lizardmen, each one topping six feet in height and all with long, flickering tongues that taste the air carefully. Two of them chase after the cab, pounding across the pavement with gusto, and I charge forward as well.

I can see the cab driver. He's the same one that John and I hitched a ride with, and as our eyes meet, I can see that he recognizes me. Quickly, he rolls down the window and pulls out the goblet, which he dangles outside.

"It's cursed!" he screeches. "Dragon curse! I heard you say it, and it's true!"

As I reach the cab, I leap up into the air, sailing over the roof of the cab with flair. The cab driver tosses the goblet into the air, and I catch it and touch my feet briefly against the roof to perform a spin then throw the goblet with all my might into the face of the closest lizardman. He's blasted backward across the street, and as I land, I draw out my Photonic Dagger. The second lizardman hisses, and I lash out, cutting him across the belly. Blood seeps through his scales and he steps back, hissing in victory, just outside the range of my knife. I shrug, draw back my arm, make the dagger grow into a sword, and slash forward. My blade cleanly removes his head, and the body tumbles to the ground.

Unbidden, my Phoenix flashes out of my pocket dimension, flames trailing off his red and golden wings.

FOOOOOOOOM!

Fire explodes across the pavement, incinerating three more of the monsters, and the bird floats down to land on my shoulder. There are half a dozen of the lizardmen left, and they all pause, then form a defensive ring around the portal, which continues to crackle and blaze with an ethereal energy. I take my stance while my Phoenix spreads his wings wide. Fire explodes on either side of me, crackling and raging.

"Better run while you still have the chance," I order them. "Back into the portal, now."

The lizardmen all look at one another. There's a long pause, and the first one actually turns around and dives headlong through the flickering energy. The others turn as well, jumping one after another through the dark energy, and I scowl.

"Hey! Come back here! I didn't actually . . . Oh, well."

My body fills with energy as I race forward, pounding toward the portal. It actually starts to close, and I give one last burst of speed, flinging myself forward just before it comes crashing shut. Interdimensional energy erupts all around me, and I'm sucked into the dungeon.

[ChaosRider: Go, Jason!!!]

[RazorEdge: That's our boy!]

[ViperQueen: That's it! Get rid of all the monsters in New York! Go, go, go!!!!]

[Originalgoth: I hope you slip and get impaled through the heart. And the gut. And anywhere else that it's *really* painful.]

[GrendleH8tr: Keep your head about you, kid. You just passed the first test. I hate to tell you, but the worst is yet to come. Keep up the good work.]

I don't know what to make of the chat, but I smile at all the responses as I come out of the portal on the other side and throw myself into the midst of the confused lizardmen. It's a new world; it's a new situation; it's . . . well, it's a lot of new stuff. That said, I'm confident that I can handle it.

I'm confident that I can *crush* it.

ABOUT THE AUTHOR

Kaz Hunter is the author of the Apocalypse Reincarnation, System Bound, and Rise of the Strongest Sovereign series. A graduate of Texas A&M University (go, Aggies!), he started writing on Wuxiaworld and Webnovel. He has since moved on.

DISCOVER
STORIES UNBOUND

PodiumAudio.com